THE TRIAL

CHARLOTTE PAGE

inked entertainment

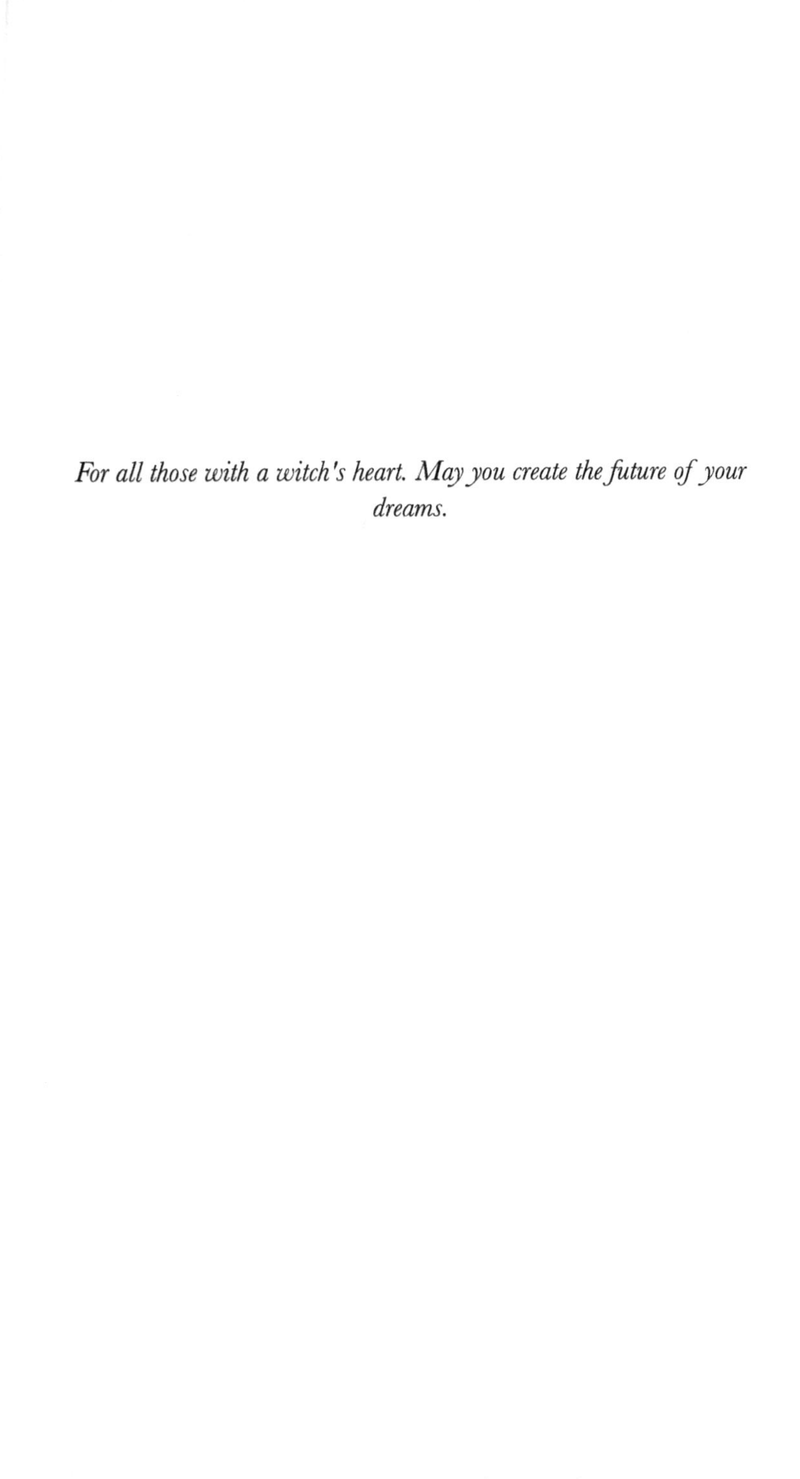

For all those with a witch's heart. May you create the future of your dreams.

PART I
MAGIC

To protect His children,
the One God created the Lighted Path,
so all those who followed Him would be safe.
But not all seek the Light,
and the children of darkness are adept at deception.
They are beautiful. They are dangerous.
They are deadly.

-The Book of Light

TWELVE DAYS AFTER

The whole town came to watch her hang.

They arrived moments before dawn, when the navy sky paled at the seams but did not yet boast the blush of morning. They stood. And they waited. The Pratchett family near the Redds, and the Carriers beside the whole of the extended Putnam clan.

Tendrils of conversation snaked through the crowd as onlookers jostled for a better view. *Will her neck snap? How long will she hang before she's dead?* A trill of hushed laughter floated over the square as the Pratchett twins wagered how many minutes her body would twitch before it fell still. Despite all the speculation, one fact remained: Blythe Bradbury would be dead before midmorning tea.

Behind the crowd, a carriage door slammed shut. The creak of metal hinges cut through the hushed murmurs. Those who stood in the back—Mr. Eliot, Dr. Hale, and an expectant Mrs. Eastey—fell silent as they caught the first sight of the witch. She looked younger than her eighteen years, smaller in the swell of the crowd. The memory of this young woman covered in blood, her eyes lit from within by a feral light, quickly replaced the stab of pity. She deserved her fate.

The onlookers parted as the witch passed, afraid to breathe the same air or occupy the same space as the condemned. Her thin hands bound in front of her with coarse rope, Blythe was but a shadow of the vibrant young woman she had been . . . before.

But before did not matter. Not when there was such an *after*.

Blythe stumbled up the stairs to the gallows. Her body seemed to strain further with each step, but when she looked over the crowd, a calm settled upon her. The blessed sun broke free of its nightly prison and bathed the world in soft golden light.

Instead of shying away from the One God's power, the witch smiled.

The front rows shuddered and stepped back, but Blythe merely stood there, her face tilted toward the sky, a row of bruises visible along her neck. Her eyelids fluttered shut. She seemed alone in the world, at peace, not a witch standing before a town eager for her death.

Behind her, the wooden steps creaked as the executioner ascended the stairs. The noise disturbed her trance, and Blythe opened her eyes, gray irises dulled by the pallor of her white skin. She twisted her wrists, tugging against the coarse rope that bound them. Beads of red welled beneath the bindings and spilled out, pooling around the wooden pendant she wore around her wrist, full of stars she'd never see again.

The blood carved a path along the length of her hands and paused. A single bead clung to her finger, afraid to let go. But since blood cannot return from whence it came, the drop of red succumbed to gravity and fell to the wood beneath her feet.

The executioner paused several paces behind Blythe. His thick arms bulged and flexed as he clenched his hands. Though most of his face hid behind a cloth mask, the gleam of his eyes and the turn of his lips spoke of a scowl. His quivering fist reached toward the heavens and grasped the hanging noose, pulling it from its hook. The rope looked thin, almost frail in his large hands, but as he placed the loop around Blythe's neck, the heaviness of imminent death settled over the crowd.

Rough twine scratched her neck and shifted higher to reveal the raw pink beneath. Her chin tipped up, a challenge to the rising sun. Or, perhaps, the pull of the noose proved too uncomfortable to bear without grimace.

A murmur broke through the square, silenced only when the steps to the gallows creaked once more.

The magistrate, William Hawthorne, paused at the front of the gallows overlooking the sea of villagers dressed in modest grays and blacks. Blythe tore her gaze from the sky to stare upon her accusers. Those who spoke out against her and those too cowardly to speak for her. Their guilt was equal in her mind. She tugged again at the ropes that bound her wrists, not strong enough to escape, but enough to feel the tear of her flesh, to cherish the bit of pain that reminded her she was still alive.

If only for a few moments more.

Magistrate Hawthorne pulled a handkerchief from his pocket and wiped at the sweat on his brow. His hands shook as they dabbed near his temples and the remaining few strands of white hair that clung to his sun-spotted head.

Winds shifted and blew from the east, tossing Blythe's tattered dress about her legs. Her hair escaped capture from the noose and framed her face, black of night against skin so pale she seemed already dead.

The magistrate unfurled the parchment. The town held its breath. Waiting. Watching. Clouds shifted and darkened, blotting out the sun.

Blythe smiled. Wide enough to catch the flash of her teeth.

Magistrate Hawthorne cleared his throat, delaying the words he had come to deliver. The words they all waited to hear. Finally, he spoke.

"Blythe Bradbury, the town courts of Brekham, under the authority of the One God, have found you guilty of the practice of witchcraft and the murder of Miss Mirabel Walcott. For these crimes, you have been sentenced to hang by the neck until dead."

Blythe scanned the crowd, her pulse visible as it hammered through the veins in her neck. The smile fell from her face when she saw Pastor Tobias Walcott. Father of Mirabel. Father of *Caleb*. She scowled to hide the grief that softened her face. She glared at the minister, her dark brows pulling together, marring her porcelain features.

"Do you wish to repent, witch? Will you admit your sins and beg the One God's forgiveness before you leave this world?" Though his voice boomed through the square, Magistrate Hawthorne's hands shook, the parchment trembling in his grip.

Blythe stared again into the sky, the line of rope and bruises visible across her throat for all the world to see. Already her white skin had turned from pink to red. Her gaze dropped to the onlookers; a commotion had broken out near the back, but she couldn't determine the cause. "I will not waste my final breaths to claim an innocence you're determined to ignore. But I do have words for you, Magistrate."

At the sound of her voice, the town grew still. A feral expression lit Blythe's face. Her eyes sparkled like stars on a crisp winter evening. Those closest to the gallows stepped back, knocking into the onlookers behind them.

Her red lips lifted to show the white of her teeth. Another drop of blood trickled down her hand and fell to the wood beneath. "My gods hear my prayers, and they smile upon me. Can you say the same of yours? Will your god punish the fools who speak in half-truths and spew forth damning falsehoods?" A rumble of thunder shook the ground. "If you do this, my gods will send you swiftly into the earth."

Lightning streaked across the sky. The heavens split, weeping upon the ground, soaking the town in rain mere degrees from snow.

"I greet my gods happily." Blythe glared upon Pastor Walcott as fresh lightning cast stark shadows across her features. "Will you?"

Without waiting for a response, Blythe stepped forward onto the dropping platform to meet her fate. The sky warred with itself, shooting lights across the sky and shaking the earth.

The commotion in the back of the crowd had moved forward, and Blythe caught a glimpse of its source.

A flash of red hair.

Panicked, green eyes.

And lips she once longed to kiss.

Though hidden by the rain, tears rolled down her cheek. "Caleb." Her gaze dropped to the wooden floor. "Forgive me."

The executioner grasped the release lever.

And pulled.

WRITTEN TESTIMONY OF BLYTHE BRADBURY

My dearest Caleb,

I am not a woman who likes to harbor regrets, but if I must confess anything, let it be this: I regret my final words to you. I didn't know what else to do. I didn't know how else to keep you safe. But knowing my bitter words might be your final memory of me . . . I had to leave you something else. Something better.

There isn't much left of my strength, but I've poured every spare bit of hope I have into this letter. Hope that you'll find it when you're ready, that it brings you comfort instead of pain. I never wanted to hurt you, Caleb. You've already endured more than anyone should be asked to bear.

I know I owe you many truths, but let me start with this. Even knowing how our story ends, I could never wish away what we had. You were more than I hoped to find in a town like this. Neither of us truly belonged in Brekham. Skeptics in a town ruled by religion. I should have known sooner how desperately in love with you I would fall.

We deserved so much longer than we got. We deserved a lifetime of memories. We deserved to grow old with your darling sister a cher-

ished part of our family. Yet even with the gallows before me, I would not trade my time with you for a hundred other lives.

Though you will not see this in time, I hope you do not come tomorrow. If I see you, I might not have the strength to do what must be done. To right the world, those responsible for your sister's death must be punished, but I cannot watch you crumble as the noose tightens around my neck.

If I see your face, I will lose every illusion of strength.

etween his father's abrasive voice and the endless trips to the carriage, Caleb Walcott's irritation rose with the blistering sun as it stretched toward its peak. He reached for a final crate of ritual candles, only to find another tucked under the carriage seat.

Caleb groaned. "How many candles could the old man possibly need?" When he finally took over as minister, Caleb would find a more efficient way to light the small church.

His father wouldn't relinquish control of the town's spiritual needs for several years, though, so Caleb sighed and hoisted the crate over his shoulder. He escaped into the cool shade of the church, where his younger sister Mirabel ran a cloth over the pews. Sixteen to Caleb's eighteen, Mirabel was too young when their mother passed to miss what their life used to be. Too young to remember mornings spent reading with her, years before their father took over the church and their lives turned into . . . this.

Before Caleb's future was bound to the church.

Setting the crate beside the rest, Caleb glanced at his

father, Tobias Walcott. The minister stretched to his full height, storing the candles quicker than Caleb could bring them in from the carriage.

"About done, boy?" The pastor's voice was gruff and cracked from too much time spent with his dusty collection of texts. "The upstairs pews still need sweeping."

Caleb bit back another groan. He hated this life. He missed his years of schooling, when he was permitted to study more than the rules of the One God. He had faith, but not enough to lead an entire town. Not enough to devote his entire future to the church.

"Just one more box, sir." Caleb gripped the simple sun charm he wore around his neck to honor the One God. Though he'd carved the charm himself only a few years prior, the wood had grown soft from frequent fussing.

Outside, the bright sun bathed the world in oppressive heat. Many believed the summer light was a gift from the One God, but as sweat trickled down Caleb's temple and disappeared under his collar, he found the heat more nuisance than gift. His red hair gleamed in the windows of the carriage as he flung open the door. He stooped for the final crate, but as he pulled, something caught and *snapped*. The bottom broke away, and candles spilled out, rolling toward the dirt road.

Spewing curses unfit for a minister's son, Caleb chased after the candles. He had only just righted himself when he heard the clopping of hooves and the jostle of a carriage. He leapt out of the way as the carriage barreled past.

"Watch where you're going!" he shouted, heart hammering in time with the horses' footfalls. *Damned fools.* The driver, a middle-aged woman with milky white skin and dark hair streaked through with silver, took no notice of him. Caleb shook his head and turned back to the church when the carriage stopped in front of a vacant house.

What is she doing there?

Caleb paused and examined the carriage. It looked newer than the one he'd spent all morning unloading. The woman had money—likely a good deal of it. So why would she move there? The house had sat empty for ten years, ever since the Sanderson family . . . died.

She must be new in town.

No one born in Brekham would move into a home with such a troubled history.

When he turned again to leave, the carriage door swung open and a vision of dark elegance emerged. The young woman looked about his age, with skin so pale he could almost make out the dusting of freckles across her nose, even from a distance. Hair as black as a starless sky hung loose to her mid-back, a rarity in a town so devoted to the One God. Most women wore their hair in braids, a modesty their god encouraged.

Caleb shivered in the hot sun. The combination of sensations was dizzying, and when the woman turned, their eyes met. The corners of her red lips tilted upward, lighting her face. But she glanced quickly away and tucked her hair behind her ears, leaving Caleb to wonder whether she had truly seen him at all. She grabbed belongings from the carriage and carried them into the house.

"Who's that?"

Mirabel's voice jolted Caleb from his thoughts. He spun, heart galloping in his throat with unnecessary force. She'd caught him watching their new neighbors, after all, not *fornicating*. "How could I possibly know? They've only just arrived."

Mirabel leaned around him for a better view, her pale blue dress fluttering in the light breeze. "We should see who they are. You know, welcome them to Brekham, like we did when Dr. Hale moved here this spring."

Caleb followed her gaze and considered the request. His heart pounded hard in agreement. *Would she be as stunning up close?*

Before he could decide, their gray-haired neighbor exited her front door carrying a platter of small cakes. He shook his head. "Mrs. Putnam has beaten us to it." Caleb stooped to pick up the last of the fallen candles. "Come on, Mirabel, I'd like to finish before supper."

Mirabel laughed, her voice ringing like the chimes that hung from their porch to ward away evil. "Why? You have no one to call upon this evening."

Caleb nudged his sister with his shoulder. Their mother's necklace, an intricate golden sun set with an amber stone at the center, winked up at him. Their father had given it to Mirabel when she turned twelve, and she hadn't taken it off once in the four years since.

"You jest, Bells, but there are no suitors calling after you, either."

Mirabel, used to his teasing, simply rolled her eyes, stalked back inside the church, and the pair returned to their duties.

~

Caleb had just finished sweeping the pews when a breathless and sweaty Mrs. Putnam burst into the church. The widow, still dressed in mourning black despite the three years since her husband's passing, clutched her pewter sun charm and reached for the doorframe to keep herself upright. Her skin was so pale the blue of her veins shone through beneath her alarm-widened eyes.

"Ma'am? Is everything all right?" Caleb abandoned the broom and approached the troubled woman.

Mrs. Putnam grasped his arm and dabbed at her brow with a handkerchief that had yellowed with age. "Yes, dear boy, of course. I simply must speak with the minister. Immediately." When Caleb didn't move fast enough, Mrs. Putnam released his arm and clapped her frail hands together. "Move along, Mr. Walcott. Go and fetch him. I haven't got all day."

"Yes, ma'am." Caleb turned and grumbled several unkind things under his breath. He had known Mrs. Putnam all his life and still her frequent demands ruffled his nerves. She'd only gotten worse since her husband's burial.

Caleb shuddered at the memory of the late Mr. Putnam's funeral service. The Walcott family hosted every burial in town thanks to their position with the church, but that meant they spent more time than most with the town's undertaker, Mr. Upton.

Mr. Upton was a strange man, more comfortable around the dead than the living, but his beady gaze lingered too long on Mirabel. It started at Mr. Putnam's service. Mirabel was only thirteen at the time, but she'd started attracting attention from the men in town.

Caleb rarely left her unaccompanied after that.

As Caleb passed the altar, his worries shifted to the minister. His father had disappeared into his private study some time ago, which usually left him indisposed the rest of the day. Caleb continued down the narrow hallway, praying the minister hadn't dipped too deeply into the sacramental wine.

He knocked softly. "Sir? Mrs. Putnam needs to speak with you."

Inside the office, a flurry of clinking glasses preceded

heavy footsteps. When at last the door swung open, the minister smelled faintly of wine.

Please don't slur. Please don't...

"What sort of services does she need?" Pastor Tobias Walcott spoke clearly and smoothed the front of his clergy robes. The minister's sun charm, passed down from pastor to pastor, hung heavy from his neck, a reminder of the important burden he carried as the spiritual leader of Brekham.

Caleb shook his head. *Thank the One God for small blessings. He's still coherent.* "She didn't say. Only that it was urgent."

The minister nodded. "Send her back. I want you and Mirabel ready to leave when I'm finished." He waved Caleb away.

It always seemed unfair to Caleb that he should follow the One God's laws so closely yet feel so much doubt—doubt that he could *never* express, to anyone—while his father gave in to his worst impulses time and time again, yet felt perfectly comfortable wearing the heavy charm and preaching about the lighted path.

There was nothing to be done about it, though, so Caleb returned to the altar and waved Mrs. Putnam forward. Using Mirabel for balance, the old woman traveled the length of the church. Her eyes darted about the room with each unsteady step.

"The minister will see you in his study. Please, follow me." He took over for his sister and led the old woman to the open door.

"Mrs. Putnam, to what do I owe the pleasure?" the minister asked, voice clear and booming despite the wine on his breath. Thankfully, Mrs. Putnam didn't seem to notice the sweet aroma.

"In private, if you don't mind." Mrs. Putnam released

Caleb and walked into the minister's study without waiting for an invitation.

His father sighed. "Help your sister. I won't be long." The hinges whined, and the door clicked shut. "What can I do for you, Mrs. Putnam?" Though the old woman wanted privacy, that was hard to achieve in the small church. The thick door only muffled words so much. Over the years, Caleb had overheard more secret confessions than he cared to remember.

If he went upstairs, perhaps then he'd escape this latest gossip. Caleb ran his fingers through his hair and turned to leave. He had taken his first step when Mrs. Putnam spoke.

"It's my new neighbors, Pastor. Something isn't right about them."

Caleb froze. He glanced down the hall and glimpsed Mirabel cleaning the final row of pews. Risking the One God's wrath, he stepped back toward the door and pressed his ear against the smooth wood.

"I wasn't aware you had new neighbors."

"I do. Mrs. Dinah Bradbury and her daughter, Blythe."

Blythe Bradbury. The name rolled around in his head and fell silently from his lips. Caleb closed his eyes, and his mind filled with her image.

"What of the husband and father?"

The old woman coughed, a wicked, rattling thing. "There is no father. Mrs. Bradbury must be the youngest widow I've ever met."

"We mustn't hold that against her. The poor man likely fell ill. It happens, as you well know."

Silence.

"Forgive me, ma'am. Please, go on. What troubles you about the Bradbury family?" His father spoke with the calm of a minister, but Caleb could hear the impatience in the rise of his words, could picture him itching to reach for his hidden drink.

"There are so many small things, Pastor, so many small pieces that together… It's as if the house remembers the Sanderson family and seeks to corrupt these women. They invited me inside and already their pantry is filled with strange herbs. And they brought cats with them. *Three of them!* And the daughter…"

Caleb pressed his ear closer to the door. *Blythe.*

"What of her?"

"She's a rare beauty, I'll give her that, so why isn't she married? She's plenty old. I daresay older than your Mirabel, who really ought to start looking for a husband, if I may be so bold. And your son—"

"My children have devoted their time to serving the One God. When He is ready for them to marry, the right suitors will present themselves," the minister interrupted.

Caleb's stomach grew sour. His father never asked his opinion on the matter, not that Caleb felt particularly interested in any of the eligible women in town. Still, it would be nice to have some say in his future, but it seemed his father planned to choose his wife, as well.

"Of course, Pastor. Please, excuse the digression," Mrs. Putnam hurried to apologize. "But there's more. I swear upon my husband's grave—may he rest in peace—I swear I saw the young woman carrying *crystals*, but she moved away with the box before I could tell for sure."

A pause. Fabric rustled.

"I will not have *witches*," she said, hissing the word, "for neighbors again, Pastor. I am a faithful servant of the One God. I walk firmly in the light. I will not tolerate heretics in my backyard. Not again."

Pastor Walcott fell silent a long time. When he finally spoke, his voice sounded grave. "That is a serious accusation, Mrs. Putnam. Let's not jump to conclusions." Chairs scraped against the wooden floor. "I will meet with your neighbors and sort this out. Have faith. The One God protects those who serve Him. He hears your concerns."

Footsteps.

"Thank you, Pastor, I—"

But Caleb didn't hear the rest. He rushed into the nave, where Mirabel had finished her chores. Between the cleaning and the heat, several strands of her light brown hair had fallen loose from the single braid she wore down her back. Moments later, the minister led Mrs. Putnam out of the church. As he waved goodbye, Caleb approached his father.

"What did she want?" He leaned out the front door and watched Mrs. Putnam shuffle across the road. Caleb risked a glance at the Bradbury house but saw no movement inside.

"Nothing. Just an old woman's superstitions." His father smoothed a hand over his clean-shaven face and chin, contemplating.

Caleb stepped through the door into the hot afternoon. "Shall we introduce ourselves to the new family? Welcome them to Brekham?"

Mirabel appeared behind them, a smile bright upon her face. "Can we, Father? We should at least invite them to services."

"Another time." The minister stepped out of the church and glared upon the former Sanderson house. Blythe appeared through her doorway to gather another crate from their carriage. "I don't want either of you consorting with the newcomers until they've come to church."

TESTIMONY OF DOLORES PUTNAM

The air inside the courtroom hung stagnant and bitter. The town crowded into the room, perched on the edge of polished wooden seats, ready to flee. Ready to fight. The smallest of sparks could set the tension ablaze.

Many in attendance had seen Mirabel Walcott's mangled body. Those who hadn't seen the young corpse had heard the story told again and again, facts warping into fiction that was somehow less gruesome than the truth. A select few men had carried the minister's daughter back to town. Days later, their skin still felt soaked in blood.

And so, the people of Brekham were eager for the witch to arrive. This trial could not give back the pious life that had been lost, but they were certain it could send someone wicked to her death.

They were certain the One God would reward such just and righteous actions.

At the back of the room, stiff hinges whined. Mr. Pratchett, father of the two most eligible young women in Brekham, entered through the wide double doors. Eleven others followed him to the jury box, where the dozen men took their seats. Like restless children, they fidgeted in their chairs and tugged at the cuffs of their freshly-pressed sleeves. They shared a series of nervous glances before settling their attention on the open doorway.

A guard strode into the courtroom next. His broad shoulders and wide, muscular back hid the witch until she stepped fully inside the courtroom. Her eyes downcast, she glided down the aisle without meeting the gaze of a single soul. As she passed what little remained of the Walcott family, she angled away from them, as if unable to bear witness to their pained faces. Already rumors circulated about the adult son, Caleb, and the twin points of heartbreak that could yet disgrace him.

The guard shoved Blythe Bradbury into her seat and lumbered away, fists clenched tight. He hovered at the edge of the court, ready should his services be required. Alone at her table, Blythe stared blankly at the wooden surface, her wrists bound with rope. Someone had scrubbed Mirabel's blood from Blythe's skin and given her fresh clothing, but brown specks were still visible on her shoes.

Despite her clean skin, no one would ever forget.

The witch had bathed in blood.

Behind the magistrate's bench, a second door opened. Magistrate William Hawthorne emerged from his chambers, followed by a tall, too-thin man. Lionel Lewis, a minister from the neighboring town of Rowley, would serve as prosecutor. They stood before the town, eyes somber, the lines of their lips grim. Prosecutor Lewis found his colleague, Pastor Walcott, in the crowd. The men nodded to each other.

It was time.

The already quiet courtroom fell so silent it was as if the townsfolk stopped breathing. As if their hearts forgot to beat. The accused tilted her face level with the magistrate's bench. Gray eyes empty. Face impassive.

Magistrate Hawthorne smoothed the last bits of white hair on his balding head. "The trial of Blythe Bradbury will now commence. Pastor Lionel Lewis has agreed to serve as prosecutor."

The magistrate paused and shuffled the parchment before him. "Men of the jury, you must swallow your fear and consider only the facts presented to you." The assembly of respected businessmen and fathers nodded as one. "Pastor Lewis, this courtroom is yours."

"Thank you, Magistrate." The thin man approached the jury, pacing before the assembly of men with his long fingers steepled before his face. "Gentlemen, you hold in your authority the power to provide justice for a woman taken too soon from this world. Over the course of this trial, I will provide evidence that Miss Bradbury is undoubtedly a witch. And I will prove, beyond any doubt, that she used her witchery to murder the minister's faithful daughter, Miss Mirabel Walcott."

Pastor Lewis paused to ensure that all in attendance had devoted their full attention. "The witnesses will discuss their encounters with Miss Bradbury's wicked magic. They will detail her relationship with the deceased, and they will provide indisputable proof that the witch killed an innocent young woman, perhaps the most righteous woman in all of Brekham."

He turned from the jury and stared out at the crowd. Mayor Eliot sat with his wife, their adult son two rows behind them. Mr. Eastey held the hand of his young wife. All the town watched. As far as they were concerned, the witnesses were unnecessary. They had already decided the witch's guilt. The trial was a formality, a requirement of their One God, a testament to their civility.

"For my first witness, I call Mrs. Dolores Anne Putnam."

Something cold flashed through Blythe's eyes. Bitter. Flecks of iron amid the gray. Then blackness. As if she were already dead inside.

At the back of the room, the frail widow rose from her seat. She ambled forward, the slippers on her feet shuffling against the wooden floor. Mrs. Putnam gave Blythe a wide berth as she passed, but the girl took no notice of her accuser.

When Mrs. Putnam settled at the witness stand, Pastor Lewis stopped before her. "Please state your name for the record." He gestured to the short woman sitting on the other side of the magistrate, a stack of parchment before her. The court recordkeeper trembled in her seat, a quill clutched in her hand.

The widow smiled at the men in the jury box. "Mrs. Dolores Anne Putnam. Wife of Cornelius Putnam, may the One God keep him in His light. I'm mother to Edwin, Arabella, and Victoria, all of whom have grown and left for neighboring towns to make lives of their own."

"Thank you, Mrs. Putnam. And how do you know the accused?" The prosecutor waved in the general direction of Blythe, but his witness never took her aged eyes off the jury.

Mrs. Putnam folded her arms beneath her breast and scowled, deepening the lines in her forehead. "When the witch arrived in Brekham, she and her mother moved in next door." Her old voice gained strength as she spoke, the rattle in her throat lessening.

Pastor Lewis paced the room with his long arms folded behind his back. "What makes you so sure that Miss Bradbury is a witch?"

"How could I live beside her wickedness all season and

be unsure? I am not yet blind, sir." She shuddered. "The moment I laid eyes on Miss Bradbury, I knew something was terribly wrong. Cats follow her around everywhere, wicked, shadowy little things. They hiss every time I step into my garden."

She harrumphed and turned away from the prosecutor. But the motion left her staring at the witch. Mrs. Putnam flinched under Blythe's scrutiny and turned to search the audience for more friendly attentions.

When the townsfolk murmured their assent, the old woman inhaled a shuddered breath and continued. "I even caught her sprinkling magical herbs around her garden. The plants grew stronger even as mine wilted and faded away. They survived through the late autumn frosts. It's not natural."

The visiting minister nodded, his fingers again steepled before him. He paced the courtroom like a hawk circling its prey. "What else, Mrs. Putnam? Surely you have proof so strong none could deny its truth. What darkness have you seen?" He leaned forward, towering over his witness. His face softened when he spoke. "You are safe to share your secrets here, ma'am. The witch cannot harm you where the One God's light shines through."

Blythe smiled. How little the foolish man knew.

Sweat trickled down Mrs. Putnam's wrinkled skin, wispy white hair glistening in the winter sunlight. She scanned the courtroom, and her thin lips stretched into a grin.

"You want proof, Pastor Lewis?" She leaned forward, boney fingers gripping the railing before her. "In the dead of night, when she thought the world around her slept, the witch ventured outside." Mrs. Putnam paused and stared upon each member of the jury in turn. "The witch plucked a mouse from her garden. The small creature sat transfixed upon her palm. And she *spoke* to the animal. Spoke to it!"

Mrs. Putnam shuddered and shook her head. "I convinced myself I had imagined it. It was dark, after all, and I'm not as young as I once was. But come morning, something had rooted through my garden and bitten every plant! I swear upon my husband's grave the witch compelled the little beasts to destroy my vegetables. And the worst of it…"

She paused, eyes wide as if she had seen her husband's ghost. "By week's end, every plant in my garden was dead."

The court dissolved into a frenzy of conversation, and Magistrate Hawthorne called for a short recess. While most stayed inside to continue their discussions, Caleb Walcott fled the courtroom. He shoved through the heavy doors and stepped into the cold morning. His breath fogged the air as he stumbled down the steps of the courthouse. His future lay in ruins at his feet, and he didn't know how to repair the broken pieces.

When Caleb reached the bottom step, he tightened his cloak around him. His breathing tore through his lungs, eyes on the verge of tears. He wouldn't—couldn't—let them fall. He had to keep moving or risk breaking apart. There was too much to do. He'd already lost his sister; he wouldn't lose Blythe, too.

So he staggered forward, running from truths that hurt as much as the witness's lies. He had known this was a possibility, had feared this outcome for months. Blythe had warned him of the small-minded people in small towns like Brekham.

Yet all that time he'd worried, never once had he envisioned this future. A world without his sister—

The first tear spilled over his lashes, and he shoved it away. He didn't have time to grieve, not if he was going to stop the trial. Not if he was going to prevent his love from wearing a noose.

Caleb turned left out of the town square, down the deserted market street. Not a single soul had stayed behind to tend to their stalls, not with the first witch trial in a decade to steal their attention. Caleb had to find a way to upend their fascination, some way to make them see the truth. Some—

"Caleb?"

The voice in the empty street, though a quiet inquiry, sent Caleb's heart racing. He turned, half-expecting to see Mirabel standing there with a smirk upon her face. His hands trembled, but he released a shaky breath when he found the voice's owner. It wasn't her. It would never be her again.

"Isaac."

Isaac Carrier emerged from behind his family's empty stall and paused before Caleb. For once, Isaac was free of soot and grease. He probably hadn't been to the smith yet that morning. "You look as if you haven't slept in days, old friend." Isaac folded his arms across his chest, shivering in the cold.

"I can't imagine why." Caleb rubbed a trembling hand over his face. His only sister—the only family he cared for—was dead. And as if that grief wasn't enough, the magistrate had imprisoned the woman he loved and charged her with Mirabel's murder. The whole town had come to watch the visiting minister prove her guilt with false witnesses. *The whole town… except for Isaac.*

A seed of hope took root in Caleb's chest. He didn't

know how to end the trial, but having an ally on his side couldn't possibly hurt.

"Why weren't you in the courthouse this morning?"

His best friend merely shrugged. "You know I have no interest in town politics." Isaac glanced around the empty street. "I wanted to pick up a few things at the market, but I guess everyone really *is* there. I'll have to try again tomorrow." Isaac turned to walk away, but Caleb reached for his arm and held him in place.

A gust of wind sent their cloaks billowing around their legs. "Is that all this is to you? Just another trial like when we were children?" Caleb released Isaac's arm and shoved him in the chest. "My sister is *dead!* Doesn't that mean anything to you?"

"I never said I didn't care." Isaac brushed his shirt where Caleb had shoved him. "But it's not as if my presence in the courthouse will undo her death."

Caleb stumbled back, the words striking as hard as a physical blow.

Isaac sighed. "Don't look at me like that. You know I meant no harm."

"Then help me." Caleb's voice shook, and he fought the tears in his eyes. Signs of weakness wouldn't help his cause. "We've been friends our entire lives, Isaac. I've given so much more than I've ever asked. Please. Please. help me."

"I'm sure the courts have it well in hand." Isaac clasped Caleb's shoulder. "Let them do their job."

That little seed of hope grew withered and brittle. "You're not listening," Caleb said, unable to hide the emotion from his voice. "You're supposed to understand me better than anyone else in this wretched town. What's changed?"

Something flashed in Isaac's eyes. "Since when do you

hate Brekham?" He stepped closer, towering over Caleb. "I am *trying* to be a good friend, but I will not indulge these delusions."

"I'm not delusional."

"No? Then tell me, what brings you to the courthouse? Do you go to ensure your sister's killer is punished? Or are you there to protect *her?*"

Caleb shifted on his feet, suddenly uneasy. Unbalanced. Isaac should have been the easiest to convince. Isaac was supposed to trust his instincts. "Mirabel deserves justice, not to see an innocent woman hang. Blythe didn't do this."

Isaac glared at him. "How? How is she still 'Blythe' to you? That woman killed your sister!" He shoved Caleb out of his way. After several paces, he turned back. "You know what? Things have changed too much between us, but that fault isn't mine."

"I've done nothing to—"

"But you have! You *chose* her, Caleb. You chose her over me, over your father, over *your sister*. You shut us out of your life in favor of a witch." He spat on the stone ground and turned away. "It seems she controls you still."

"Don't walk away from me. I will prove her innocence! I will prove it, and then *you* will be the one begging for my forgiveness. You'll be the one admitting your delusions."

Isaac didn't turn around. He didn't pause. He kept walking, his soft reply carried through the empty market by the wind.

"I'm sorry, old friend."

irabel pushed through the mid-week market, weaving effortlessly through the thicker afternoon crowd. It wasn't yet autumn, so the stalls consisted mainly of local foods and wares. Traders from other villages wouldn't arrive for a few weeks yet. "Come on, Caleb, hurry up! Father needs me to rehearse for the service tomorrow."

"Your sister is a terror. Please, tell me you realize that," Isaac Carrier whispered to Caleb as the pair fought to keep up with the young woman.

"Come on, Isaac, she's not that bad." Caleb skirted around a pair of children as they ran after each other using loaves of bread as swords. Their shoes slapped noisily against the cobblestone. The main square was one of the few places used heavily enough to justify something sturdier than dirt roads. "But I'm glad you could sneak away from the forge long enough to come with us."

"I expect to be rewarded for my sacrifice," Isaac grumbled, picking through a cart of fresh fruits. Despite trying to clean up, Isaac still smelled faintly of burning metal, and there was a smudge of grease along his collar. Yet no one dared say anything about the tiny bits of disarray in his appearance. Though slightly shorter than Caleb, Isaac's entire frame was layered with impressive musculature from a lifetime of blacksmithing. He had a strong jaw and straight nose that Caleb had overheard more than one girl admiring to her friends after church services.

"Caleb!"

"Coming, coming." Caleb hurried after his sister, his childhood friend on his heels. Despite being separated in the crowd, Caleb kept a clear view of Mirabel's path.

Mirabel paused at a vegetable cart and scanned a selection of onions. She reached forward, plucked one from the middle row, and inhaled deeply. "This will be perfect in the soup I'm planning."

Caleb wrinkled his nose at the tangy sweet smell. "How much?"

The man behind the cart, skin browned from all the time spent outdoors in his fields, rubbed at the stubble on his chin. "Two for a copper."

An objection rose in his throat, but Mirabel whirled on him before he could speak. "Don't be cheap, Caleb. Pay the man."

"I'm not cheap. I'd simply prefer to spend coin on food we all like."

Mirabel propped her hands on her hips, and for a moment, she looked so much like their mother that Caleb was stunned into silence. His sister took his quiet for permission and snatched the bag of coins from his waist, paying the merchant herself. Mirabel added two onions to her basket and flashed Caleb a smug grin before disappearing into the crowd.

A low chuckle escaped Isaac's lips.

"What?"

Isaac's brown eyes flashed in the sunlight. "If the ladies of Brekham knew how easy it was to change your mind, Mr. Walcott, they'd line the streets for your attentions. And your coin."

"A preacher's son doesn't exactly have a lot of coin to spare, Carrier." Even so, Caleb's face burned under his friend's scrutiny. Despite his mediocre financial prospects, being in line to take over the church gave him a measure of respect he wasn't sure he deserved. Not that he had time to consider marriage prospects, thanks to his father. "Besides, it was *you* the ladies truly vied for this summer. Did anyone ever fully capture your fancy?"

Caleb's attempt at mockery only resulted in a smug grin.

"One most certainly did."

"Really? And who is the lucky lady?"

Isaac glanced around them, short blond hair gleaming in the sun. When he seemed sure no one of concern stood nearby, he leaned closer to Caleb and whispered, "One of the Pratchett twins."

"Which one?"

"Does it matter?"

"You, sir, are a terrible gentleman." Caleb laughed and searched the market for his sister, but she had disappeared among the crowd.

Instead, he spotted Mr. Pratchett and Magistrate Hawthorne deep in conversation as they headed toward the courthouse. Laughing. The young widower Amos Eliot, Mayor Eliot's only son, skirted around the edge of the crowd, eyes fixed on the ground before him. Dr. Oliver Hale, new in town since spring, bartered with the local apothecary while Mr. Upton, the tall, lanky undertaker, talked excitedly behind him, as if trying to strike up a friendship with the far more personable doctor. Finally, Caleb caught sight of Mirabel at Mrs. Eastey's stall.

Isaac reached for Caleb's arm when he made for the flower stand. "I know I promised to keep you company, but Mr. Pratchett just disappeared into the courthouse."

"And?"

"And that means the twins are likely alone. They may require my… company."

"You're incorrigible, Isaac."

His friend grinned. "I know."

Caleb considered him. "Fine. Bells and I are nearly finished anyway. I'll see you at the next service?"

"Of course. You are the greatest friend a man could ask for." Isaac flashed a smile and weaved his way out of the market.

"Stay in the light, Isaac!" Caleb called after him, but Isaac didn't slow. His friend would be in a world of trouble if any of their fathers found out about his intentions. The One God didn't allow unwed adults to explore such forbidden pleasures. Of course, not everyone followed those rules, but being found out was still catastrophic. If he were wise, Isaac would be looking for a wife, not trying to bed half the eligible women in town.

Caleb shook his head and caught up to Mirabel at the flower stand. "Good afternoon, Mrs. Eastey." Caleb inclined his head to the woman who lived beside the church. "Did you have a nice time away?" Mrs. Eastey and her husband had only returned the previous night from a trip to the nearby town of Rowley.

"I did. However, your sister seems determined to take my finest flowers for nary a copper." Despite the sharpness of her words, her tone was kind.

"I'm confident we can come to an agreement, ma'am." Perhaps the late summer heat had addled his good senses, but Caleb simply reminded his sister to pay a fair—but reasonable—price.

As Mirabel haggled with Mrs. Eastey, a flash of loose black hair caught his attention as it fluttered in the soft breeze. The wind shifted directions, and the hair parted to reveal the face of a dark angel. Her porcelain skin was tinged with pink at the bridge of her nose, and light freckles dusted the apples of her cheeks.

Blythe.

Her name echoed through his mind, first in Mrs. Putnam's paper-thin voice and then in his own. *Blythe Bradbury.* The young woman whose mother made the grave error of moving into the Sanderson home. The woman he had yet to speak with since she arrived, despite her proximity. Blythe and her mother had neglected religious services for two weeks. And though they dressed in the same style as the other women in Brekham—high collars, hems that nearly brushed the ground, and sleeves that extended past the wrist even in the worst heat—there was something undeniably different about the Bradbury women.

There were already rumors about why they refused to bind their hair into *appropriate* styles. Caleb didn't believe any of them.

"Caleb? Caleb!" Mirabel pulled at his sleeve, flowers in her other hand. "Where has your mind gone?"

Caleb spared a glance for his sister before returning his attention to their mysterious new neighbor. "What? Nowhere."

Mirabel peered around him. "Oh look! Isn't that the young woman we saw a few weeks ago?"

"Who is that, Miss Walcott?" Mrs. Eastey shaded her eyes from the glaring sun.

"She and her mother moved in across the street while you were away." Without waiting for Mrs. Eastey's response, Mirabel stepped toward Blythe and glanced back at Caleb. "We should introduce ourselves and welcome her to town."

"Wait!" Caleb reached for her elbow and held Mirabel in place. He lowered his voice so Mrs. Eastey wouldn't hear. "Father said not to talk to her until she comes to church."

"And how will she know she's welcome unless we invite her?" Mirabel paused, but before Caleb could summon a worthwhile rebuttal, she pulled from his grasp. "Stay here if you like, but I'm going."

Mirabel eased through the crowd, coming to a stop before Blythe. Caleb watched his sister fuss with the end of her braid as she introduced herself to the forbidden woman. A strange pressure built in his gut until he found himself moving forward without conscious decision. Caleb tried to convince himself that he was only being polite, but he couldn't deny the way he felt drawn to Blythe, as if someone had tethered them together and now pulled the cord taut.

He paused just behind his sister. A safe distance—an *appropriate* distance—from Blythe. "Good day."

Blythe tilted her chin up to meet his gaze, exposing her slender neck. A bright smile softened her face. "And to you."

Their gazes held and locked, and Caleb lost himself in those gray eyes. Never in his life had he been so completely undone by the mere presence of a woman.

They stood in silence until Mirabel cleared her throat. "This is my brother, Caleb Walcott. I promise, he's normally a bit better at conversation." She shot him a dirty look. "But only a bit."

His cheeks flushed with heat as Blythe laughed, but he managed to step closer and hold out a hand. Blythe rested her fingers against his palm, and he pressed a kiss to her smooth skin. His heart pounded hard in his chest, shoving blood further south than it should go. "It's a pleasure to meet you."

"The pleasure is mine, Mr. Walcott. I'm Blythe Bradbury." She took back her hand, almost reluctantly, and considered him a moment. "Walcott... Are you the pastor's son?"

Nervous and made unsure by the sudden coolness of her expression, by the sudden retreat of her smile, Caleb nodded. "I am."

Mirabel glanced between them and rocked forward on her toes. "We saw you and your mother move in a few weeks ago. We were helping our father at the church."

Blythe's dark eyes seemed calculating as she examined Caleb's face. "I thought you looked familiar." She tucked a wayward strand of hair behind her ear. "A rare comfort in a town full of new faces."

Except, she didn't sound comforted. She sounded on edge. Cautious. Inside, Caleb yearned to reassure her, but of what? He *was* the minister's son. There was no way to deny reality. And it was strange... Normally, that knowledge created quite a different reaction. He cleared his throat. "Would you care to join us for the next service?"

"Please, say you'll come." Mirabel stepped past Caleb and grasped Blythe's thin hands. "You must. You can sit with Caleb while I play piano for the service. That alone is worth the attendance. I'm really quite good." Mirabel smiled broadly. "Your mother is welcome to join us as well."

Blythe settled her attentions on Mirabel and squeezed her hands. "Mother will be delighted. We'll be there."

Blythe released Mirabel and stooped to retrieve her basket. She nodded goodbye. "Until then."

Caleb's heart lodged in his throat, stealing his speech. He waved at Blythe's retreating form and watched her slip away.

But just before the swell of the crowd swallowed her, Blythe turned back to the Walcott siblings, her earlier smile returning. "Save a place for me."

And then she was gone.

~

Pastor Walcott's service the next morning seemed never ending.

Caleb twisted in his seat with each footstep, each cough, each creak of the old church. Halfway through the central prayer to the One God, Mirabel glared at Caleb so sharply from where she sat at the piano that shame burned his face. He managed to calm his repeated glances toward the entrance, but he hardly heard a word the minister said. He might care more for the service if his father would let him lead—or at least write—a sermon once in a while. How was he supposed to guide the people of Brekham if his father didn't *teach* him anything?

When the minister concluded his teachings and dismissed the assembled townsfolk, the seat beside Caleb was still empty.

Blythe had missed the entire service.

The church emptied as people returned to their lives. Isaac waggled his brows at Caleb before trailing after the Pratchett family, one of the twins glancing back to see if he followed. Playing the part of the dutiful son and future pastor, Caleb bid farewell to each of their parishioners.

When they were alone, Caleb and Mirabel straightened the pews and counted the donated coins. Pastor Walcott retired to his study, where Caleb imagined his father drinking through the rest of their wine stores. He hoped he wouldn't need to rouse his father later. The minister often woke swinging.

Mirabel headed for the stairs.

"Where are you going?" Caleb slid the last of the holy books into place. They still had to run a dusting rag over the entire nave. The One God required complete cleanliness in His churches.

"I thought I should straighten the upstairs." She placed her foot on the first step.

Translation: she wanted to play the ancient harpsichord. If she pressed the keys lightly enough, the minister wouldn't overhear Mirabel's one great indulgence, her one deviation from the One God's teachings—she composed songs that had nothing to do with Him.

Caleb sighed. "Fine. Go ahead." Mirabel raced up the stairs without so much as a thanks.

In his sister's absence, Caleb sank into one of the rear pews. He'd mistaken Blythe's politeness for true interest. He'd let himself imagine her there with him, sitting by his side for the duration of the service. With her there, the horrible wooden benches wouldn't feel so hard, and the minister couldn't stop Caleb from seeing her again, outside the church.

And he so wanted to see her. It was a constant ache in his chest, this knowing that they were connected somehow, if only he had the opportunity to discover it. He needed to know why she cooled so suddenly when she realized his connection to the church.

A soft knock sounded at the door. Caleb ran a hand

through his hair and pushed off from the pew. "You may enter."

The knock came again.

He crossed to the entrance. "The door is unlocked. I said you could—" The words died on his lips when he saw her standing on the front steps wearing a cream-colored dress with fine lace details at the cuff of her sleeves. "Miss Bradbury. The service ended quite some time ago." Caleb shifted in the doorway.

"I know." Blythe's cheeks were pink, but Caleb couldn't tell if the color came from her tardiness or too much time in the sun. "Mother kept me busy all morning, and I couldn't get away. I came to apologize to you and your sister."

Caleb glanced back into the church, but Mirabel was already shut into the small room upstairs. "I'll tell her you stopped by."

"Might I come in?" Blythe glanced past him into the church, but something akin to worry clouded her expression. "I thought, perhaps, you could tell me more about Brekham."

At the back of the church, glass shattered. Caleb flinched and stepped outside, pulling the door shut behind him. "Walk with me instead?" When she nodded, Caleb offered Blythe his arm and held his breath.

Blythe let her hand rest against his bicep and followed him behind the church to the cemetery. She paused at the wrought iron entrance. "Should I read anything into this location, Mr. Walcott? A cemetery is strange place for conversation."

"I don't mean to be morbid." Caleb stepped past the entrance and turned back to wait for Blythe. "I simply…" Caleb paused. In truth, this was the place he felt safest from his father's drunken wrath, but he couldn't say that. "I find a peace here. It's where my mother rests."

"Oh." Blythe looked as if she might say more. Instead, she simply followed Caleb into the cemetery and to his mother's grave. The headstone's carving had smoothed with time, but the One God's symbol was as clear as the day the marker was set. Caleb grasped the charm he wore around his neck and noticed that Blythe didn't seem to have one. At least, not where he could easily see.

"Is that her?"

Caleb nodded. He wasn't entirely sure why he'd brought Blythe there. No one ever came to this place with him. Not Isaac. Not his father. Not even Bells. Yet it seemed right somehow that Blythe was there, like his mother would approve.

Blythe brushed her fingers along the top of his mother's headstone. "Ten years… How old were you?"

"Eight." Caleb twisted his hands together. "Mirabel was six."

"What happened to her?" Blythe stepped closer, her gray eyes searching his. An unseasonably cool breeze kicked up around them, tossing her loose hair into the space between them. "I'm sorry, that was overly forward. You don't have to say."

Caleb shook his head. "I don't mind. It was a long time ago." Despite his assurances, his chest clenched at the memory. "She was quite ill, but the sickness took her quickly. I don't think she suffered long. At least, it felt too fast as it happened."

"I'm so sorry." Blythe rested a hand on Caleb's arm. Even through his shirt, the heat of her skin branded him. "The fates can be cruel, stealing loved ones well before their time."

Tension bloomed in Caleb's chest, and he shrugged off

Blythe's touch as the long-buried anger rose within him. "Fate had nothing to do with it. Witches poisoned her."

Pain rushed through him as the memories surfaced. His mother had fallen ill, and everything seemed to happen so fast after that. She seemed to get better, then suddenly, she was gone. The witches responsible hanged for their crimes, but it didn't matter. His mother had already left him. His father clung to the One God with every bit of strength he possessed.

And Caleb's future was sealed.

"I should have known better," Blythe murmured behind him.

Her bitter tone shocked him, and he turned away from the grave. "I don't follow."

"Mother warned me not to trust a preacher's son, especially not in a town as small and narrow-minded as this."

"I don't—"

"What proof do you have, Mr. Walcott?" Blythe crossed her arms beneath her chest. "What supposed magic ripped your mother from this world?"

"I—"

"There are a hundred ways to die young. Accidents. Weaknesses of the heart. Consuming the wrong berry." Blythe's voice rose with each example, tears glittering in her eyes. "What proof did you have besides your own grief? What proof allowed you to cry witchcraft and sentence an innocent woman to death?"

Caleb had no ready response for her. No one questioned the truth of his father's claims. No one cast doubts on cries of witchery. He wanted to assure Blythe that his father had proof before the accusations were made, but... Caleb couldn't remember ever hearing it.

I was young, Caleb assured himself. *The minister wouldn't have shared the details with a child.*

But then another memory surfaced. Mrs. Putnam bursting into the church the day Blythe and her mother moved in.

I will not have witches *for neighbors.*

Mrs. Putnam was so quick to point fingers. Based on what? A well-stocked kitchen? Caleb looked at Blythe with new eyes, absorbed the defensive way she held her body, the tears she fought to keep from falling. How often have such rumors plagued her?

"I think..." Caleb faltered. He had never expressed doubt, had never given voice to those words. Yet if she was brave enough to question him, he could interrogate his own past. "I think it's easier, sometimes, to blame others. If we don't, we have to admit the One God failed us. Or admit that we don't know Him like we believe we do."

Overhead, clouds moved in to cover the sun. "And what is it *you* believe, Mr. Walcott?" Blythe's voice trailed up his spine

Caleb shivered, and for the first time, spoke his most secret truth.

"I don't know."

Blythe smiled at that. It was a slow, careful thing, like the blooming of a rare flower. "Those are dangerous words, coming from a pastor's son." Yet she said it with no judgement. If anything, Caleb felt as though he'd passed an unplanned test.

"Can I trust you to keep my secret?" His heart pounded loud in his chest, and he was sure all of Brekham could hear it. Though he felt exposed, the sensation was electrifying.

"Perhaps," she said, but that smile only bloomed brighter. "Until we meet again, Mr. Walcott."

She stepped past him and walked carefully between the headstones, each blazing with the One God's sun. At the iron entrance, Blythe paused and looked back at Caleb, where he remained by his mother's grave.

"It's a gift, you know, that you can visit your mother like this."

"Yeah?"

Blythe nodded and turned back toward the road. "I wasn't so lucky."

TESTIMONY OF PRUDENCE EASTEY

*W*hile the court recessed for the midday meal, word of the first witness's claims spread through town. The onlookers hurried home to share news of Mrs. Putnam's accusations, to delight in the retelling of the damning evidence. Neighbors told friends and children told their classmates.

All who could spare the time raced to the courthouse for the next witness, another of the witch's neighbors. When the jury filed back to their seats, not a single chair in the courtroom remained vacant.

Even Caleb Walcott had returned, looking paler than when he had stormed out. He sat beside the older Walcott, behind the witch.

"Do you keep to the light of the One God, Mrs. Eastey?" Prosecutor Lewis paced before the packed room, his attention fixed on the young woman sitting at the witness stand. He pulled at his crisp white cuffs. Straightened his starched shirt.

Mrs. Eastey nodded, her brown eyes darting to glance at the Bradbury witch. With a shudder, she returned her attention to the embroidered handkerchief in her hands. "Of course, Pastor Lewis." The corner of her lips twitched upward. "I wouldn't live mere paces from the church if I wished to hide from His light."

Soft laughter filled the courtroom, but it didn't warm the frigid air. Nothing could. Not with winter fast approaching. Not with a witch—a creature fueled by the wicked dark of night—in the room.

Pastor Lewis folded his hands behind his back and inclined his head to the witness. "Is it safe to assume then, Mrs. Eastey, that you shall speak only the truth before the court? You have, after all, sworn by the One God to do so."

"Of course, sir." Mrs. Eastey ran a hand over her braided hair, smoothing the frizzing edges. "I remember… I remember what we all saw that night." She cast another fleeting glance at Blythe. "I will do everything I can to protect the town from such wickedness."

A murmur of agreement rolled through the crowd.

Yet Blythe? She studied the table before her like it was a shield, like if she sat still enough, none would see her. The gentle rise and fall of her back as she breathed was the only sign that she was flesh rather than stone.

"Thank you, Mrs. Eastey, but it is not that night I wish to discuss. First, we must hear about your initial meeting with the Bradbury family." He resumed his pacing. "How many days had the witch been in town before you met her?"

"About two weeks, sir."

"Why so long? Weren't you eager to meet the new family on your street?" He paused before the jury. "Surely you were curious about the new occupants of the Sanderson home."

Prudence Eastey fussed with her handkerchief. "My

husband and I were out of town, traveling to the local markets." She looked to the back of the courthouse where Thomas Eastey smiled and nodded for her to continue. "I didn't realize we had new neighbors until Miss Walcott told me one afternoon at the market."

"The victim introduced you to the witch?"

"Not exactly, sir. Miss Walcott noticed Miss Bradbury in the market and mentioned that the family had moved in across the street from me." Mrs. Eastey shuddered. "I didn't meet the young woman until the next day."

The minister nodded, his shoes punctuating time as he paced the wooden floor. "Mrs. Eastey, please tell the court what you saw when you first visited the Bradbury home."

"It was horrible." Her voice came out a whisper. "There was so much shouting."

"Shouting?" Pastor Lewis asked as a murmur worked through the public gallery. Heads bowed together, in pairs of twos and threes, to share in whispered conversation.

Save for two men.

Pastor Tobias Walcott glared at the witch seated rows ahead of him. He looked older than his years, his hair rapidly graying. His son, Caleb, stared without seeing, tears sparkling in his green eyes. Grief for his dead sister, perhaps, or pain over his own failures. Possible, still, that the witch possessed his mind, twisted his grief for her benefit.

Magistrate Hawthorne sighed and pinched at the bridge of his nose. "Let's continue, Mr. Lewis. Please."

"Yes, Your Honor." The prosecutor returned his attention to his witness. "Continue, Mrs. Eastey."

After releasing a shaking breath, Prudence nodded. "I baked a pie for the Bradbury women to welcome them to town and apologize for not visiting sooner. I brought it over to their house, but when I knocked upon the front door, no one answered. As a youth, my family often preferred to use the kitchen door, so I went round the side of the house." She paused and fussed with the handkerchief in her hands.

Pastor Lewis parted his lips to speak, but Prudence found her voice. "As I passed their large window, the one above the side garden, I caught sight of the Bradbury women. They stared at each other with such venom in their eyes." She shook her head. "I have never seen such anger shared between mother and daughter. It's unnatural."

"Did you hear what they said? Could you make out the meaning of their disagreement?" The minister stepped forward and leaned over the witness stand. "What proof do you carry of her witchery?"

"Her mother snatched something from Miss Bradbury's grasp and told her daughter to be careful. She said… She said it wasn't safe for them to make nice with men of the church." Prudence gripped tight to her handkerchief. "Mrs. Bradbury told her daughter to keep to herself. She said they would have to leave if they were discovered." Mrs. Eastey shook her head and twisted the wedding ring about her finger. "The elder witch knew they would be caught."

"And where is the mother now?" Pastor Lewis asked, though the gleam in his eyes said he knew the answer he sought.

"Disappeared." Mrs. Eastey raised her chin and fixed her stare on the accused. Her voice hardened, and the quaking ceased. "Her mother has fled, her carriage gone missing since the night of the murder. Mrs. Bradbury was so disgusted with her daughter that she disappeared into the swells of oncoming winter."

The witness sneered. "May the One God have mercy on her impure soul."

NOW

he courtroom was empty, save for him. Caleb welcomed the silence, the loneliness of the barren room. At least alone he didn't have to hide the war inside himself.

Caleb lowered his head and cupped his hands behind his neck. If Mirabel could see him like this, she would usher him into the kitchen and make tea for them both, teasing him until he mustered a smile. Guilt tore at Caleb for the thought. He should have done more to protect her. He should have cherished Bells more while she was still alive. If he listened close, he could almost hear her laughter in the wind or one of her many melodies in the chorus of voices outside.

But he would never *really* hear her laugh again.

She was gone. Forever.

Stabbing heat stung his eyes, but Caleb squeezed them shut. He wouldn't shed another tear. He had cried himself dry the night he found her, and he didn't have time to grieve. He had to find the truth. Because what he saw that night, the shock of Blythe injured, her dress covered in his sister's blood…

Caleb's stomach rebelled at the memory, and his throat tightened to block the rising bile. There was another explanation. Blythe would never hurt his sister.

They had been friends.

Conviction finally drove Caleb to his feet. His love was innocent, and he would find proof so strong that no one in town could disagree. Not even his father.

With burning purpose flooding his veins, Caleb left the courthouse. Yet when the outside world slammed into Caleb, it overwhelmed his senses. The sun was too bright, the wind too bitter. And the noise. Noise everywhere. Horses clopped past, pulling rickety wagons, the wheels creaking as they turned. And everywhere, the murmur of voices. Hushed whispers of gossiping townsfolk. The callous shouts at pack animals and small children. It took every ounce of control to stop his hands from crushing over his ears to drown out all the *noise*.

Instead, Caleb shielded his eyes from the harsh afternoon light and hurried around to the back of the courthouse, heading for the exterior entrance to the basement cells.

Outside the door, he paused. He traced the worn wood and thick metal bolts with his fingertips. He rested his forehead upon the wood. Another bitter wind blew through the town, tearing at his clothing and biting his skin.

Caleb pressed against the door, wishing he could go to Blythe's cell and get the truth from her lips. Instead of the resistance he expected, the metal lock fell to the ground in pieces. A tremor of fear mixed with anticipation. Someone had come before him. Someone had broken the lock.

He pushed the door open and stepped through.

Cold. Dark. Damp. That was his first impression of the

dungeon-like hallway leading toward the basement cells. Fear squeezed his heart like a winch, and a heavy weight pressed against his chest, as if slabs of granite slowly crushed him.

A bright memory lit the hallway better than the nearly-spent torches. Mirabel and Blythe, together in the market, their faces alight with laughter. The image seared his mind. Caleb managed a step forward. Then another. And another. With each step, his resolve hardened. But as he turned a corner, he found a man sprawled upon the floor. Caleb froze, but when the man didn't move, he crept forward and knelt, pressing his fingers against the man's neck.

His pulse beat steadily, yet he did not wake. This close, Caleb could make out the One God's sun on the man's uniform. He was one of the guards.

Someone else was *definitely* here.

He continued forward, careful to quiet his steps, and paused when he heard voices. A woman talked in hushed tones. A second voice contained muffled sobs.

Caleb eased toward the edge of the stone wall and peered around the next corner. Blythe stood inside the small cell, tears streaming down her face. She clutched at the bars even as she sagged against them. She looked defeated in a way Caleb had never seen.

Before her, standing tall and impassive, was Dinah Bradbury, Blythe's supposedly missing mother. She had the same pale skin, dark hair, and delicate features as her daughter. For a moment, Caleb wondered how Mrs. Bradbury had broken in and subdued the guard, but then he remembered all Blythe could do, and fear tightened his throat.

He withdrew behind the cover of the wall and closed his eyes, willing his ears to capture their conversation.

"I warned you this would happen," Mrs. Bradbury said, her voice harsh and full of condemnation. "I *told* you to stay away from that boy. The stars warned you about the church. You had nothing to gain and everything to lose." A pause. Footsteps paced back and forth. "Why couldn't you listen to me, Blythe, just this once?"

"Mother—"

Caleb stiffened at the sound of Blythe's voice. Never in all the months he knew her had she sounded so utterly *broken*. He ached to go to her, but he didn't know what Mrs. Bradbury would do to him. Did she blame him for his sister's death? For Blythe's imprisonment?

"Enough." Mrs. Bradbury's voice lashed out with the intensity of the pastor's fists. "It's too late to beg for my forgiveness. If you are old enough to ignore my warnings, you're old enough to face the consequences alone."

Silence spread. Then—

"Wait! Mother, please!" Something thumped against the stone floor.

"I will not delay and risk walking to the gallows with you." Hard soles scrapped against stone.

"You can't leave me here!" Metal clanged. "This is your fault as much as mine. *You* brought me here. *You* chose this gods' forsaken town."

"And yet I'm not the one on trial. I followed the rules." Fabric rustled, like the billowing of a cloak.

"No, please." The metal clanged again. "Take me with you. Don't leave me here alone." A sob cut off whatever Blythe meant to say next.

A long, soft sigh floated through the halls. "I cannot wait, dear daughter. Your mistakes give me no choice but to follow the rising sun."

"They'll kill me. You must know that. If you leave, you might as well walk me to the gallows yourself."

The silence that followed was so long and so absolute that Caleb wondered whether Mrs. Bradbury had simply vanished and taken her daughter with her.

"You walked yourself there already, dear daughter."

The quick shuffle of feet drew near, and Caleb scrambled back the way he had come. But he didn't make it far before Mrs. Bradbury rounded the corner. She paused when she saw him. Her gaze swept over his face, appraising.

"Leave." She kept her voice low, too quiet for her daughter to hear. "You'll only make things worse."

Caleb shook his head. "You may wish to abandon her, but I will not."

Her eyes flashed, a trick of the dying torchlight, but she didn't contradict him. She didn't strike him down.

Mrs. Bradbury swept passed Caleb with a face of stone. He turned to watch her go, but Caleb saw no indication of regret as Dinah Bradbury passed the unconscious guard and disappeared around a corner, leaving her daughter to die.

TWELVE WEEKS BEFORE THE MURDER

Caleb stood before the town square where the late summer harvest festival was in full swing. Mr. Pratchett, head of the merchant council, had brought vendors—and, more importantly, customers—from all the nearby towns. Brekham was filled to bursting with people and fresh harvest. Though the crowd overwhelmed his senses, he was grateful for an excuse to escape the church.

Beside him, Mirabel vibrated with anticipation. "Can you believe Grace and Verity pulled this off? It's beautiful."

While Mr. Pratchett brought business to Brekham, his twin daughters were the minds behind the elegant sun charms hanging in each stall and the garlands of flowers strung between them. The town square seemed to burst with possibilities.

"Don't get so taken by the decorations that you over-spend at the first vendor." Caleb handed his sister a small bag of coins so she could enjoy the festival without his constant supervision. "We'll meet at the fountain and leave together."

Mirabel rolled her eyes. "I'm not a child, Caleb. I don't need to be escorted home."

"Promise me, Bells. You know how Father gets."

"Fine." She weighed the bag in her hands, already scanning the square for the best vendors. "Try to have a *little* fun while you're here. I know how hard that is for you."

"Bells——" But she was already gone, weaving through the crowd to shop until her purse ran empty.

Alone in the square, Caleb wandered aimlessly through the stalls. The locals who recognized him from church greeted him warmly, and he cursed his red hair. The rare coloring made him conspicuous in a crowd, even when he wished to move anonymously through the world. Eventually, he found his way to an aisle of metalworkers and stopped in front of the Carriers' stall.

Isaac and his father were the only blacksmiths in Brekham, but their work surpassed even those smiths from much larger communities. Their booth boasted gleaming knives and sturdy farming tools. They had recently expanded to include custom charms and rings, pieces Isaac gave to the women of Brekham to encourage more amorous evenings. Ironic, given how many of the pieces contained the One God's sun.

Caleb greeted the older Carrier with a firm handshake. "Could I borrow Isaac for a moment?"

The master blacksmith looked like he might disagree, and the line at his booth wasn't short, but there were benefits to being the preacher's son. Mr. Carrier nodded and relieved Isaac of his duties.

Once the pair were away from the booth, Isaac slung his arm around Caleb's shoulders. "Thank the One God. I was about to lose my mind to boredom."

Caleb rolled his eyes. "How could you be bored? Your stall was the busiest in the row."

"Not everyone enjoys work." Isaac spotted the Pratchett twins. Though their dresses *technically* met the One God's modesty requirements with the long flowing skirts and high neckline, the bodices were exceptionally tight. Isaac smiled roguishly at the sister on the right.

"I see you figured out which twin you're courting."

"Indeed." Isaac released Caleb's shoulder but stayed close to whisper, "Unless she betrays her sister by looking at me so."

Caleb whirled on his friend but kept his voice low. "You still can't tell them apart?"

"Can you?"

"Well, no." He lowered his voice further. "But I'm not the one courting them. Shouldn't you figure that out before you woo the wrong one?"

Laughter floated across the square before Isaac could respond, and Caleb returned his attention to the honey-haired Pratchett twins, whose beauty was rivaled only by their talent for tall tales and a heightened sense for decoration. Their cousin and constant shadow, Miss Edonie Redd, had joined them. Miss Redd's eyes grew wide, and she turned to stare at Caleb and Isaac.

Isaac, despite his bravado, looked away and busied himself with the variety of soft fabrics offered at the nearest stall. A flush of red creeped up his neck.

"For your sake, friend, I hope you haven't courted both sisters." Caleb clapped Isaac on his wide, muscular back. "Even I couldn't talk you out of that one."

Isaac looked a bit green.

"Have you spoken to their father yet? You ought to get his blessing before you take this any further," Caleb pressed, enjoying the way his carefree—and often careless

—friend squirmed. "Mr. Pratchett has a lot of power, what with him leading the merchant council and all. He could ruin your father's business if he learned of your indiscretions, especially since they're *his* daughters you have your eye on."

Isaac groaned. "Don't act so scandalized. Just because you're too wed to the One God to take interest in marriageable women, doesn't mean we're all so chaste. Besides, it's not as if I can approach Mr. Pratchett about his daughter when I don't know which sister I'm there to beg permission…"

Caleb's stomach soured as he waited for Isaac to continue. It always felt wrong, like an itch beneath his skin, when others made assumptions about the depth of his piety. Mostly, because it *should* be true.

Except, it wasn't, and Caleb didn't know how to fix the doubts that clawed at his heart.

When his friend still hadn't continued after several moments, Caleb waved a hand in front of Isaac's face. "Carrier? Where has your mind gone?"

"Where was *she* when I chose the twins?"

"Who?" Caleb turned to follow Isaac's hungry gaze and found a familiar face in the crowd. *Blythe.* She was dressed more simply than the Pratchett twins, yet the deep auburn dress clung to her delicate curves as the wide hem brushed the tops of her shoes. Caleb's heart sped when she glanced in his direction, and he prayed for her to spare him a smile, something—anything—to show that she'd forgiven him for the strange turn of their last conversation, but she must not have noticed him in the crowd. She did nothing to acknowledge his presence.

I wasn't so lucky.

Those were her parting words, and Caleb had wondered ever since what had happened to Mr. Bradbury.

If his death was one of the accidents Blythe described to him. Why couldn't she visit his grave? Was it too far away or was there no body to bury?

Grace, or perhaps Verity—Caleb wasn't sure which twin it was—approached Blythe and struck up a conversation, her sister and Miss Redd close behind. Blythe greeted them each with a soft smile, but even across the distance, Caleb could sense her unease.

"Perhaps it's a good thing I haven't spoken to Mr. Pratchett," Isaac mused, drawing Caleb's attention. A predatory smile pulled at Isaac's lips as he watched Blythe.

A flush of anger burned in Caleb's veins. "You don't even know her name."

"Do you?"

"Yes, I do. Miss Bradbury moved in near the church." Caleb's words sounded defensive, even to his own ears, but he couldn't stop himself. "You already have both twins after your affections, Isaac. Leave her be."

Isaac cocked his head to one side, watching the young women as Blythe extracted herself from the trio and moved to another aisle. "Why, Caleb? Have you laid claim on her?"

"What? No, of course not. I—"

"Then stay out of my way, old friend."

"Isaac, wait!"

But Isaac was already crossing the square, a wolf stalking its prey. Caleb watched his friend, jealousy and propriety and a feeling he couldn't name warring within him. Finally, cursing colorfully under his breath, he chased after them.

Caleb rounded the corner into the next aisle just as Isaac stopped before Blythe. Isaac flashed his most winning smile and reached for her hand. "I've heard such wonderful things about you, Miss Bradbury. It's a pleasure to meet you." He bent forward and kissed her hand. "My name is Isaac Carrier. Perhaps you've heard of my family's smithy?"

Blythe yanked her hand from Isaac's touch, her cheeks flushing a furious red. "Are the gentlemen of Brekham always so forward, Mr. Carrier?"

If Isaac felt the harshness of her words, he didn't show it. "Only when the ladies are as lovely as you."

Blythe scowled, seeming immune to the charm most Brekham women swooned over. "Mind your tongue, sir." She wiped the back of her hand against the dark folds of her skirt.

"Or what?" Isaac asked, all mirth. "Will you mind it for me?"

"I'll carve it from your face."

Her words left Isaac speechless, a first in all the time Caleb had known him. He seized the opportunity and gripped his friend's arm. "Enough, Isaac. Apologize to Miss Bradbury."

Blythe's eyes flashed in the sunlight, and she leveled her steely gaze on Caleb. "I didn't ask for your help, Mr. Walcott." She turned on her heels. "Good day, gentlemen."

Her words cut like a whip, leaving Caleb disorientated and confused. He thought Blythe had warmed to him that day in the cemetery, after things had gone sour. What if he misread? What if her smile had been one of pity or politeness?

No. Isaac must have said more than Caleb had heard.

"What did you do?" He shoved Isaac's shoulder, letting his frustration and the sting of rejection bleed into the motion. Not that it did much good. A lifetime of shaping hot metals left Isaac much, *much* stronger than Caleb could ever hope to be.

But Caleb didn't wait for a response. He took off after Blythe, weaving through the crowd.

"Miss Bradbury, wait." He called out to her as the distance between them shrank. "I'm sorry for my friend."

Blythe didn't even look at him. "You can tell a lot about a man by the company he keeps."

"I've known Isaac since before we could walk."

"And yet you still keep him around?" Blythe whirled on him, a flush of color rising along her cheeks. "That man belongs in a barn with the rest of the dogs."

Though he was equally irritated with Isaac, he felt a sudden defensiveness for his friend. "I swear, he's not usually like that."

"They never are, not around the people they respect. Excuse me." Blythe brushed past him. "I've had enough of today's festivities."

"At least allow me to escort you home," Caleb said, hurrying to keep pace with her. "I'm heading back to the church anyway."

Blythe tilted her face to look at him, but he couldn't read her expression. "Will Mr. Carrier be joining us?" She stared past Caleb, and he turned to follow her gaze. Isaac stood beside the baker's stand with his broad arms crossed against his chest. Scowling.

Caleb shook his head. "Not unless you prefer he did."

Blythe considered him a moment, time moving with an artificial slowness that threatened to tear him apart. Finally, she nodded. "After you, Mr. Walcott."

He couldn't contain the grin that spread across his face. He also couldn't miss the look of betrayal on Isaac's face as he led Blythe away. The back of his neck tingled, and whispered conversations sprang up as they passed the Pratchett twins. Grace frowned deeply. Verity shielded her eyes from the sun as she turned back to look for Isaac. Or, perhaps, he had the twins reversed.

Once the cobblestone streets gave way to dirt roads, Blythe broke the silence. "I can handle fools like Mr. Carrier on my own. I have before."

"I never said otherwise."

Blythe shook her head and kicked a pebble in their path. "Even so. I don't need your protection. Or your pity."

He paused in the middle of the road. "Is that what you think this is?"

"Isn't it?" Blythe stopped a few paces ahead and turned back. "Why else?"

Caleb ran a hand through his hair, his palms slick with sweat. He'd never been this kind of nervous before. It was equal measures unsettling and exhilarating. "May I speak openly?"

"There's nothing to stop you."

"I wanted a chance to speak with you in private." Caleb resumed his progress toward the church, and Blythe kept pace with him. "I haven't forgotten that day in the cemetery. I'm so sorry, Miss Bradbury."

His words hung in the air between them. Caleb expected Blythe to accept his apology, but instead, she studied him with an intensity that made him shiver. "And what, precisely, are you apologizing for, Mr. Walcott?"

A hollow pit formed in his stomach. This felt like another test, a moment when fate could smile upon him or smite him into the earth. And worst of all, he didn't know the correct answer. His fingers itched to reach for his sun charm, but somehow, he knew that would be a mistake.

"I've thought about what you said, about the gift of my mother's close grave." Caleb watched Blythe's reaction carefully, not wanting to cause her further pain with the reminder. When she glanced at him expectantly, he continued. "I had never considered alternative outcomes. I'm sorry you don't have the same opportunity to commune with your father."

Blythe raised a single brow, and Caleb felt the sharp, hot pang of failure. "Is that all?"

"No," Caleb rushed to add, but the word came out more question than statement. "I also…" He trailed off, unsure how to continue. Caleb remembered the sudden turn of Blythe's mood. He knew what topic caused the change, and yet he still didn't fully understand *why*.

And without that understanding, how could he apologize with any sincerity?

"When I mentioned the cause of my mother's death, you were adamant that witches had nothing to do with it." Caleb measured each word, careful not to imply accusations where he meant none. "Why were you so sure?"

Blythe stared up at the sky, where gray clouds had moved to block the sun. A dangerous omen. "My mother and I have traveled more than most, and in places like Brekham, where the religion of the One God is prominent, we've heard stories of witches. Women who shun the sunlight, who invite demons into their beds, who wreak havoc on the health of parishioners and well-tended fields." She scoffed, as if Caleb's fears—the fears shared by everyone he knew—were foolish. "In all our travels, I have never once crossed paths with a woman capable of the fanciful charges levied against her."

Caleb bristled at the explanation. "You speak as though witches belong in the realm of imagination." He'd been to the last trial in Brekham. He'd watched two women hang for what they did to his mother.

"Don't they?" Blythe asked, stopping to look at him fully. "What motive could a so-called witch have to murder your mother?" Blythe must have noticed Caleb flinch, because when she spoke again, her voice was gentle. "Having someone to blame might soothe the harsh edges of grief, but isn't it more likely that a natural illness took her? There is so much that our doctors cannot yet cure."

"But the courts found them guilty. They hanged two women for witchery. If they were innocent—" Caleb's throat tightened, and his stomach lurched. He had never considered their innocence a possibility. Even now, it was almost too awful to bear.

"I have seen more women killed for accusations of witchery than I care to remember." Blythe shivered and turned to continue toward her home, wrapping her arms around herself. "That's why Mother wouldn't let me attend your father's service. It's why I'm not supposed to speak with you now. She thinks if I get too close to a minister's son, it's only be a matter of time before I'm accused myself."

"I would never let that happen," Caleb said, an unexpected ferocity in his voice.

Blythe glared at him. "I'm not a damsel in need of rescuing, Mr. Walcott."

"I'm not looking for a damsel."

"Aren't you?"

Caleb wanted to deny her words, but his fierce reaction shocked even himself. "I respect your desire for independence. I only hope to have some place in your life." There was something about Blythe that filled him with courage and terror in equal measure. Something that made him want to bare his soul and pray she didn't find it lacking. "But should you ever require my assistance, you need only ask for it."

Blythe continued with him down the street. "And if I reject your friendship?"

"Then I shall wallow in my misfortune where you won't have to see it."

She laughed, a magical sound that filled the air with mirth. Caleb's entire body warmed with embarrassment, but when she turned to look at him, there was no mockery in her expression.

"I'm sorry," she said at last, "it's been a long time since someone has surprised me. Men so rarely accept my boundaries, let alone with such earnestness."

"Does that mean you'll accept my friendship?"

Blythe traced the edge of her dress sleeve as they walked, smoothing it over her wrist, the contrast of colors like rich wine against fresh snow. "I'm out of practice at having friends. Ever since Father died, Mother and I have moved with each turn of the year. At first, I tried to make friends with my new neighbors, but we never stayed long enough for it to matter. By the third or fourth move, I stopped trying. What's the point in making friends if you never see them again?"

"That sounds lonely."

"It is." Blythe shrugged. "But it makes leaving easier."

Her words carved a hollow space in his chest. Though Caleb often wished for moments of anonymity, he couldn't imagine such a solitary life, where no one knew him deeply.

The ache of such loneliness made Caleb want to reach for her, to trail his fingers down the length of her arm, but he kept his hands firm at his sides. He would respect her boundaries where so many others had failed. "Do you want the same life here, in Brekham?"

"I don't know," Blythe said, yet the words were earnest. They didn't cut as they could have. "I do enjoy your company, Mr. Walcott, when it's just the two of us. But knowing you will make it harder to leave."

His mind flooded with a hundred rebuttals to her claim, but he held his tongue. Up ahead, the church steeple came into view. They were close to saying goodbye, and they spent the next minutes in silence.

When they reached her home, Blythe paused, training her charcoal gaze on him. "A year is a long time."

Caleb nodded, unsure where her thoughts were headed. "It is."

"And you would understand if later I changed my mind."

"Of course." He would promise anything, if only it meant she'd linger longer on the lawn. If only she'd continue talking with him.

She smiled, soft and almost shy. "I'll think on your offer, Mr. Walcott. Until we meet again."

"I'll count the hours," he replied, but perhaps too soft for her to hear. She disappeared into her new home.

Into the Sanderson house.

Caleb forced himself to turn around. Forced himself to return to the church. As he passed through the threshold, he was surprised to find his father semi-coherent, sweeping the aisle. Pastor Walcott greeted him with a grunt. Then a raised brow. "Where's your sister?"

Caleb cursed and spun on his heel, darting back out the front door. He raced to the fountain at the town square, where he'd promised to meet Mirabel.

~

Mirabel sat on the edge of the fountain with a basket of bread, cheese, and cured meats beside her. She searched the crowd for her brother, but when she couldn't find him after several minutes, she snatched the sweet pastry she'd bought for him and bit into the gooey fruit center.

"Be careful, Miss Walcott," a voice said as a glob of fruit dribbled down her chin. "You don't want to ruin that fine figure of yours."

Mirabel wiped the mess from her skin and glared up at the man, scowling when she recognized her neighbor. "My figure is no concern of yours, Mr. Eastey." She set the rest of the pastry in her basket and stood, noting with a terrible chill the way the man's gaze tracked her movements. "How is your wife? Feeling well so far?"

Mr. Eastey shrugged. "Well enough, I suppose. Do you need someone to accompany you back to the church?"

"No." The word came out more sharply than she intended, though not as harshly as she felt inside. "My brother is here. Caleb would be very cross if I left without him." She backed away from her neighbor, backed away from the hungry look in his eye. So many of the town's men were like that, and the unbridled desire made her skin crawl. "Good day, sir."

Mirabel turned sharply on her heel and weaved through the crowd, away from the fountain. Ever since she'd turned thirteen, men in town stared at her chest and watched the sway of her hips. She should be used to it by now, but when their attentions came unexpectedly, it was harder to brush aside.

Harder still when the men were married with children on the way.

She stopped in front of an empty vendor's booth, away from the rest of the crowd, and turned to make sure Mr. Eastey hadn't followed. She wanted a moment of solitude before she resumed her search for her brother.

"…and who does she think she is, stealing away Isaac's attention? Mr. Walcott's, too."

Mirabel stilled her breath. Who had stolen her brother's attention? When? He was always at the church. Mirabel inched closer to the corner. The woman speaking sounded close, like she was in the next aisle.

A second voice replied, "Dear cousin, you scandalize yourself. Is Mr. Carrier truly 'Isaac,' already?" The voice snickered.

"Hush, Edonie. This is serious. Grace is courting him, or they *should* be courting by now."

With this third voice, nearly identical to the first, Mirabel placed the trio of women. Twins Verity and Grace Pratchett, and their cousin, Miss Edonie Redd.

"We *are* courting," Grace insisted. "More than courting, we——"

"You what, dear sister?" Verity's tone seemed almost reproachful. Until she giggled. "Was Edonie right? Have you truly scandalized yourself, Grace?" A pause. "You have! See how she blushes? You best hope father doesn't discover your dalliances."

A strange heat worked through Mirabel's body It was wrong to spy on others, the One God's teachings were clear, but what Miss Pratchett alluded to… Even Mirabel's father couldn't forgive such a transgression. She should leave. She didn't want to know anything more—but what did the women know of her brother?

Grace's voice wavered like she held back tears. "It doesn't matter now. You saw how he approached Miss Bradbury. He chased after her like a dog with a bone. If I didn't know better, I'd swear she enchanted Isaac to steal him away from me."

"Don't be such an alarmist, Grace. She walked home with Mr. Walcott, not your Isaac. Mr. Carrier will come around. Our father is very wealthy," Verity said.

Caleb walked her home? Betrayal blanketed Mirabel's skin

like a cold mist. Her brother had specifically asked her to wait for him.

Edonie snorted. "As if Mr. Walcott could steal attention away from a man like Mr. Carrier."

"Hush, Edonie," Verity snapped. "Mr. Walcott has his… qualities. He is the minister's son after all."

One of the women huffed out a breath. "Yes, and he has even less coin than the Carriers."

"Perhaps Miss Bradbury desires a man of the church."

Mirabel snorted a laugh. If only these girls knew how little her brother cared for the church. He faked it well enough, but Mirabel was a true believer. She could sense his reluctance. She noticed the slight pauses she was sure covered deep-rooted doubts. Caleb only studied to take their father's place because he didn't have other options.

At least, he didn't have any *easy* options. There were always choices—for men. Mirabel cared more for the church than Caleb ever would, but she could never take over for their father. She was destined only for a loveless marriage and a brood of children she didn't want.

"Who's there?"

Uh oh. Mirabel turned to examine the stall beside her, but it was too late.

The three women rounded the corner in an instant, coming to a sudden halt before Mirabel.

"How long have you been standing there?" Grace asked.

Mirabel could always tell the twins apart. The differences were subtle—Grace had the sharper nose and more angled jawline—plus now, Grace's face was flushed red with embarrassment and, possibly, shame.

Smiling at the women a few years her senior, Mirabel ignored the question. "Good afternoon, Misses Pratchett. Miss Redd."

Verity stepped closer until Mirabel had to crane her neck to meet her stare. "What do you know of Miss Bradbury?"

"Umm…" Mirabel glanced past Verity, wishing Caleb would return, wishing he hadn't forgotten her. Why had he taken Miss Bradbury home and left her—his *sister*—behind? "I know only that she lives near my father's church." Perhaps a reminder of the One God would calm the women interrogating her.

It did not.

"Why was she talking to your brother? What interest does she have in Mr. Carrier?" Grace stepped beside her sister. Identical faces glared down at her.

But Mirabel wasn't so easily intimidated. She may not have much, but unlike her brother, *she* had inherited a backbone. She smiled at Grace, all false sweetness. "It seems not as much interest as Mr. Carrier has in *you*."

Grace's mouth fell open. Panic widened her eyes. Though she tried to speak, nothing passed her moving lips. Her twin, however, was less easily ruffled.

Verity's eyes sparkled with malice, and she edged in closer, forcing Mirabel back a step. "You will forget what you heard, Miss Walcott, or so help me—"

"Or you'll *what*, Miss Pratchett?" Mirabel pushed forward into Verity's space this time. "Have you forgotten whose father serves the One God? Imagine the trouble there would be if I told him what I heard today."

Grace stumbled like she could faint at any moment. Edonie gripped her elbow, ready should her cousin collapse.

"Why you rotten, little…"

"Mirabel!" Caleb's voice carried above the noise of the busy festival. "Bells, where are you?"

She smirked at Verity. "I'm so sorry, Miss Pratchett, but I must leave. My brother is looking for me."

Verity backed away and reached for her sister. Grace brushed away tears. "Please don't say anything, Miss Walcott. Please."

The feeling of victory washed out of her. Brekham wasn't an easy town for women, no matter if they wished for marriage or not. "All you had to do was ask, Miss Pratchett. Your secret is safe with me."

Mirabel left the three women behind and returned to the fountain, where she found her brother waiting. His cheeks were red from the sun, redder even than his hair. "Come along, Caleb," she said by way of greeting and handed him the half-eaten pastry. "I took a bite as payment for your abandonment."

Caleb accepted the treat but winced at her words. "I'm so terribly sorry, Bells. I have no excuse for my negligence."

She waited to see if her brother would mention Miss Bradbury, but he said nothing. A strange feeling curled in her gut, an emotion she couldn't name, and she followed him back to the church without mention of the brewing scandals she'd overheard.

*C*aleb lingered in the hallway, a statue of shattered heartstrings and cracked hope, only long enough to be sure Mrs. Bradbury was gone. To be sure the guard would not wake. As soon as he felt secure in their privacy, with the sounds of Blythe's heartbreak still echoing off the stone around him, he made his move.

He hurried down the hall toward the cell, but with his haste came noise. His boot found a loose stone and sent it skittering across the floor. He cringed at the sound, and his heart nearly stopped when her voice lashed out.

"Who is it? Who's there?"

The harshness of her tone couldn't cover the tremor of fear. A hard knot formed in his chest. He ached to call out, to reassure her, but the knot pressed against his lungs until it hurt to breathe. Caleb wanted to close the distance to his love, but found he couldn't. It was as if Mrs. Bradbury, without his knowing, had conspired to keep him away from her daughter.

"Coward!" she shrieked. "Show yourself or be gone with you!" Metal crashed against metal as she shook her locked door. "Be gone with you," she whispered again, a plea. It crushed his already mangled heart, and he fought his stone-like limbs.

He stumbled when his legs finally moved, nearly toppling to the ground. Once he was moving, though, he couldn't stop. It felt as though Blythe drew him forward by an invisible thread, pulling harder and harder until he couldn't fight it a second longer. She was just beyond the corner. Another step.

Shock spread across her face at the sight of him. Her eyes grew wide, and she collapsed into tears. "Caleb?" Blythe sagged against her cell, holding onto the bars to keep herself upright. Grief strained her words. "Have you come to kill me?"

With careful steps, Caleb crossed the distance between them. He stopped short of touching her, some small warning niggling at his mind. "Of course not."

"Then why?" Blythe wiped at the tears, but more fell to take their place.

Seeing her like this, Caleb couldn't stop the hand that reached for her, couldn't stop the fingers that brushed along the side of her face and trailed her jaw. He had to fix this. She hadn't done the things everyone said. She was innocent, and he would find proof beyond the truth in his gut. "Can you think of no other reason?"

Blythe leaned into his hand. Tears spilled over her lashes and onto his skin, tiny pinpricks of warmth. "They mean to kill me."

"I know." He leaned forward so their foreheads touched between the cold metal bars. Something electric spread across his skin at the feel of her. He wished so desperately for the bars between them to disappear. He wanted to hold her in his arms while he promised to fix everything. "You are not alone, Blythe. You are never alone."

He tilted her chin skyward and captured her lips with his. Caleb kissed his beloved with all the urgency and grief wrapped around his broken heart. Blythe returned the kiss, but only for a moment. She pulled away, fresh pain twisting her features.

The look she gave him reminded Caleb so much of his sister's fear after one of their father's drunken rages. The memory drew Mirabel's face to mind, first with her eyes alight with laughter. Then, in a flash, the lifeless stare of her corpse.

"Mirabel…" Her name fell from his lips like a reflex. It hung in the air. A question he wouldn't ask. An accusation he could never make. A prayer to return to a better time. Caleb would give anything to remove that final memory of his sister from his mind.

Blythe reached for him through the bars. "I am so, so sorry, Caleb. I know she meant the world to you."

He took her hand, placed it over his heart. "The town may believe my father's lies, but I know you did not do this." He paused. In the distance, rats scuttled across the stone floors. Their squeaky voices sent chills down his spine. "I will find the truth."

"No, Caleb, you can't. I—" Blythe pulled her hand away and clutched it to her chest. Pain flickered across her brow.

"Hey," Caleb soothed, reaching through the bars to hold her free hand. "I made you a promise. I am yours until my dying breath. I will fix this."

"Caleb, please. You're not listening." Blythe pulled away and stepped out of reach, hands clenched into fists. "You cannot save me."

"So, help me. Tell me what you remember of that night."

Blythe dropped her gaze to the hard stone floor. "What if I am not worth saving?"

"Of course you are." Caleb wrapped his fingers around the cold bars. "Please, Blythe. Whatever happened, I need to know. I can search for evidence, and when you explain to the court what really happened, I'll have proof. You just have to tell me—"

"But there's nothing!" A sob caught in Blythe's throat. "All I remember is being at home with my mother and then waking up *here*." She gestured to the cell, fresh tears spilling down her cheeks. "I have no proof, Caleb. It might have been me."

"It wasn't," Caleb said, as much to reassure himself as her. He remembered clearly the violence wrought upon Blythe when Mirabel was discovered. He should have known her memory could be compromised. "Please, just try to remember. It might take time, but you have to try."

"It won't make a difference." Blythe exhaled in a huff. "The jury has already cast their judgment. They will only twist my words to their own ends."

"But we must do something."

Her eyes gleamed, shining almost black in the dim light. "I never said I would do *nothing*."

*M*rs. Sanderson rocked in her chair, the needles clicking in her hands as she knit. Eight-year-old Caleb sat by her feet, soaking in the warmth of the fire. His father had recently gifted him with a grown-up copy of the *Book of Light*, full of the One God's complete teachings. He held the leather-bound book with care. It was too heavy to hold, so he rested it against his crossed legs.

"Mrs. Sanderson? Why can't unmarried women be near children?" He'd never heard of such a thing before. Was Miss Sanderson, Mrs. Sanderson's daughter, breaking the rules by spending time with him and his sister, Mirabel? He glanced across the room, where the unmarried woman was helping Mirabel improve her sewing.

"What's that, dear?" The old woman, who smelled of apples and cinnamon, paused in her work and leaned forward to read over his shoulder . She fell silent for several moments before finally clearing her throat. "Being *with child* is different than being near them."

"But what does it mean?" he insisted.

She ruffled his red curls. "I think that's a question better answered by your parents." Mrs. Sanderson rocked back, the chair squeaking against the floor as she resumed her knitting.

Heat flushed Caleb's cheeks. He didn't like being wrong. Not knowing things made him feel itchy and too hot, but he knew better than to contradict his elders.

"Ouch!" Mirabel, who had recently turned six, shouted and threw her sewing project to the floor. "I hate this!" She stuck a bleeding finger in her mouth.

"Miss Mirabel, we can't throw things when we get upset. Sewing takes patience and practice to master." Miss Sanderson retrieved the abandoned fabric and needle, her long blonde curls brushing against the floor.

Mirabel scrambled away and crossed her arms. "I don't want to practice sewing. I want to play music!"

Mrs. Sanderson continued rocking in her chair, undisturbed. A soft chuckle escaped her lips.

Caleb set his father's book aside and rose to his feet. "Bells, you must be nice to Miss Sanderson. Mother said so."

"Mother lets me play the harpsichord." Mirabel stamped her foot, growing dangerously close to a full tantrum. "It's not fair. I want to go home."

"We can't, Bells. Mother isn't feeling well." Caleb tugged at his sister's arms until she uncrossed them. "I'll read to you until Father retrieves us. Would you like that?" He had also brought along a children's version of the *Book of Light*. Mirabel always loved those stories.

Mirabel studied her pricked finger and glanced back at Miss Sanderson, who was still holding her sewing things. After a long pause, Mirabel pulled on her twin braids and nodded.

Caleb returned to his place in front of the fire, and

Mirabel settled beside him. He reached for the thin, cracked book that used to be his and flipped back to the first page. He glanced over at Mirabel, whose tiny face flushed with heat, and focused his attention on the words in the book. "Before the One God shed his light on us, we lived in darkness. He—"

Bang!

The front door burst open. Winter winds whipped through the house, carrying swirls of snow. Caleb shivered and wrapped his arms around Mirabel, shielding her from whatever danger had arrived.

Mrs. Sanderson stood from her rocker and set her knitting aside. "Mr. Walcott? Is everything all right?"

At the mention of his father's name, Caleb released Mirabel and stood. He shivered when he saw the man in the doorway. He looked like his father in all ways except one: his expression was harsher than Caleb had ever seen. "Papa?"

His father stormed into the house, face pinched and eyes bright with tears. Father scooped up Mirabel, who squirmed and cried in his grip. Caleb held his father's outstretched hand, trembling.

Pastor Hawthorne stood on the other side of the door with a cluster of men from town.

"What's happening? Where's Mother?" Caleb shivered in the cold air, wishing for his cloak. But it was on the other side of the room, and his father was dragging him toward the open door.

"She's gone."

Mirabel stopped squirming. "Where did she go? Can we go, too?"

"No." Their father shook his head, and tears spilled down his cheeks. "Death has taken her from us."

Caleb's breath caught in his throat. Death? No, his

mother couldn't be gone. She was on the mend. Everyone promised she was getting better. They said she just needed a few days' rest without her children. Tears stung in his eyes, and he buried his face into his father's side before they could fall.

"I'm so very sorry for your loss, Mr. Walcott." Mrs. Sanderson stepped forward, arms outstretched to offer comfort. "My daughter and I can watch the children while you tend to your affairs."

Father yanked Caleb away. "Stay back, *witch*. You will not harm more of my family."

Mrs. Sanderson went pale at his words. "Mr. Walcott, you can't possibly believe I had anything to do with your wife's death. I tried to help her."

The younger Sanderson woman rushed forward. "Mother would never hurt her. Or the children. You must know that!"

"Do not lie to a servant of the One God!" Father's voice boomed through the room, and Caleb had to stop himself from clasping his hands over his ears. "I know you hastened my wife's death with your moon-cursed teas and dark rituals."

"We did no such thing," Miss Sanderson argued. "Perhaps if her husband had a more tender hand, she wouldn't have fallen ill!"

"Enough! Pastor Hawthorne, please take these wretched women away." Father turned his back on the Sanderson women, pulling Caleb roughly by the arm to follow. "Don't believe the witches' lies. They poisoned my wife as surely as they'll poison my children against me."

"But they didn't do it, Papa. Mrs. Sanderson would never hurt us. She's nice." Caleb tried to pull his arm free, but his father's grip only tightened.

"See? Already the witches have corrupted my son!"

Pastor Hawthorne and nearly a dozen men swarmed into the house. "Bind them!" Pastor Hawthorne shouted, and the men tied rope about the ladies' wrists. "Gag them and bring them to the magistrate. We must prepare for the trial at once."

Mrs. Sanderson tried to protest, but one of the men tied a cloth scarf across her mouth, so she couldn't weave any other dark curses with her words. Her daughter squirmed and fought, shoving her elbow into the gut of one of the men, but others took his place and pushed the girl out of her home.

In an instant, they were gone.

His father forced Caleb to attend the trial. It lasted only two days.

Caleb watched as the Sandersons hanged.

ELEVEN WEEKS BEFORE THE MURDER

For ten years, Caleb tried to forget everything that happened in the days and weeks after his mother's death.

The arguments with his father.

The pain of a palm across his face.

Watching two women dangle from coarse ropes.

But ever since he'd walked Blythe home from the harvest festival, memories had invaded his waking moments and stalked his dreams. Despite all the years he tried to forget, Blythe's reminders brought the past into razor-sharp focus. Including his embarrassing misunderstanding about what it meant for a woman to be *with child*.

Yet more than his embarrassment about unwed mothers, Caleb remembered Miss Sanderson's bitter accusation.

Perhaps if her husband had a more tender hand, she wouldn't have fallen ill!

Caleb hadn't known then what the younger woman meant, but now as an adult, he understood the implication. Though he was no stranger to his father's rage, he'd always thought the anger was born of his mother's death. He never saw any marks on his mother, and the pastor never laid a hand on Mirabel.

Isn't it more likely that a natural illness took her?

There is so much that our doctors cannot yet cure.

Blythe's words followed him like a shadow, knocking his understanding of the past off balance He needed to know the truth of his mother's passing, but he had few options at his disposal. Caleb couldn't speak to the pastor—that would only lead to a black eye and bloody nose. Asking the new town doctor wouldn't do any good, either. Caleb couldn't risk his father learning about his questions, never mind that the doctor wasn't around when Mother died. Furthermore, Isaac had fallen ill recently and demanded the doctor's full attention.

But there was one place Caleb could search.

The small enclave at the back of the courthouse couldn't be called a proper library, but the little room housed the only public collection of texts in town. Four rickety wooden shelves held unsorted stacks of books, dumped there when a relative passed and those remaining had no use or space to keep them.

Rumor had it, the previous doctor's medical collection had ended up here.

Somewhere.

Caleb searched the stacks of old tomes, each covered in more dust than the last, brushing cobwebs away to better read the cracked spines. Somewhere in this mess of secular texts, Caleb would find his answers.

The first two bookshelves turned up nothing useful, and Caleb maneuvered his way around the small table in the center of the room. At the third shelf, he passed over thick journals that charted the weather and crop cycles, disregarded a collection of recipes that were hardly legible, until around the back of that third shelf, he finally found the medical texts.

There were too many to carry back to the church or across town to his family's small home, so he gathered as many as he could and turned to take them to the table.

"Mr. Walcott?"

The soft voice startled Caleb, and he nearly dropped the books to the floor. He secured his grip, and when he peered around the stack, his heart gave a sudden lurch. "Miss Bradbury? What are you doing here?"

"I could ask the same of you." Blythe reached out and took the top few books from Caleb's arms, unblocking his view of her. "I've been here several times this month, but it's the first I've seen of you." She turned and set his selections on the table.

Caleb followed, trying desperately to think of something clever to say. "But it all looked untouched. There's dust everywhere." He stifled a cringe. So much for clever.

Blythe didn't seem to mind, though. She slipped toward the back of the room. "That's because the best titles are over here." She disappeared behind the farthest shelf and reappeared with a thick book covered in cracked, graying leather. A smile quirked at her lips as she settled in one of the three chairs at the table. "You do know it's usually best to read one book at a time, right?"

Warmth creeped up Caleb's neck, but Blythe's tone was light, and he took the seat opposite her. The last time he'd seen her, she promised to consider his friendship. Perhaps this was where they could start. "Mind if I join you?"

"So long as your mountain doesn't topple over on me." She opened her own text and settled in to read, her loose hair falling forward to cover half her face.

Caleb opened the first of the medical texts, looking for

something that would explain his mother's illness and sudden decline. Yet he couldn't keep his attention focused on the words and inked images. He found himself glancing up each time Blythe turned a page, watching her slender fingers brush along the aged paper. The way her brow creased with concentration. The way—

Blythe looked up from her reading and tucked her hair behind one ear. "Perhaps the customs are different in Brekham, but in most places I've been, it's considered rude to stare."

"I'm sorry." Caleb lowered his gaze, even though there was no bite in Blythe's words. "I was simply curious..."

"About?"

"What brought you to our tiny library."

Blythe sat up straighter in her chair, like she was steeling herself for an argument. "I want to know how it works."

"How what works?" Caleb raised his gaze to Blythe's and let his book fall shut.

She smiled, and it was like the unfurling of a rare flower. "Everything." The word came out more breath than substance, but when Caleb returned her grin, Blythe leaned close. "I want to understand it all. Why the moon and stars cross our sky. How to predict an oncoming storm. The histories that brought us to where we are today. I don't want anything to be beyond my comprehension."

"I don't think it's possible to know everything," Caleb said, enchanted by Blythe's naked ambition, "but I'm inspired knowing you intend to try."

This time, it was Blythe who looked away. Blythe who had color creep into her cheeks. "And what of you?" she asked, pointing to his stack of books. "What is it you want to know?"

Caleb reopened his medical text. "Nothing quite so

extraordinary as your pursuits." Nerves twisted his insides, his words weighed down by the past he sought to understand and the friendship he so wanted to endure. "I'm looking for answers about my mother's death."

His whispered words hung between them.

Slowly, Blythe reached forward and rested her hand on his. "I hope you find the answers you seek." She held his gaze for one second, two, and then her attention flicked away and she withdrew her touch. She returned to her book, to her studies.

Caleb tried to do the same. He flipped through page after page, but nothing left an impression.

Nothing but the feel of her hand on his.

TESTIMONY OF THE BREKHAM TRIO

For the second day of the trial, the morning witnesses—the Pratchett twins and their cousin, Edonie Redd—asked to testify as a group. They swore to Magistrate Hawthorne that they feared for their safety and would only speak up if they could take the stand together.

The magistrate agreed after thorough assurances that the women would maintain the level of decorum appropriate for court. Though they promised to cause no trouble, a sour note hung to the air as the jurors settled into their seats. Some wondered if their testimony was appropriate, with the twins' father sitting among the jury. Yet no one dared speak while the three women huddled together along the right side of the aisle.

Moments later, Blythe trailed into the room behind her guard. The rough twine that bound her hands shifted, revealing a wooden amulet carved with the One God's sun. Perhaps, some thought, the witch hoped to curry the One God's favor. Perhaps she wished to convert.

It was too late to save her from the gallows, but perhaps

their merciful god would cleanse and embrace her in death.

Caleb glanced over his shoulder as the witch approached, and Blythe shifted her gaze. When their eyes met, something flashed between them. There was no fear. No tension. The rest of Brekham faded into dust, irrelevant in the face of their connection.

The moment ended when Blythe passed the minister's son and returned her attention to the magistrate at the head of the courtroom. Her eyes gleamed with silver: dark, dangerous, and unafraid.

There was nothing so dangerous as a witch who greeted her executioners with no fear in her heart. Everyone knew that. Many in attendance noticed the shift in Blythe's posture, and they held their breath. Watching. Waiting.

Finally, as Blythe settled onto her chair, the air cooled and the court relaxed.

The magistrate cleared his throat. "Pastor Lewis, please call your witnesses. My back aches, and I have no patience for delay this morning."

The prosecutor stood and straightened imagined wrinkles on his vest. "Gentlemen of the jury, today I present to you Misses Verity and Grace Pratchett and Miss Edonie Redd. Born to the most respectable of your local families, these young women were raised to be friendly, accommodating, and kind. Unfortunately, they had the grave misfortune of trying to share that warmth and light with Miss Bradbury. Before they discovered her wickedness, of course. This morning, they will detail harrowing stories of the witch's power, used in broad daylight, with no concern for the One God's laws." He motioned to the girls, and they stood.

The Pratchett twins wore their dark hair in intricate

braids pinned tight to the base of their skulls. Edonie's auburn hair fell in a single plait over her right shoulder. The young women glided down the aisle, keeping as much distance between them and the witch as possible.

Caleb leaned forward, elbows resting at his knees. He rubbed his temples and watched women he'd known since childhood settle behind the witness stand.

Pastor Lewis resumed his usual pacing. "Ladies, you saw Miss Bradbury on several occasions this autumn, correct?"

The girls nodded. Verity spoke a soft "yes" to the jurors.

"And when did you first suspect her witchery?" The prosecuting minister twisted his wrists. They popped and crackled in the silent court.

Grace wet her lips and glared at the accused. "We first noticed she was odd at the harvest festival, but being generous children of the One God, we tried to welcome her."

Verity nodded. "She kept her distance, like she thought herself above us, and whenever anyone approached, she answered before they could voice their question."

"It was as if the witch plucked the knowledge from their minds," Edonie finished. The plainest of the trio glanced at her cousins, and they nodded their agreement.

The prosecutor tilted his head. "Are you saying Miss Bradbury possesses the ability to read our thoughts?"

"We are," Grace said.

"It was only the *first* sign of her witchery," Verity added.

Caleb curled his fingers into fists so tight his hands trembled. Had his father not been at his side, he might have sprung from his seat to contradict the witnesses. No one had the power they suggested. No one.

"Is there more? What other proof can you present of Miss Bradbury's guilt?" Pastor Lewis leaned against the railing and considered the jurors before him. "Explain to these men what you have seen."

The girls were silent a moment, until the sound of shuffling fabric shifted through the air. Edonie jolted as if kicked. Her face reddened, and she cleared her throat. "She… she bewitched the men of Brekham."

The Pratchett twins nodded. "They *all* fawned over her," Grace said.

"They fell over themselves to escort her home," added Verity.

In the back of the court, heads bobbed in agreement. Many had witnessed the town's men—both young and old —paying closer attention to Blythe than other woman her age. The minister's eyes grew dark. He glared at his son. The town knew who had ultimately escorted Miss Bradbury home after the harvest festival.

Grace scanned the captive courtroom. "And one time, I…" Her voice grew quiet. Around her, the court went silent and still. They hardly dared to breathe for fear of missing her next words. "I saw her *curse* one of the finest young men in Brekham."

Pastor Lewis froze. The man knew something of a witch's curse, had personal experience of the pain it could cause. He approached the witnesses, face ashen with fear. "Tell us, Miss Pratchett. Whom did she curse?"

Grace leveled her gaze on Blythe. "She cursed Mr. Isaac Carrier!" Her arm flung out, and though he had not attended any previous sessions, she pointed out Caleb's best friend, where he stood near the back of the room.

Isaac rose from his seat. "Miss Pratchett speaks the truth!" He pulled up the sleeve of his shirt. "I tried to speak to Miss Bradbury at the market, but she muttered something and turned away." He held a scarred arm up for all to see. "The next day, I was taken with pox. I was confined to my home for a month."

The courtroom erupted. Isaac glared at Caleb before nodding solemnly to the girls on the witness stand. The villagers squirmed in their chairs, distancing themselves from the witch and the boy she had cursed. The magistrate banged his gavel upon his bench, but the hysteria grew louder.

Caleb stood and leaned over the railing that separated him from the accused. "Say something, Blythe. Set the record straight." His voice was thick with worry. "Show them the truth."

Blythe twisted in her chair as the minister yanked Caleb back into his seat. She met his eyes, but slowly, she shook her head.

It was not yet time.

The sun sank on the western horizon, painting the sky in reds and golds. Caleb swept the last bit of dirt into the dustpan his sister held. The minister had tasked them with cleaning the church—again—while he traveled to the neighboring town of Rowley to meet with Pastor Lewis and other local clergymen.

Mirabel stood and emptied the dust into a bin. "I'm surprised you're still here, Caleb. I thought you'd abandon me the moment Father left," she said, her back to him. "You're hardly around anymore."

"What do you mean? We're together most hours of the day." Caleb went upstairs and returned the broom to the supply closet, guilt climbing up his ribcage. He hadn't realized Mirabel noticed his near-daily absences. She was always busy at the piano when he slipped away.

"Don't do that," she said, following him up the stairs. "Don't fake confusion with me. I've seen the way you disappear the moment father isn't paying attention." She studied him, lips flattening into a thin line. "You're visiting *her,* aren't you?"

"I don't—"

"Miss Bradbury. I heard the twins talking about you two at the harvest festival."

Though Caleb said nothing, his burning cheeks were answer enough.

Mirabel tossed the dust pan into the closet. "It's true, isn't it? You *are* seeing Miss Bradbury."

"It's not what you think, Bells."

"Of course it isn't. I don't know *what* to think. Since when do you keep secrets from me?" Her lower lip trembled, and she crossed her arms against her chest. "Do you think I'll run to Father to spill your secrets?"

"Bells, no." Caleb rested his hands on his sister's narrow shoulders. "Of course I don't."

"Then why?" Mirabel gripped their mother's necklace, rubbing her thumb along the rare amber stone.

"There's simply nothing worth sharing. I've been visiting the library. Occasionally, Miss Bradbury is there as well."

In truth, it was more than occasionally. Caleb had seen Blythe nearly every day since that first encounter in the small room. They talked about everything, enclosed in that little world of books. Blythe shared highlights from her current obsession—studying the constellations—and Caleb explained the most plausible medical explanations for his mother's death, though he was certain he hadn't found the exact cause yet.

"Library?" Mirabel released their mother's necklace and tilted her head. Since when do we have a library?"

Caleb chuckled and closed the closet door, leaning against the sturdy wood. "I suppose calling it a library is too generous. It's that tiny enclave off the courthouse."

"Oh." Mirabel's brow crinkled. "So, what happened

tonight? With Father gone, there's nothing stopping you from… whatever it is you're doing at the *library*."

"We read, Bells. That's it. And with Father gone, someone had to watch over you and tend to the church," he said. But when his sister glared at him, Caleb sighed. "She had other obligations tonight."

"Oh?" Mirabel flashed him a crooked grin. "And what might those be?"

"I didn't ask." Caleb crossed to the other side of the balcony and leaned against the railing. His mood, already low from cleaning, grew sour. He had, in fact, asked Blythe why she needed to cancel their usual plans, but she hadn't given him a clear answer.

Mirabel peered out the stained-glass window and sighed dreamily. "I bet she has a romantic evening planned with one of the other Brekham men. Someone brave enough to ask for more than a reading partner." A laugh danced off her lips. "I bet she's with Isaac! Sally saw them talking at the market yesterday."

Caleb gritted his teeth until his jaw ached. Isaac had only just recovered from his sudden illness. What was he doing wandering the market to talk with Blythe? Especially when he was *supposed* to be winning over Miss Pratchett after his absence. "It's none of my business," Caleb said, even as he felt the bitter sting of rejection. "Miss Bradbury may choose her company as she pleases."

"Perhaps she chooses the company of no one," Mirabel mumbled from the window.

"Come on, Mirabel. We should get home."

"No, Caleb, wait." Mirabel motioned toward the window. "Look."

With a sigh, Caleb crossed the room and glanced out the window. The stained glass painted the outside world in hues of purple and blue. Outside, Blythe headed toward the forest behind the church, guided by the light of the full moon.

Where is she going? Why didn't she tell me?

"What Miss Bradbury does in her own time is her business, Bells. Let's go." When Caleb turned, Mirabel was nowhere to be found. *By the One God's light…* "Mirabel!"

Caleb raced down the steps as Mirabel disappeared out the back door. He hurried after her, the chill of night harsh against his skin even as the moon illuminated the path before him. He caught Mirabel by the elbow at the edge of the forest. "What are you doing? You can't chase after strangers in the forest."

"She isn't a stranger." Mirabel yanked from his grip and straightened to her full height, which wasn't much. She barely came up to Caleb's shoulders. "Miss Bradbury is a neighbor of the church, *and* you admitted to spending time with her yourself. I'll be fine, Caleb."

"I'm still responsible for your safety. You shouldn't wander the forest alone."

Mirabel cast him a withering look and continued into the trees. "And what of *her* safety? What kind of neighbors would we be if we left her to die out there?"

"Have you considered that she might want to be alone?" Caleb asked as he hurried to keep up with his sister. Overhead, the leaves had begun to blush red with the arrival of autumn. "If she wanted company, she would have asked for it." *She could have invited me.* "Father would skin us alive if he knew what we were doing."

"You worry too much," Mirabel whispered. "Now, hush. Or else she'll hear us."

Easy for her to say. Father never raised a hand against Mirabel. Instead, he channeled all his drunken rage onto his son. Not that Caleb would have it any other way. He'd take three times the abuse if it kept his sister safe. He dodged the tree branches as best he could, but still a few tore at his cloak and whipped at his face.

The silence between the Walcott siblings grew heavy, the forest filled with the hum of insects and the rustle of scurrying animals. As they worked deeper into the thicket of trees, another sound joined the chorus of nature.

Soft chanting swept through the trees, an airy voice Caleb had to assume belonged to Blythe. Who else would visit the forest in the dark of night? Ahead of him, Mirabel paused, clinging to a thick tree. She peered around its trunk, and Caleb shivered. The air around him felt thick with energy, like the charge before a storm. Except… not a single cloud dotted the sky. The stars had shone brightly outside the forest, before the branches covered their tiny lights.

Caleb settled beside Mirabel and peered around the tree.

Blythe stood in the center of a clearing. Around her, white candles burned in a circle. She tilted her face to the exposed sky, her black hair cascading down her back. She held her arms out, palms up, as quiet words spilled from her lips. She looked ethereal. Powerful. Magical.

And magic meant danger.

"Bells, go back to the church," Caleb whispered, his voice barely audible in the tiny space between them.

"Why?" Mirabel eyes were fixed on Blythe. Color rose in her cheeks, deep enough that it was visible in the dark of the forest.

Caleb tugged his sister away from the edge of the trees. "It's not safe. You need to go back to the church."

"But if you're staying—"

"Go. Now." His words were harsh as anger burned inside him. All the hours he'd spent trying to find a medical cause for his mother's death, all the times Blythe had insisted those tried for witchcraft were innocent, and yet *this* is what Blythe did when she was alone? Did she think him a fool?

Mirabel placed a hand on his arm. "Caleb…"

His sister's touch softened the edge of his anger. But why wasn't Mirabel afraid? She studied the *Book of Light* just as much as he did. She should recognize the signs.

Unless… unless she did and wanted enough proof to charge Blythe herself.

A tremor of fear snaked through his anger. Caleb nudged his sister back the way they'd come. "Go. And not a word to anyone about what you saw. Promise me."

Tears sparkled in Mirabel's eyes. "Why don't you trust me?"

"Bells—"

"Forget it." She turned and stalked away through the forest, returning to the church. To safety.

Caleb rubbed his hands along his arms. *I'm sorry, Bells.* He hated to see her angry with him, but better angry than in danger.

Better angry than to witness any more of Blythe's treachery.

aleb waited.

And waited.

Time stretched on, and Caleb kept track only by the depth of stiffness in his limbs and the growing flame of anger in his heart. He should have known something was wrong the moment Blythe defended the Sandersons. Her empathy for the witches should have been a warning bell. He was a fool to let Blythe convince him to reopen old wounds, to dive back into the pain of his mother's death.

In the clearing before him, Blythe tilted her face toward the heavens and whispered promises to the night sky. Her voice rose to a crescendo—though Caleb couldn't make out the words. Blythe raised her arms like she meant to embrace the moon. As she flicked her wrists, a gust of wind kicked up and tore through the branches, making the leaves rattle and dance.

Her candles flickered but remained lit.

When Blythe lowered her arms and turned to face Caleb's hiding spot, her skin glowed with the light of the full moon, a silvery sheen across already pale skin. She danced from candle to candle, moving through the circle as if to music only she could hear. Her body glided with fluid grace, like a river winding through a forest, as her loose hair swung with wild abandon behind her.

There were so many little signs that Caleb should have noticed. The loose hair. The lack of a visible sun charm around her neck or wrist. The way she kept herself separate from nearly everyone else in town. Each piece fit together into a damning puzzle.

Blythe's ritual beneath the moon confirmed it.

She had to be a witch.

Caleb squeezed his hands into fists. In the clearing, Blythe arched her back, exposing her slender throat to the sky. He hated that a part of him still searched for a different explanation, something that wouldn't send her to the gallows.

The gallows…

Could he truly send her there?

Blythe spun around the circle, faster and faster, and the energy in the forest intensified. The small hairs on the nape of Caleb's neck raised as goosebumps prickled his skin. He rubbed his arms and noticed that the stiffness had eased from his legs. Which was… strange.

A moment later, Blythe flung her arms toward the sky and the static feeling disappeared in a rush. Caleb stumbled forward, leaning against the tree that served as his hiding place. His body felt like a dishrag that had been wrung dry. Wilted and exhausted. He watched as Blythe blew out her candles and gathered them up into a cloth bag. As she walked to the eastern edge of the clearing to hide the bag beneath a bush, Caleb's mind went to his mother. His anger stirred again, and he flung himself away from the tree.

Branches snapped beneath his feet as he pushed into the clearing. "What kind of fool do you think I am?"

Blythe whirled around, a panicked scream catching in her throat. When she spotted Caleb, she clutched at her chest. "Caleb, I— What are you doing here?" she asked, voice trembling with fear.

He ignored the sound of his given name on her lips. "Did it amuse you," he said instead, taking a cautious step toward the witch, "to watch me fall for your lies? Was my pain nothing but a joke to you?"

The witch shook her head. "I never lied. I—"

"Don't." The word punctured the shrinking space between them, and Caleb stopped. Grief tightened around his heart, shoving aside his anger. "You let me believe that innocent women hanged for a crime they didn't commit. You let me research my mother's death as if the cause wasn't already known. And all the while, you were..." Caleb faltered, unable to say the words aloud.

"I was *what*, Mr. Walcott?" A sharp edge entered Blythe's tone, and when Caleb glanced up, her posture was ramrod straight. She held his gaze with a fierceness that shocked him. "If you have an accusation to make, spit it out."

"You could hang for what I saw tonight."

This time, it was Blythe who stepped closer. "Is that what you want? Another woman dead at the hands of the Walcott family, all because you're afraid of stories meant to frighten children into minding their parents?"

Caleb bristled at her tone, but he didn't back down from the challenge in her gaze. "I don't want your death. I want answers."

"About what?"

"Everything." When Blythe scoffed at his response, Caleb stepped forward until there was mere inches between them. "You ridicule our beliefs, you claim witches don't exist, and yet I find you performing a ritual beneath the full moon. And don't try to deny it," he added quickly when she parted her lips as if to speak. "I *felt something*. I know it was more than a dance. There was power in this clearing, power that doesn't come from the One God."

Blythe studied him for several moments before speaking. "And this makes me a witch in your mind."

"I have no other word for it." A twinge of irritation stoked the embers of anger within him. "And if you would stop talking around the issues and simply *explain* what I saw—"

"Or what? You'll run home to your minister father and have me sentenced to death?" Blythe crossed her arms and shoved past Caleb, walking toward the edge of the forest. "I will not let you blackmail me into exposing every piece of my life. I have never hurt anyone, and I never will."

Caleb chased after Blythe's retreating form. "And after your lies, I'm supposed to accept that?"

"I will only say this once more," Blythe said, whirling around so fast to face Caleb that he nearly crashed into her. "I have never lied to you, and I don't intend to start now, but I cannot tell you the things you wish to know. If that means Mother and I have to leave Brekham, so be it."

"Leave?" Caleb's heart gave a painful lurch. "Why would you leave?"

Blythe raised an eyebrow. "I'm certainly not going to stick around so you can have me killed."

Another twinge of pain tightened Caleb's chest. "I don't want your death."

"So, what will you do then, without the answers you crave?" Blythe tilted her head, considering him. "Men like you don't allow women like me to live in peace."

"Men like me?"

"Ministers' sons. Followers of the One God." Blythe paused, worrying at her lower lip. "What will it be, Mr. Walcott? Do Mother and I have to leave or can we safely stay in Brekham?"

Caleb weighed his options. The minister would be furious if he ever found out Caleb hid a secret like this. Furious enough to leave a patchwork of bruises and maybe even a few scars. But if he explained what he saw, the Bradbury women would surely hang, and Caleb didn't want that, either.

And then there was the issue of what little Mirabel had seen...

"Mr. Walcott?"

"I'm sorry, Miss Bradbury. I don't know."

Blythe fell back a step. "Well then, I suppose it's best if we keep our distance going forward."

Caleb hated the thought, but he nodded anyway. "I think that's wise."

"Right." Blythe ducked her head and swiped her hand across her cheek. She turned and walked a few paces before ultimately pausing to glance over her shoulder. "I really wish you hadn't followed me tonight," she said softly, her words gentle like the babbling of a brook. "I quite liked spending time with you."

As Blythe slipped away through the trees, Caleb felt the stab of her words. He felt the loss of their blossoming friendship as it withered on the vine. As it sprouted thorns that dug into the flesh of his heart.

He stood alone in the woods until the coolness penetrated all the way to his bones and he was sure Blythe was safe in her home. Then, finally, the minister's son walked back to the church, trying and failing to quell the unwelcome hurt in his soul.

The townsfolk filled the church to bursting It was warmer than normal for spring, and the crush of bodies added to the heat in the air. Sweat trickled down Caleb's face, and he pulled at the collar of his scratchy dress shirt. He sat in the front row with his sister, watching their father on the raised platform.

Pastor Hawthorne was now Magistrate Hawthorne. His predecessor had passed away. In a few moments, their father would cease to be a student of the One God.

He would become Pastor.

Magistrate Hawthorne dipped his aged thumb into oil blessed by the One God's sun and pressed it against his successor's forehead. "Do you, Tobias Walcott, swear to uphold the laws of the One God, to be His vessel, and to lead the people of Brekham along the lighted path?"

Tobias Walcott bowed his head. "By the One God, this I swear."

"Then drink of our holiest wine," Magistrate Hawthorne said, tipping the chalice toward the new pastor.

"Drink and become our Pastor. Guide us as we serve the One God."

Caleb's father reached for the chalice and drank deeply of the wine. A little dribbled down his chin, and he wiped it away, red staining the cuff of his white sleeve.

Applause broke out beside Caleb, and he hastened to join the growing cacophony of approval. He clapped until his hands hurt. Mirabel joined for a moment but gave up and gripped the edge of the pew, her feet swinging back and forth above the ground.

The rest of the night rushed by in a blur of food and celebration. Many of the townsfolk congratulated Caleb, and at first, he couldn't understand why. *He* hadn't done anything extraordinary. When he asked Mr. Carrier why everyone was so proud of him, Isaac's father explained that Caleb was next in line to run the church. That his life was going to change, too.

His father hadn't told him that. Caleb had been studying the *Book of Light* for years, but grow up to be a pastor himself? Didn't he get a choice?

Caleb knew better than to ask any of that aloud. Instead, he focused on the food and the best part of the evening: hanging out with Isaac. The boys—eleven-years-old and feeling on the cusp of manhood—snuck upstairs away from the other children. But eventually, even Isaac needed to go home, and Caleb was left alone in the rapidly emptying church.

A church that would someday be *his*.

As the sun dipped low in the sky, Caleb bid farewell to the Pratchett family—the last to leave the church—and went back inside to search for his sister. He found Bells asleep in one of the pews, twin braids spilling over the side. Caleb grabbed his cloak from near the door and draped it over her. He scanned the empty room for signs of his father, but he was not in the nave, nor was he on the raised platform.

Caleb wandered down the dim hallway. "Papa?" No one answered, but Caleb noticed a flicker of candlelight under the study door. "Papa, are you in there?" Glass clinked. A chair skidded across the floor.

When Caleb swung open the door, he found his father slumped over his new desk, a near-empty glass of wine in his hand. His father brought the chalice to his lips and drained the rest of the red liquid.

"Papa? Can we go home now? Bells is already asleep and…" Caleb trailed off as his father refilled his drink. "I thought the wine was only for services?"

His father sat up straighter, glass still in hand. He turned and glared at Caleb.

"Papa?" Caleb shrank back toward the hall.

"It's Pastor Walcott now, boy. Do not question me." He hurled the chalice toward Caleb, and it shattered against the wall. Cold wine soaked Caleb's shirt, and bits of glass bit at his bare hands and cheeks. With a final bleary-eyed glance at his son, the minister hunched over his desk and reached for the bottle. His fingers traced the edges of a charcoal drawing of his dead wife.

Caleb slunk out of the room, shaking the shards of glass from his clothes. Tears stung in his eyes, but he sniffed and brushed them away.

When he returned to the nave, he found Mirabel sitting up and shrugging away his cloak.

"Come on, Bells. We should get home before dark." He grabbed his cloak from where it had slipped to the floor and swung it on.

Mirabel rubbed her eyes and plopped to the floor. "Where's Papa?"

Caleb tightened his cloak and swiped at the wetness beneath his eyes. "The minister will meet us at home."

TESTIMONY OF PASTOR TOBIAS
WALCOTT

"Gentlemen of the jury, today I call forth my final witness on the matter of witchcraft. His testimony is infused with the light and authority of the One God, and he will prove that Miss Bradbury's heart belongs to the dark, that in her veins flows the wickedness of unnatural magic."

Pastor Lewis, dressed in a suit as gray as storm clouds, stood before the court as a poet before his audience. His dark eyes were bright behind his spectacles, which glinted in the afternoon light.

"I call forth... Pastor Tobias Walcott."

Blythe stiffened. Though her body didn't move, her gaze shifted to follow the minister as he took the stand. The man had aged a decade in the days since his daughter's death, the lines on his face deeper than his years. The gray at his temples seemed to climb higher into his hair with each breath.

The pastor angled his body toward the witch and glared at the son who sat behind her. The old man seemed incapable of any expression other than those married to anger or pain.

Magistrate Hawthorne nodded to the prosecutor. "Proceed promptly, Pastor Lewis. My wife would like me home for supper."

With a nod, the prosecuting minister turned to his witness. His lips curled into a gentle smile, one designed for the bereaved. "I'm certain all in attendance know you well, sir, but please, state for the record your connection to this case." Pastor Lewis nodded at the small woman on the other side of the magistrate, her quill already flying across her parchment.

Brekham's minister cleared his throat, finally turning away from his son. "I serve the One God and keep the people of this town on the lighted path." Silence fell when he stopped speaking. The room appeared to shrink as those in the gallery leaned forward for a better view.

When his witness did not continue, Pastor Lewis prompted him further. "And the deceased? What is your connection to Miss Walcott?"

Pastor Walcott dropped his gaze. Grief pulled at his features, and he rubbed his hands over his face. "She is— she *was* my daughter." His voice cracked as he corrected himself. When he looked up, he glared daggers at Blythe. "And the witch *murdered* her."

Pastor Lewis paced before the witness stand. "We shall address the murder in due time. First, share with the court your proof of Miss Bradbury's witchery. What have you seen of her magic?"

"Nothing."

"Nothing?" The prosecutor stumbled in his pacing. When he turned to stare upon his witness, a bead of sweat ran down his face.

"You heard right, Minister. *I* witnessed no such proof."

Pastor Walcott paused and settled an icy stare upon Blythe. "But my son did."

Blythe's head snapped up, and she twisted in her chair. Her haunted eyes shifted between the aging minister on the witness stand and the young man sitting behind her, but Caleb couldn't meet her stare. His eyebrows arched skyward, lines creasing his forehead. Confusion and horror pulled at his expression as he shook his head, like he couldn't believe what he was hearing.

The prosecutor stepped toward the jury, his worry replaced by a delighted, devious smile. "Your son? What did he tell you?"

"The boy said nothing to me, but he keeps his secrets poorly hidden. I'm sure the witch has claimed his mind. She makes him forget where his loyalties *should* lie." The minister reached into the folds of his clergyman's robes and withdrew a thick book. "But he *wrote* about the witch's power."

Whispered conversation erupted through the court-house. Friends and neighbors whispered theories across the pews. The hum of their words drowned out the shocked expletive that slipped from Caleb's lips. Their attention diverted to their own conversations, no one saw Blythe twist again in her seat, her eyes filled with betrayal, screaming a silent *How could you?* at Caleb.

Bang! Bang! Bang!

Magistrate Hawthorne slammed his gavel hard against his bench. The crack of wood silenced the crowd. Caleb's hands balled into fists. Blythe's eyes seemed to glow in the dying sunlight.

The pastor opened the journal to an earmarked page. "Shall I read a passage?"

"No!" Caleb shot from his seat, fists shaking at his

sides. "You cannot steal my words and twist their meaning!"

"Sit down, young man." Magistrate Hawthorne motioned to the guard at the edge the courtroom. "Sit, or I will have you removed."

Caleb sat. Trembling. But with rage or fear only he knew for certain.

"Please, proceed." Prosecutor Lewis nodded to his witness.

The minister held the book before him, but he studied each man on the jury, one by one, as he spoke. "The entry is dated a little over two months ago. Before my daughter —" His voice broke. Pastor Walcott cleared his throat and pressed his fingers beneath his eyes. "Before the incident."

Pastor Walcott cleared his throat and began to read.

"Never in my life have I met a woman as frustrating as her. Never have I been more conflicted about what I've witnessed, about things I've been raised all my life to believe are true. There's no denying the power she wields, yet if I were to tell anyone what I saw, the town would call for her death. Simply writing that mere possibility feels dangerous and carves at my heart. I—"

"Stop!" Caleb stood and rushed the witness stand. "That's *private!*" The guard blocked his path to his father. "You have no right. There is no proof in those pages." He struggled against the larger man, but he didn't have the strength to overcome the guard's muscular bulk.

The magistrate scowled. "This court has the right to *all* evidence against the witch. I would think you, of all people, would want her punished for her crimes."

"But she didn't do it!" Caleb twisted and reached for his father, but he couldn't shake the guard's grip. He spun back toward Blythe. "Tell them! Tell them they have it wrong." The guard twisted Caleb's arm behind his back. He cried out in pain. "Tell them, Blythe, please," he begged. "Don't let them send you to the gallows for something you didn't do."

"Remove Mr. Walcott from the courtroom." Magistrate Hawthorne slammed his gavel over and over, but the noise could not dispel the pandemonium engulfing the townsfolk.

"No! Blythe, please—"

The witch watched in silence as the guard dragged Caleb through the crowd and out the door.

WRITTEN TESTIMONY OF BLYTHE BRADBURY

efore I continue, please know that I do not blame you for this end.

You tried so hard to clear my name, no matter my warnings that it would do no good. I do not fault you for the things you wrote. I hate that these men twist your love for me into something wicked. They are the wretched ones, and the universe will see them punished, if not in this life, then in the next.

Tonight, you begged for answers, and I regret than I did not give them to you. I thought I was protecting you. I thought it would be easier on your heart if you discovered the truth on your own, but I should have told you all I know. I should have trusted you. I'm so very sorry, Caleb.

During my days in this cell, I have wondered what might have happened if Mother had picked a different town. Though my life would be poorer for it—even if it were longer—I think perhaps your life would have been simpler. Surely, your sister would still be with you.

Though, perhaps, the same villains would have found another way to break your heart.

NOW

Bitter wind assaulted Caleb's face as the guard threw him down the courthouse steps. Caleb's legs gave out beneath him, and he fell, palms sliding across the cobblestone street. Loose stones tore at his flesh, peeling back layer after layer of skin. The wet heat of blood coated his hands, turning his stomach.

Caleb stumbled back to his feet and wiped the blood on his trousers, further tugging at the torn skin. Ripping it. Tearing it. He spun back toward the courthouse as the doors slammed shut. The heavy bolt clanged into place, keeping him out.

Despite the lock, Caleb still raced up the steps. His arms and hands throbbed. Blood trailed to his fingertips and dripped to the ground. His shredded palms protested as he gripped the cold metal handles and pulled.

The door shuddered but did not give way.

He was trapped outside while his father persecuted the girl he loved. While the minister used *his words* to hammer the final nails into her coffin.

How did he find my journal?

Shame and regret infected Caleb as he retreated down the steps. Blood dripped from his fingers, and already his hands felt stiff. He had been a fool to write the things he witnessed, more foolish still not to destroy the pages after he knew the truth.

If the court twisted his words to damn Blythe…

No. It wouldn't come to that. Even if Blythe remembered nothing of that night, Caleb could still find a way to save her. She would not rot in a cell while Mirabel's true killer walked free.

The thought struck home somewhere deep inside Caleb, drawing fresh fury into his veins. Someone had *murdered* his sister, and yet their life hadn't changed. They still traveled the streets of Brekham like they had done nothing wrong. It wasn't enough to save Blythe. Mirabel deserved justice. She deserved to have her killers punished.

Caleb looked to the sky, but this time, the One God's sun brought no peace. He longed for the moon. He longed for the thick blanket of night. *I will find who did this to you, Bells. I promise.*

But first, he had to return home and destroy anything else the minister might try to twist against him. Caleb would destroy every item in his room is that's what it took.

Halfway home, the clopping of hooves startled Caleb from his thoughts. His father's carriage thundered past, but the driver pulled hard on the reins, drawing the horses to a stop. A moment later, the door swung open on creaking hinges, and Pastor Walcott leaped to the street.

Caleb swallowed. Hard.

His father approached with unbridled violence in his eyes, but they were in public. They weren't hidden behind the walls of the church or their home. Surely the minister wouldn't—

Pain exploded across Caleb's face.

"You disgraceful, insolent fool!" The minister swung again, but Caleb was ready this time, and he ducked out of the way. "Mirabel was your *sister,* and yet you defend her killer!"

"Blythe is innocent." Caleb fought the urge to rub his sore cheek. His lacerated hands would cause more pain than they eased. "You protect the true killer by pursuing this witch hunt."

The minister grabbed Caleb's collar, dragged him forward, and punched him square across the jaw. "Do not speak to me of witch hunts, boy." He released his hold, and Caleb's knees buckled beneath him. The minister kicked out, catching Caleb along the hip. "I did not raise you to fall for a witch's tricks. You were supposed to follow the One God's light. You were supposed to protect your sister. You useless... wretched... child." The minister punctuated each insult with a swift kick to the ribs.

"That's quite enough, Pastor Walcott."

The unfamiliar voice stalled the minister's wrath long enough for Caleb to drag himself upright. Dr. Oliver Hale stood between them, an unexpected but welcome shield. The doctor held himself tall, even against the town's religious leader. "I think it's best if you return home, sir."

"This is a family matter."

"I should hope not." Dr. Hale glanced over his shoulder at Caleb, his gaze full of understanding. "Such abuse has no place inside the home. Sir."

Caleb held his injured side and watched as his father's face burned red with what Caleb could only hope was shame. Though he had no reason to believe it, he still wished to think the minister regretted all the years of hidden violence. All the years Caleb was forced to tread lightly and measure each word before it reached his lips, no matter how useless his attempts at preventing the minister's wrath were.

"So be it," the minister said at last, turning on his heel and returning to the carriage. With one foot on the step, he turned back to his son. "You will not enter my home until you've denounced the witch and begged the One God for His forgiveness. Perhaps not even then." Without a glance spared for the doctor, the minister disappeared inside the carriage and the driver spurred the horses on.

As Caleb watched his father leave, a strange emptiness opened inside him. His father was wrong. About Blythe. About the truth of Mirabel's death. His father knew nothing of the inextricably linked griefs that tore Caleb apart inside. And though he loathed the minister as much as he loved him, Tobias Walcott was the only family Caleb had left. It hurt to lose him.

The doctor pushed a dark curl out of his face and watched the carriage disappear down the lane. Once it was little more than a speck in the distance, he turned his attention to Caleb. "Are you all right?"

"I'll be fine. I'm used to his fits of rage." Caleb pulled his hand away from his side, but the movement tugged at his damaged palms. He couldn't hide his wince.

"That does not look 'fine,' Mr. Walcott. You're hurt." Dr. Hale gently took hold of Caleb's wrist and examined the injured skin. A moment later, the doctor nodded a little to himself. "Come with me. I need to dress the wounds before infection sets in."

Caleb cautiously followed the older man. "Why are you helping me?" Everyone else in town hated him, shunned him. His father. His best friend. Everyone.

"I'm a doctor, Mr. Walcott, I tend to those in need. Currently, *you* are the one who needs me most."

Before Caleb could object, the pain in his hands

burned and his ribs throbbed, reminding him of the truth of the doctor's statements. So, he followed him back toward town.

He would let Dr. Hale tend to his injuries, and then he would sneak into the church and review what little he knew about his sister's death. In the morning, he would begin his *own* investigation.

No matter what it took, he would discover the truth in time to save Blythe.

Even if it meant losing the only family he had left.

PART II
ASSOCIATION

Take care in the character of your friends,
for their shadows can overcome even the brightest of paths.
-The Book of Light

When Caleb returned to the church, Mirabel stood in the doorway, hands on her hips, waiting for him. He tried to enter, but she moved to block his path. Again. And again.

Finally, Caleb sighed. His strange encounter with Blythe had left him weary. He didn't have the energy to fight with his sister, too. "Please, it's late. We should close up and return home."

Mirabel lowered her hands from her hips, but before Caleb could fully feel relieved, she crossed them against her chest. Caleb braced for her reply. He knew that stubborn stance well enough.

"I'm not going anywhere until I get the truth." Mirabel glared up at her brother. "All of it."

"Fine," Caleb said, turning to sit on the steps. He ran his fingers through his hair and searched for a lie that would put an end to this whole affair. Though he'd never considered himself adept at deception, he had hidden plenty from his family over the years.

So Caleb spun an elaborate fiction, mixed with the

little bit of truths he'd come to know about Blythe. He told his sister about Blythe's father, how she wasn't able to visit his grave like they could with Mother. He explained how Blythe grieved often, but for the anniversary of the death, she wanted someplace private to visit him. How the whispering they heard was a young woman desperate to talk with her father again.

His story moved Mirabel to silent tears and whispered apologies, and he hated himself for lying. Hated himself more for wishing his version of events were true. It would make things so much simpler. Instead, he was embarrassed at having believed a witch's lies and angry that he didn't know what to do about this new truth.

For a week, the memory of the forest ritual taunted Caleb. He dreamed about Blythe's dance, of the moonlight radiating off her skin. He dreamed of his mother, too. Of her death. During his waking hours, he reminded himself that the Sandersons killed his mother. That Blythe's protest about their innocence couldn't be true. Yet in his dreams, his subconscious supplied more mundane, medical explanations for the truth.

Whatever her motives, Blythe had awakened a curiosity he couldn't ignore. If there was another explanation for his mother's death, if there was a non-magical cause, he had to know. Which meant he needed to return to the library.

Yet with a father like Pastor Walcott, Caleb couldn't simply disappear the moment he chose. There were sermons to write that the pastor would never deliver. He tried to compel his father to use one of his homilies, but all he got for his trouble was a black eye. Still, he wrote them as requested. Delivered townsfolk to his father's study for guidance. Memorized passages from the *Book of Light* lest his father try to doubt his faithfulness and blacken Caleb's other eye, as well.

As the sun inched toward the horizon, the Walcott family returned home, and the minister disappeared into his room with a large bottle of wine. Caleb passed through their small kitchen to grab a muffin. The house was too small for a formal dining area, so a rickety table and chairs sat along the wall opposite the sparse cupboards.

Mirabel stood by the stove, chopping more of those cursed onions. She glanced over her shoulder at him. "You're going to spoil your dinner."

"That bitter bulb is already ruining it." Caleb bit into the muffin and bursts of apple and cinnamon sent him reeling into the past. Their mother had made this recipe often. When his sister glared at him, Caleb relented. "I'm going for a stroll. I'll be back in time for dinner with plenty of appetite."

"You had better." Mirabel glanced toward the doorway that led to their father's room, sadness smoothing out the annoyance on her face. "I don't want to eat alone."

Caleb crossed the room and embraced his sister, kissing the top of her head. "You won't, Bells. I promise. I'll be back soon." And then he slipped down the narrow hallway with peeling white paint, into the main foyer, and out into the cool night.

The walk to the courthouse was brief, but Caleb's breath fogged the air and his arms prickled with cold even through his shirtsleeves. He wouldn't have long to search, but he had to do *something* to quell the nagging thoughts that stole his sleep at night.

When he slipped into the small enclave and wove past the first two shelves, he found a stack of familiar books sitting on the table at the center of the room. A candle burned beside them, illuminating the stained pages in a yellow glow.

Caleb's stomach cramped as a fresh chill worked down

his spine. "Is someone here?" Even as he asked, part of him knew the answer. He could feel her presence like a hook in his chest, and no one else frequented the small library as far as he knew.

A moment later, Blythe appeared from around the next set of shelves, another large text in her hands. For the first time since she'd moved to town, her dark hair was bound into braids, and her pale blue dress looked faded compared to the jewel tones she usually wore. She looked like a shadow of herself, and a small voice inside told Caleb it was his fault.

"Sorry," Caleb muttered, backing away. "I didn't expect to see you. I'll leave."

"No. Wait." Blythe hurried to the table and set down the text beside the others. "I'm glad you came."

"Why?" The question spilled out before Caleb could think better of it. He braced for Blythe to yell at him, to beg him to keep her secret. Instead, she simply slipped into the chair and motioned for him to sit across from her.

Nerves made his heart jumpy and erratic, but Caleb sat across from the witch. He tried to remember the Blythe from before he found out, curious and full of life and unafraid to challenge him.

His chest ached. He hadn't realized how much he'd missed that version of her. How much he'd missed the excitement in her voice as she shared her latest discoveries while he toiled uselessly with medical texts.

The same medical texts Blythe now had open before her.

She spread her fingers across the pages of the book, yellowed with age and candlelight. "Though you have little cause to trust me, please believe that I never meant to hurt you. I didn't mean to dredge up painful parts of your past or reopen old wounds."

Caleb forced himself to breathe slowly, to keep his words even. "Yet still you did."

"I know." Her words came out rushed, and they almost sounded apologetic. "Which is why I wanted to help you find answers. And I think…" She paused, her gaze dropping to the book between them. "I think I may have found something."

A feeling akin to hope jolted inside Caleb. "What is it?"

Blythe glanced up, meeting his gaze for the first time since he stepped into the small room. Worry creased her brow, and Caleb fought the urge to touch his swollen and blackened eye. "Did your father do that?" Her words whispered between them, but Caleb couldn't bring himself to confirm the truth. His father might swing his fists more often than any man should, but Blythe was the one he should fear.

"I wasn't sure I was right," Blythe continued when Caleb still didn't speak, "but if that *is* his work, you'll want to see this." She turned the book to face him and slid it to his side of the table.

Caleb skimmed the pages. He had seen them before—germ theory and the dangers of infection. Many of the symptoms matched his mother's illness, the fever and chills, but he'd never seen his mother injured. Not even from a kitchen knife.

"If the pastor laid hands on his wife the way he does his children," Blythe said, each word spoken with an unexpected tenderness, "it's possible infection set into one of the injuries."

"No." Caleb shook his head, but his entire body went cold. His hands trembled where they rested beside the book. "That can't be it. The pastor didn't start—he wasn't like this until after she passed. He never hurt her."

Slowly, Blythe reached across the space between them

and held his hand. Her skin was smooth and warm against his, steadying and unnerving all at once. "You were young. Children so often miss these kinds of things."

Perhaps if her husband had a more tender hand, she wouldn't have fallen ill!

No. He refused to believe it. His father was many things, but he had never hurt anyone but him. Caleb was sure of it. The pastor couldn't be the reason Mother was gone. It wasn't possible.

Caleb stood from the table, pulling his hand from Blythe's touch. "I have to go."

Blythe followed him to the door. "Caleb, please. I didn't mean to hurt you. I only wanted to provide the answers I know you crave."

"I asked for explanations," Caleb said, whirling around, ignoring her use of his given name. Ignoring the way it made his traitorous insides stir with unwelcome longing. "That night, in the forest. You had no answers then. Now, instead of explaining yourself, you accuse my father of murder?"

"That wasn't my intent. I—"

"Unless you have *those* answers for me, we have nothing left to discuss." Caleb waited for Blythe to respond, but she dropped her gaze as tears sparkled in her dark eyes. Her grief—whether real or for show—tugged at his heart. He had to get away before he relented. She was the danger here. Not him.

Caleb stepped through the threshold that separated the library from the rest of the courthouse. "Goodbye, Miss Bradbury."

And this time, when he left, Blythe did not follow.

*W*armth enveloped Caleb when he crossed the threshold into Dr. Hale's home, but even that comfort was overshadowed by the simple signs of the doctor's wealth. While not the grandiosity of the Pratchett home, Dr. Hale's place was far larger than Caleb's and the furnishings much nicer. There was nothing threadbare or worn about the place, though the furniture stylings were simple. The wooden chairs were free of ornamental adornment yet expertly made.

The doctor left Caleb standing in the entryway while he crossed into the sitting room to prod the burning embers and add more wood to the fireplace. The logs crackled and caught fire. Flames danced along the bark, twisting and reaching, consuming all in their path.

"...Mr. Walcott?" Dr. Hale waved a hand before Caleb's face.

Caleb tore his gaze from the fire. "Sorry. I lost myself there for a moment." He flinched as his hands throbbed anew with pain.

"This way." Dr. Hale ushered Caleb through a small

but tidy kitchen and into a side room where a wooden table stood at its center. Along the counters, glass bottles filled with liquids of all colors gleamed in the candlelight, mocking him with their cheery hues. Caleb turned to leave, but Dr. Hale blocked his escape.

"You can take a seat." The doctor gestured toward the table. "I need a good look at those hands."

Caleb passed a display of thin blades. A shudder worked down his back.

"I know the room looks intimidating, but I don't have space to store my supplies anywhere else." Dr. Hale brushed that same curl from his forehead, his pale skin and dark hair reminding Caleb a bit of Blythe. "Here, let me get your cloak." The doctor eased it from Caleb's shoulders, careful to keep the thick fabric from brushing his torn skin.

Seated on the table, Caleb stared at the woodgrain on the floor rather than meet the doctor's eye.

Dr. Hale didn't seem to take offense at his patient's quiet, focusing instead on his work. He gripped Caleb's wrists firmly and turned his palms skyward. He prodded the fleshy parts with soft cotton, sending throbbing pain all the way up Caleb's arms. Caleb winced, but his curiosity overtook him, and he raised his gaze to watch the doctor work.

"You may want to avert your eyes." Dr. Hale's voice preceded the touch of cold metal.

Despite the warning, Caleb couldn't help but look. A hooked instrument eased into his skin, and Caleb watched, fascinated, as the doctor pulled bits of stone from his hands. He'd read plenty about medicine over the past season, but to see the skills in action was something else entirely.

Stones *plinked* inside a small bowl, and when all the

debris was removed, Dr. Hale tossed the tweezers in after them. "Brace yourself."

Caleb watched as the doctor poured a clear liquid over his hands. For a brief moment, less than a heartbeat, he wondered what all the fuss was about, until the alcohol set fire to his nerves. He bit back a scream as the liquid ate away at the clotted flesh, reopening the wound, stinging and burning at the insides of him.

"Sorry. I know it's uncomfortable, but it's necessary." The doctor's voice might have soothed him if it was not followed so swiftly by another pour of the alcohol. The liquid fire scorched over his second hand, and Caleb could no longer suppress his grimace.

But soon the fire died away, replaced by the steady warmth of the doctor's fingers as he dabbed his hands dry with fresh cotton. Dr. Hale covered Caleb's palms with a thick salve that numbed his skin, and wrapped bandages around the wounds.

When he was done, the doctor glanced up from his work. "Better?"

Caleb nodded.

"Good." The doctor smiled, dimples forming despite the thinness of his angular face. "Time for tea."

Dr. Hale was out of the room before Caleb could decline the offer. Alone, his worries about Blythe's future, his fear that the words in his journal may be her end, circled in his mind. He needed a plan. He needed to get back to the church and figure out where to begin.

Caleb slipped from the table and grabbed his cloak. There *must* be a way to save Blythe and find his sister's true killer. He couldn't waste time on tea.

"Where are you going?"

"There are matters that require my attention." Caleb tried to move past the doctor, but Dr. Hale stood in the only doorway out of the room. "I'm grateful for your help, but I have a lot to do and not nearly enough time."

The doctor parted his lips to protest but sighed and stepped out of the way. "Is there anything more I can do to help? Do you have a place to stay?" He paused, holding the cups of tea closer to his chest. "I heard your father…"

"I can stay at the church." Caleb brushed past the doctor. He needed to find the truth, to understand why so many witnesses spoke lies against his love. Why Mrs. Putnam, Mrs. Eastey, the Pratchett twins, and Isaac would — *Isaac.* Caleb clenched his jaw and paused in the doorway. "Do you know Isaac Carrier?"

"I do." Dr. Hale sipped from one of the cups.

"Did you treat him for pox?"

Dr. Hale tilted his head to one side, but his expression grew cautious. "Why do you ask?"

"Isaac blamed Miss Bradbury for cursing him." Caleb watched the doctor, but no recognition lit his face. "During the trial. Don't you remember?"

"I haven't attended." Dr. Hale shook his head. "I'm sure Mr. Lewis will require my testimony soon enough, but I don't want the other witnesses to influence what I remember of the night I examined your sister's body." He took another sip, but then seemed to remember who exactly Caleb was. "I'm terribly sorry, Mr. Walcott. I didn't mean—"

"No. I understand." Caleb slung his cloak around his shoulders and hurried for the front door.

"Mr. Walcott, wait." The doctor called after him loud enough that Caleb turned. "I cannot confirm whether I treated Mr. Carrier, but I can say this. There are causes other than witchery that might make a young man come down with pox." Dr. Hale stared at Caleb then let his gaze fall to Caleb's groin. "Reasons your father, in particular, would find immoral. Do you understand?"

Caleb nodded. Isaac was never one to delay pleasure. "Thank you. Truly."

And he meant it. When this was all over, Caleb would return the doctor's kindness. But for now, Caleb slipped into the cold night with new purpose.

He needed to visit an old friend.

Music danced through the Walcott sitting room, soaring from the piano with each strike of Mirabel's fingers. The sound was the most luxurious thing in the tiny one-story home, most of the wooden furniture passed to them from the previous minister. The piano had been their mother's, and it was the only bit of wood in the house that was still polished to perfection. Mirabel made sure of that.

As Caleb listened from their threadbare couch, only half-reading the worn copy of the *Book of Light* in his lap, Mirabel's fingers strayed from religious melodies to pluck out a song of her own design. He marveled at her creation, the ebb and flow of harmony and dissonance, of quiet lament and raging sorrow. It was breathtaking.

But it was also getting rather loud.

"Watch your volume, Bells," he cautioned from the couch, glancing down the hall to their father's bedroom and study. "You know how he gets." Though not expressly forbidden in the One God's rules, Pastor Walcott hated secular music. He had warned Mirabel more than once to keep her musical talent within the One God's light.

Mirabel rolled her eyes, but her fingers didn't miss a single key. "You worry too much."

"I worry exactly the right amount," he mumbled before letting his gaze drop back to the book. He'd read the words so many times over the years, the letters swam in front of his eyes like meaningless symbols. Caleb had more cause to worry than Mirabel could ever know. It had been nearly a week since his last trip to the library. Six days since Blythe pointed blame at his father. He wouldn't—couldn't —believe she was right, but he could hardly think of anything else.

As Mirabel played, Caleb let himself get lost in his sister's music. He let Blythe's theories and his own fears slip away, and his eyelids drifted shut. Somewhere deeper in the house, wood creaked. Percussive beats grew closer. A shadow blocked the light, and when the pungent reek of wine assaulted his senses, Caleb finally registered the danger.

He shot to his feet, but he was too far from his sister. The minister stumbled to the piano and slammed the lid shut, cutting off the music mid-melody. Mirabel screamed and clutched her hands to her chest.

"How many times have I told you not to play such filth in my house?" The pastor's rage couldn't fully hide the slur to his words.

Tears rolled down Mirabel's cheeks. "It's only music."

"Do not contradict me. Not in my house!"

"But Father, I—"

Caleb's chest clenched as his father raised his fist, and his body reacted faster than his mind. He rushed the minister, grabbed the raised hand, and wrenched the arm behind his back. His father grunted as Caleb tugged harder, and they both stumbled away from the piano.

Mirabel trembled in her seat, eyes wide with horror.

Perhaps if her husband had a more tender hand, she wouldn't have fallen ill.

Caleb tried to shake Miss Sanderson's words away, but with his sister terrified before him and his father cursing and screaming and threatening to beat him senseless, he could hardly think of anything else.

The depth of his ignorance knew no bounds. His stomach clenched, and he feared he might be sick.

Pastor Walcott went slack in his arms, then twisted violently to one side, breaking Caleb's hold. Caleb didn't have time to react before the minister lashed out with his fists. The initial swing connected with Caleb's eye, which had only just finished healing. The second split his lip. Caleb tasted blood.

"Lay hands on me again, boy, and I will *break* you." Pastor Walcott spit in Caleb's direction.

Caleb had weathered his father's abuse for years. He could handle anything the old man dished out, but he would not let his sister suffer.

"If you hurt Mirabel," Caleb said, wiping the blood from his lips, "I will destroy you. All of Brekham will know your secrets. They'll know how much of their money you waste on wine. You will never lead another sermon."

The minister stumbled, catching himself on the arm of a chair. "No one would believe you."

For the first time in months, Caleb held his father's stare. "Care to find out?" With each breath, Caleb's lips and eye pulsed with pain, but he refused to be the first to look away. Finally, the minister's gaze fell to the floor, and Caleb turned to his sister. "Bells, grab your cloak."

The piano bench screeched against the wooden floor as

Mirabel stood. She flinched at the noise, her hands still trembling as she crossed to the front door.

"If you leave now, don't bother coming home before dawn." The minister shoved away from the chair and stumbled back down the hall toward his room. "A night in the cold will teach you both some respect." The bedroom door slammed. Glass shattered.

Caleb took the cloak from his sister's shaking fingers. He settled the soft, black fabric over her shoulders and hugged her close. "Ignore him," he whispered, pressing a kiss to the top of her head. "How are your fingers?"

"They're fine," she said in the quietest voice Caleb had ever heard. "He missed."

"Good." Caleb pulled on his own cloak and swung open the door, leading his sister out into the cold.

~

*L*eft out in the cold, autumn night, Caleb didn't know where to go. A wind kicked up, tugging at his hair, biting his exposed skin, and Mirabel shivered beside him. Caleb tucked her under one arm, and led her away from their home.

Once she was somewhere safe and warm, he could crack open their past and explore the dangerous truths whispering at the back of his mind. Already, betrayal pulsed through him, causing more pain than his split lip and throbbing eye.

"Caleb?" Mirabel leaned closer as they walked down the vacant street. The rest of the town was already shut in for the night.

"Yeah?"

"I'm sorry." She sniffed and wiped her sleeve across

each cheek. "I should have listened when you warned me. If I had played more softly…"

"No, Bells." Caleb stopped and took his sister's hands in his. "You mustn't blame yourself. The minister's actions belong to him alone." When Mirabel nodded, Caleb continued east down the dirt road.

After a few minutes, Mirabel spoke again. "Where will we stay tonight? The church?"

"No." He couldn't have Mirabel at the church, not when his every step led him toward a dangerous woman and even more dangerous answers. "Your friend, Miss Fredrick. She lives near here, right?"

Mirabel nodded.

"Do you think she'd take you in for the night?"

His sister grinned, light returning to her eyes. "I think so. Sally has been begging me to visit for ages, but I've been so busy at church." She paused, worrying at her lower lip. "What excuse shall I give?"

"Tell her…" Caleb trailed off. He wanted to lay their family secrets bare and bring shame to his father, but if he did, he'd lose his only leverage. He also couldn't predict the collateral damage that would befall Mirabel. Or himself. "Tell her father was overcome with divine inspiration and needed intense quiet for his communion."

"But that's not true." Mirabel shot him a worried look as they neared Miss Fredrick's house. "We can't lie."

"We can't very well tell the truth, either." Caleb paused in front of the house. "Do you need me to walk you to the door?"

She shook her head and tugged on the edge of her braid. "I'll be fine."

"I'll come fetch you in the morning." He pressed a kiss to her forehead, waited in the dark to ensure Mirabel was welcomed inside, then hurried to his next destination. With each step, his mind played memories on a loop. Miss Sanderson's accusations. Rows of text about infection and injury. Blythe dancing beneath the full moon, the air static with power.

By the time the church came into view, Caleb's body ached from running. He didn't stop at the church, though. He crossed the street and bounded up Blythe's front steps. The wooden planks creaked under his weight, the sound so much louder than when he was there as a child. No one had ever bothered to fix the little porch.

At the front door, he paused, his heart pounding a panicked rhythm against his chest. Caleb raised his hand to knock, but fear held him still as stone. What if she cursed him? What if she found his appearance at her home repulsive? He had no right to expect anything else, given the way he'd spoken to her at the library. Caleb had brushed her help aside, had refused to believe, and the whole time, she'd been right.

Probably.

Caleb squared his shoulders and forced himself to knock. His cold knuckles ached from the contact, and the sound that emanated was deeper than expected, as if the door were twice its size. The silence that followed was heavy. The waiting agony.

A stronger breeze picked up, and dry leaves rustled on their branches. Each heartbeat seemed to last an eternity, until—

Footsteps approached. The door muffled a gasp, and then the locks shifted open. Blythe opened the door, just enough for Caleb to see her face and the dusting of freckles along the bridge of her nose.

Her slate eyes narrowed. "Mr. Walcott, what are you doing here?" Her words were cautious and laced with suspicion. "I thought we had nothing left to discuss."

Caleb ran shaking hands over his face. All his composure cracked and fell away. "I didn't want to believe it, but I..." He dropped his hands and struggled for a steady breath. "I think you're right. I think my father did something."

"Oh." Everything about Blythe softened—her posture, the tension around her eyes, the set of her jaw. She opened the door more fully, eyes widening when she took in the state of his face. "What happened?"

It hurt too much for even a sarcastic smile. He could barely grimace. "I think you know."

"You should come in. Quickly, before you let out the warmth." Yet the way her eyes darted from side to side spoke of her true concern.

Come in before someone sees you.

Caleb stepped through the threshold and rubbed his hands along his arms to warm himself. It was strange, being back in the Sanderson home after so many years. It looked much the same—gleaming hardwood floors and a grand staircase at the back of the foyer. To his left, the fireplace he used to sit beside to read was crackling with burning logs. To his right sat the dining room, with a table large enough to seat eight. "Is your mother home?"

Blythe shook her head. "Mother is away on an errand. She's due back later this evening."

In another reality, Caleb might be embarrassed to know that they were alone. The town gossips would surely have dozens of theories if they found out, but none of that mattered. Not when Blythe was a witch and his father tried to hurt Mirabel and might be the real reason Caleb's mother was dead.

Panic rushed up his chest again. "My entire life was built on a lie. The Sandersons *died* because of it. How did you know? How did you figure it out?"

Before Blythe could answer, a piercing whistle split the quiet. They both flinched. "Come. I'm making tea." She passed through the dining room to the kitchen at the rear of the house, glancing over her shoulder when Caleb didn't follow. "Tea fixes most things."

"I don't need tea, Miss Bradbury. I need answers." Even so, he followed her into the kitchen, where a kettle whistled until she removed it from the stove. He watched as she prepared two cups of tea, adding sugar to both. "Ms. Bradbury, please. How did you know it was him?"

Blythe set the tea on the counter beside him and turned to open an upper cupboard. She pulled out a black and white stone mortar with matching pestle and several glass vials filled with dried herbs. "I didn't know for sure," she said at last, measuring pinches of the herbs and placing them in the mortar. "I'm still not positive. I cannot see into the past, Mr. Walcott."

She flashed him a grin over her shoulder, and he noted that her hair was loose again, falling like waves of night down her shoulders. Caleb tried to return the expression, but his split lip burned in protest. He tasted blood again.

"You didn't deserve this," she said, grinding the pestle into the herbs. They crunched under its weight.

"Maybe I did." Caleb reached for the cup of tea, letting the heat warm his skin. "You don't know what happened."

"No one deserves that kind of abuse. No one." Blythe set down the pestle and carried the mortar to where Caleb stood at the edge of the counter. "May I?" She pointed to his tea cup, and when Caleb nodded, she lifted it over the pestle and poured a few drops into the crushed herbs. A tangy, earthy smell filled the space between them.

"As for your questions," Blythe continued, "all I did was read. The passages I found made sense. Infection is a common cause of death in the places I've lived, and after I saw what your father did to you…" She shrugged. "It seemed to fit."

"You make it sound so simple."

"I know it's not." Blythe dipped her fingers into the mortar and stirred the mixture three times. "Especially when the family is your own. Nothing about family is simple."

Caleb leaned against the counter, gripping tight to the tea cup, as if the tiny bit of stoneware could tether him to a less painful reality. "I wish he had died instead of her. Does that make me terrible?"

"It makes you human."

"Human," Caleb echoed, raising his gaze to Blythe. "And what of you? Can you change the past? Could you alter my history?"

Blythe tensed. "You grossly overestimate my power."

"But you do have power," he pressed. "I saw it. I *felt* it. There are some things you can do."

"Far less than stories would have you believe." She wiped her hands on a towel and then dipped her thumb into the mixture. "But I could show you, if you want."

Caleb fought eighteen years of instincts. His body told him to run, to flee from the witch who offered to show her power, but his curiosity held him in place. Somewhere deep inside, beneath skin and muscle, he trusted her. Like she had once told him, he wanted to know *everything*.

He nodded and closed his eyes as Blythe leaned close. Her bare fingers brushed his cheek. "This may sting, but only for a moment," she whispered and pressed her herb-covered thumb to his lips.

At first, all he noticed was the touch of her skin against his, but then his lips started to tingle.

Then burn.

Caleb gasped and tried to pull away, but Blythe held firm. "It'll only last a moment," she promised, resting her other hand against his chest. "Breathe with me." She inhaled deep, and Caleb forced himself to follow. He squeezed his eyes tight and breathed. In and out. In and—

The burning shifted into an intense, agonizing itch. And then finally, everything stopped. All he could feel was Blythe's thumb as she brushed away bits of now-dried herbs. When he opened his eyes, he found her smiling at him.

"Better?" When Caleb simply stared at her, Blythe pointed to the window above the kitchen sink. "See for yourself."

Cautiously, Caleb walked to the window and peered at his reflection, made possible by the dark night outside. The split on his lip, that had so recently tasted of blood, was completely healed. In the reflection, he saw Blythe approach.

"We have little gifts," she said, speaking with a deliberate slowness. "Small things that make life easier, tricks that help our gardens grow, and recipes that can heal small hurts. There's no reason to be afraid."

"Where does it come from?" Caleb turned and found Blythe standing closer than he expected. She smelled of fresh herbs and moonlit skies.

She flashed the shadow of a smile. "It's a long story, and I don't fully understand how it all works."

"I want to hear it," he whispered, the words filled with a reverence he couldn't hide. "When you're ready, and on your terms, but I want to know." Caleb felt that strange sensation again, like something drawing him closer to Blythe. He reached out and tucked a strand of loose hair behind her ear.

Blythe leaned into his touch, letting her hands fall to his waist. "You're not going to send me to the gallows?"

Warmth bloomed inside Caleb's chest, and he threaded his fingers through her hair. It felt like silk in his hands, and he leaned forward until his forehead rested against hers. Every place they touched defied the One God, but Caleb couldn't bring himself to care. "I will keep your secrets safe."

"Including this one?" Blythe asked as she raised onto her toes, bringing her lips only a single breath from his. Caleb could feel the heat of her body so near his…

And then there was no distance at all.

Caleb wasn't sure which of them ultimately closed the gap, but it didn't matter. They were kissing, her lips soft and warm against his. Their first explorations were gentle and hesitant, but then Blythe wrapped her arms around his neck, pulling him closer, kissing him deeper. Harder.

The longing tore at his insides, destroying all the walls he'd built against this kind of connection. He couldn't get enough of her. The taste of her lips. The delicious press of her hands against his throat. They stumbled backward and knocked into the counter. One of the tea mugs fell and shattered on the floor.

The noise startled them apart. It left them gasping for air.

"I am so sorry." Caleb rested a hand against the counter as heat flamed his face. "Let me help—"

Blythe rested a finger over his lips. "Don't apologize, Caleb." She raised onto her toes and pressed another kiss to his lips. "I'll clean it later."

"Blythe, I…" He forgot his words as she leaned her hip into his, pressing against visible proof of his desire. A low moan rumbled in his chest, and he leaned forward to kiss her again. He would never grow tired of this.

"Blythe, darling? I'm home." Mrs. Bradbury's voice carried in from the front of the house. "I thought I told you to keep this door bolted?"

This time, it was Blythe who pulled away first. Her rosy cheeks went stark white as she shoved him toward the back door.

"I'm so sorry. I shouldn't have come. I didn't think..." His whispered apologies wouldn't form a coherent thought. Because he was *not* sorry they had kissed. He was only sorry her mother had returned home. His body already ached for the press of Blythe's skin against his.

"Hush. And I told you, no apologies." Blythe swung open the back door, and Caleb stumbled into their dark garden. She paused before closing the door, a smile warming her features. "I'll find you tomorrow. We'll talk then."

Without waiting for his response, Blythe closed the door.

Caleb grinned like a fool the entire way back to the church.

WRITTEN TESTIMONY OF BLYTHE BRADBURY

et me not digress too far. I know what truths you seek. Though it is perhaps too late, I offer them to you now. That night in the forest with Mirabel... Caleb, it is so hard to even write the words. I do not wish to break your heart, but you deserve to know. If you are not ready, you can tuck this letter away for another time. You get to decide.

If you are ready, if you feel you can bear this weight, I will do my best to share the truth without doing you harm.

I did not raise a blade against your sister. I did not take her life. Yet neither am I wholly innocent. Whether you ultimately deem me innocent or guilty, I shall bear the weight of your decision. I know how you cherished your sister, and I will weather your hatred, from the grave if I must, if that's what you need to heal.

My memory is still hazy in parts, but someone came to my home. There was begging and threats, and then I agreed to do something altogether foolish and reckless and wrong.

I agreed to weave magic at the behest of another.

For that alone, I deserve fault for her death. I should have known better than to agree. My memory is sharp enough to know I tried to protect her. The moment she arrived is clear in my memory. I tried to turn her back to the church. I tried to send her away.

But I wasn't fast enough.

For nearly a week after their kiss, Caleb found little moments to steal away to see Blythe. Between his father and her mother, there was never enough time to be alone. Even the tiny library felt precarious, too exposed to do more than lock fingers while they read.

But today, today would be different.

Caleb was alone in the church, his family busy with other things. He was technically there to carve wooden amulets with the One God's sun symbol to sell. Instead, he watched the Sanderson house from the second-floor window, his carving mostly forgotten in his hands. Mrs. Bradbury was to leave that afternoon and travel to Rowley. Blythe wouldn't say why her mother was going, only that she wouldn't return until the following morning.

They would finally have the luxury of time and privacy.

Downstairs, the front door burst open, slamming against the wall. The sound startled Caleb so much he nearly stabbed himself with the carving tool. His mind raced with possibilities—was it the minister coming to blame him for something new or one of the townsfolk in dire need of advice while his father was unavailable? Caleb pressed the carving tool into the wood, continuing to work on the One God's symbol.

Someone cursed and closed the door with more care. "Caleb!" Isaac's voice echoed through the church, slowing Caleb's speeding heart. "Where are you?"

"Upstairs!" he called, finishing the curve of the sun. Caleb's focus slipped moments later, and he resumed his watch out the window. Mrs. Bradbury's carriage was in the yard now, a horse tethered to the front. It wouldn't be long before she left.

"Where is the terror?" Isaac asked, stopping beside the window. "What are you looking at?"

Caleb rolled his eyes. "My sister isn't a terror. Mirabel is spending the day with a friend." Guilt tugged at Caleb's ribs. Mirabel had been spending more time with Miss Fredrick ever since their father's outburst. Caleb needed a better way to protect her from the minister, but he hadn't figured out *what* to do yet. At least she was safe with her friend.

"Good." Isaac brushed flecks of wood from the window seat and sat opposite Caleb. "Because I need your help."

"Please tell me you haven't mixed up the twins again." Caleb set down his carving and brushed the bits of curled wood from his clothes. "There are some social knots even I can't help you unravel."

Isaac let out a humorless laugh. "No, I settled that weeks ago. I gave Grace a necklace and asked her to wear it for me always. She hasn't taken it off since." Isaac grinned, a bit of his usual mischief shining through. "Problem solved."

"You, sir, are a terrible gentleman." Movement outside caught Caleb's attention, and he turned to look more fully out the window. Mrs. Bradbury finished loading a basket into the carriage and returned to the house. His heart thudded in his chest. Soon, she would be gone. Soon, Blythe would be in his arms.

"I know," Isaac said, his tone suddenly solemn. "That's why I need your help."

Mrs. Bradbury emerged from the house. For a moment, Caleb thought he caught sight of Blythe's dark hair before the door closed, shutting her away. Mrs. Bradbury headed for the carriage, her deep blue riding dress frillier than anything Blythe ever wore. She reached the carriage and climbed into the driver's seat and—

Isaac smacked his arm.

"What was that for?"

"I'm trying to ask for your help, and you're busy daydreaming out the window." Isaac scowled. "What's gotten into you?"

"Nothing," Caleb said, perhaps too quickly. "I'm sorry. What did you need?"

Despite his outburst only seconds ago, Isaac stared as his lap. "I… I wanted to know if you could convince your father to marry Grace and me."

"Marriage?" Caleb grinned. "Why, Carrier, I never thought I'd see the day."

Isaac smacked him again. "This is serious, Caleb."

"Fine, fine. It shouldn't be any trouble. Once summer comes—"

"We cannot delay that long." Isaac stood suddenly and paced the small second story of the church. "I can't wait months and months to make Miss Pratchett my wife."

Caleb focused on his friend, even as every part of him begged to look outside, to see if Mrs. Bradbury had gone.

"You know how my father is. At best, he might wed you in the spring, but the *Book of Light* says summer is best. Weddings held when His sunlight is weak are doomed to fail. You know this."

Isaac ran his fingers through his hair. "There has to be another way."

"Unless one of you is on your deathbed, you'll have better luck convincing the minister to admit to his own failings." A horse whinnied outside, and Caleb glanced out the window. The carriage slipped out of view. Mrs. Bradbury was finally leaving. "I know winter seems to last forever, but the wait will be worth it." He stood and approached his friend. "Now, it's my turn to beg your assistance."

"Aren't you supposed to fix my problems before asking for favors?" Isaac grumbled, but he didn't pull away. "What is it?"

"I'm calling on Miss Bradbury today, but my father can't find out." The words spilled out in a rush, and it felt incredible to finally tell his friend. He couldn't tell him everything—he'd never betray Blythe's confidence—but telling Isaac even that much made it all seem more real.

Isaac scowled. "You're abandoning me in my time of need to chase after some woman? Do you know what the other women in town say about her? There's a reason she moved into the old Sanderson house."

"Don't act as if you didn't abandon me all summer to woo the Pratchett sisters." Caleb checked out the window once more to ensure Mrs. Bradbury had truly gone, all the while trying to suppress the sudden rage at Isaac's insinuation. But he wouldn't lash out like his father. Ever. "And the townsfolk know nothing about her. If you care for me at all, you'll stop these hateful rumors."

"Fine." Isaac slumped onto the window seat and fiddled with Caleb's half-carved sun charm.

"And if the minister asks where I was today?" Caleb pressed, pulling Isaac back up.

Isaac grumbled and followed Caleb down the stairs. "You were at my house all day," he promised.

"Thank you, Isaac. Truly." Caleb threw on his cloak and led Isaac outside, locking up the door. He paused, desire and anticipation making him dizzy. In a moment, he would be alone with Blythe. In a moment, they'd have nothing but time.

"Go on, then." Isaac shoved him forward and headed for his own house. "See you around, Walcott."

~

Caleb had barely raised his hand to knock when her door swung open.

Blythe wore a simple dress, a shade darker than the flush of pink on her cheeks, and her hair was once again loose around her shoulders. A shy grin tugged on her lips. "Caleb."

He returned her smile, her voice warming him despite the chill in the air. "Blythe." Before he could step inside, she reached for his hand and pulled him into the grand foyer, closing the door behind him. Heat pulsed from the place where their skin touched, and he reached with his free hand to brush the hair from her face. He breathed in her scent of fresh herbs and cloudless nights. "I've missed you."

"But you're here now." Her voice was like rich honey in a perfect cup of tea. Blythe raised on her toes and leaned into him, pressing her lips against his. Her touch set him aflame with desire, and Caleb wrapped his arms around her, deepening the kiss. She was all warmth and soft curves against him.

When she pulled away, Caleb was breathless.

"Come. I want to show you something." Blythe twined her fingers through his and led him up the grand staircase. In all the times Caleb had visited as a child, he'd never once seen the second floor. At the top of the steps, they turned right and stopped before a closed door, the wood-grain smooth from years of gentle touches.

Blythe paused, her fingers resting on the handle. "Before we go in, I want to make my intentions clear. You may hold me close. You may kiss me. But this isn't an invitation to do anything more than we've already done."

Caleb's heart raced at the thought of what *more* might entail, but he nodded. There would be time for more later. They had a lifetime of more ahead of them. He pressed a kiss to her temple. "Of course."

Blythe opened the door and led Caleb inside her bedroom.

Though he had never given this room much thought, it looked every bit as he might have imagined. There were books everywhere. A scattering of parchment littered a small desk tucked into the far corner. On the walls, Blythe had hung charcoal drawings of strange shapes marked with tiny dots.

"What are these?" he asked, approaching the wall to examine the images closer. One in particular caught his eye. Unlike the others, overtop the straight lines connecting a series of dots, someone had sketched a figure in a flowing dress leaning forward to point at the right edge of the page.

"They're constellations," Blythe said, using the unfamiliar word like it was commonly known. She came to stand behind him and wrapped her arms around his waist, resting her head against his arm. "When I can't sleep at night, I draw them until I grow tired."

"Constellations?"

"Patterns in the stars." Blythe released Caleb and came to sit on top of her desk. "Didn't your father teach you?"

Caleb shook his head. "The minister finds all parts of the evening sky distasteful. He says they're an affront to the One God and the sun with which he blessed us." He stepped closer to the desk, letting his hands rest on either side of Blythe's hips. "I'm sure that sounds ridiculous to you."

"It does," she agreed, then laughed when Caleb grimaced. She pressed a quick kiss to his cheek. "I didn't say I found *you* ridiculous. Your father's notions are woefully outdated, especially given that the sun is merely a star closer than all the others, close enough to provide light and warmth."

Though he hated to admit his ignorance, his confusion must have shown on his face. Blythe riffled through the pages on her desk until she found a brown leather book and flipped through the pages, giving Caleb a brief introduction to the wonders of the night sky.

"She's my favorite," Blythe said several minutes later, pointing to the picture that had drawn Caleb's eye. "She's called the Traveler, and she reaches for the Eastern Star. Mother and I have journeyed under her watch since Father died, moving forever east, trying to find a place to call home. One day, we'll follow the Traveler across the sea."

Blythe reached for Caleb, drawing him closer. "Mother says there are incredible universities there." She paused to press a kiss to his lips. Another to the hollow beneath his jaw. "I could study for decades and still have more to read."

Her excitement filled the air, and she kissed him again,

deeper this time, her fingers twining through his hair. Caleb sighed into the kiss and leaned closer, savoring the soft tug at his hair, the warmth of her lips, the press of her chest against his. He would never tire of this, and as his body begged for more, Caleb kept Blythe's earlier intentions front of mind.

But as Blythe's teeth pressed against his lower lip, her story about the Traveler sank in deeper.

"Wait." Caleb pulled away, panic threatening to cut off his air. "Please tell me you're not leaving Brekham."

Blythe wiped her thumb across her lips and wouldn't meet his gaze. "I don't want to leave."

"There's a difference between not wanting to leave and actually staying." Caleb held her hand gently in his and silently pleaded with her to look at him. "Blythe, please. Tell me you'll stay."

"I'm not sure I'll have a choice." Blythe leaned into him, resting against his chest. Caleb held her in a fierce embrace. "Ever since Father died... You have to understand, it's hard for two women to survive alone in a new community. Rumors eventually run us out of town. Or, rather, we leave before they can. Over and over and over."

Caleb's chest ached. For Blythe. For himself. For the rumors already brewing in town at the hands of his best friend's beloved. "How long?"

"I wish I knew." Blythe pulled away and wiped a stray tear from her cheeks. "It's usually my fault that we have to leave. Rumors are hard to quell when there's some small truth to them. Mother does better at hiding who we are, but I..." She paused, the shadow of a smile crossing her lips. "Well, *you* already found out about me."

Fear crawled up Caleb's spine. "I will never share what I know. Ever."

"I know." Blythe touched his lips, the same place she'd

healed the week before, and slipped off the desk. "I trust you, Caleb."

He watched as she crossed the room and paused before the bed. "Is there anything more I can do?"

Blythe perched on the edge of her mattress. "For now, simply stay. When the sun sets, I'll teach you how to read the night sky."

NOW

"Isaac!" Caleb banged on the Carrier family's front door, wincing as the shock sent throbs of pain to his bandaged hands. Isaac wasn't at the family forge, and Caleb didn't know where else to look. Through the windows, candlelight flickered. "Isaac! Answer the door."

Caleb glanced around the small front porch where he had played often as a child. But the toys of their youth no longer cluttered the weatherworn wood. He paced faster, paused to pound again on the door. To his right, a flutter of curtains caught his eye. *Isaac.*

"I know you're in there," he yelled, banging on the door again. "Open up before I do something we'll both regret." If he kept this going much longer, the whole town would come running.

Silence followed his demands, but the tension in the air felt different. Caleb held his breath. Inside, the heavy lock slid free, wood scraping along wood, and the door creaked open.

Isaac stood inside the foyer, the opening only wide

enough to show half of his face. But when his eyes settled on Caleb, they narrowed to slits.

"What do you want, Walcott?"

"I want to know why you lied. Your illness had nothing to do with magic, *Carrier*." He drew out the last name like it was an insult, but the effect fell flat.

"Try proving otherwise. The court believes the witch cursed me." Isaac tried to close the door, but Caleb shoved his boot in the way.

"But you and I both know that isn't true." Caleb leaned his shoulder against the door and eased it open a few inches. "What would your parents think, if they learned their son lied before the visiting minister?"

"Perhaps you should ask them. They've gone to *your home* to console Pastor Walcott." Isaac shifted his weight to look Caleb in the face. "He lost his only son to a witch today."

Caleb froze, the verbal jab landing harder than he could have anticipated. He couldn't find his voice, had no words to respond, because Isaac was right. As far as his father was concerned, he had no children left. "Fuck you, Carrier," he snapped, vision blurring, and then shoved his way into Isaac's house.

Isaac scrambled back, but when Caleb entered the home, he paused. Isaac stood before him, disheveled in a way Caleb had never seen. His hair was a mess, his shirt hastily tucked in, the top buttons undone. If not for the alertness in his eyes, and the bright sun in the late after-noon sky, Caleb might have guessed Isaac was asleep when he arrived.

None of that mattered. Caleb needed the truth.

"What have I done to turn you against me? Why do you suddenly hate me so?" His voice rose in volume and pitch, but Caleb didn't care. They were alone. "Why would you condemn my love to death?"

"Because she's a *witch!* Why can't you see that?"

"That doesn't mean she did anything to hurt my sister." Caleb shoved Isaac with all his strength, but Isaac barely moved. "Why make things worse for her? We're friends. You should be helping me!"

"Like you helped me?" Isaac scoffed. "How many times did I ask for your help only to be abandoned in favor of Miss Bradbury?"

"I—"

"You had your chance, Caleb. You chose wrong." Isaac ran his fingers through his mussed hair and fastened the undone buttons of his shirt.

Realization over Isaac's state of disarray dawned, turning Caleb's vision red like the morning sky. "She's here, isn't she?"

"I don't—"

"Miss Pratchett. She's here." Caleb shoved past Isaac to search the house, but Isaac grabbed his wrist and held fast. Caleb tried, and failed, to break the hold. He whirled on his friend. "You can't help me prove my love's innocence because you're too busy bedding yours? How could you—"

"Isaac?" A female voice carried through to the main room. "What's taking so long? My parents expect me home before dark."

Isaac froze, his brown eyes wide with alarm. Though his lips moved, no sound came out.

A moment later, one of the Pratchett twins emerged from Isaac's bedroom, her hair and clothing similarly out of sorts. Her bun was loose, half her hair fell in curls down her back. She stumbled when she saw Caleb and hurried to straighten her skirts.

"I need a minute, Grace—Miss Pratchett. Just one minute more." Isaac's voice shook, and he shifted his weight, putting himself in front of Miss Pratchett, blocking Caleb's view of her.

But Caleb still saw when Miss Pratchett rested a protective hand across her stomach. He saw how her clothes clung to the small bump. Remembered Isaac's request all those weeks ago.

"She's carrying your child, isn't she?" Caleb asked, and the way Miss Pratchett blanched and reached for Isaac's arm was confirmation enough. "That's why you wanted my help. That's why you wanted my father to marry you before winter. You needed to wed before the baby could reveal your transgressions."

Guilt clawed at Caleb's throat as he voiced the words. Isaac and Grace were far from the only ones in Brekham to break that particular law of the One God, and he didn't wish to see either of them shamed by the town, but he wouldn't let them hurt Blythe to hide their own deviation from the lighted path.

"Caleb, please. You can't say anything. It would ruin us both."

"I don't want to," Caleb admitted, but he turned away from the tears slipping down Grace's cheeks. "I have no desire to see you hurt, but I will tell all of Brekham unless you recant your lies. You will set things right in the court, Carrier, or so help me—"

"But it would make no difference," Grace said, voice shaking with fear. "Miss Bradbury *is* a witch. Nothing we say will save her from the gallows."

"That doesn't mean you can spread lies and make things worse!"

Isaac pulled away from Miss Pratchett and rested his hands on Caleb's shoulders. "Please, Caleb. Even if our friendship means nothing to you, don't do this to her. Grace doesn't deserve this. *Please.*"

"You have two days to convince Pastor Lewis to put one of you on the stand." Caleb stepped away from Isaac and pulled open the door. "Two days, Carrier, or the whole town will know."

⁓

*C*aleb wandered Brekham for hours, trying to come up with a plan to find his sister's killer. Trying to assuage his guilt over the ultimatum he'd leveled against his only friend. By the time he returned to the church, his father had already locked him out. Caleb stared up at the stained-glass windows feeling lost and alone under the watchful eye of the moon. It was too cold to sleep outside and too late to return to Dr. Hale's to see if his earlier offer was genuine.

Across the street, the lights were already off inside Mrs. Putnam's house—not that Caleb would seek refuge there. The old woman was the first to testify against Blythe and had suspected her from the moment she moved into the old Sanderson home.

His gaze drifted to the right, where Blythe's home stood silent and dark. Blythe had only invited him over a handful of times. Would she care if he stayed there now? Dinah Bradbury had already fled Brekham, so at least she couldn't mind his trespass.

With his cloak pulled tight against the cold, Caleb hurried across the street. He glanced again at Mrs. Putnam's home, and the Eastey house, too, but their windows were shuttered, and no lights flickered around the frames. The world around him seemed asleep.

Still, Caleb avoided the front door, instead slipping into

the garden around back. He gripped the doorknob with aching hands, but it wouldn't turn. He tried again, harder, in case it had simply frozen shut, but Mrs. Bradbury must have locked up before she abandoned her daughter.

Caleb blew on his hands to warm them and searched for a way inside. He spotted a spade beside the wilted, frost-burned herb garden. *Forgive me*, he thought as he used the spade's handle to break open the door. Inside, moonlight illuminated a small expanse of kitchen that looked unchanged since he'd been there last.

Behind him, something rustled in the garden. Caleb jolted and turned toward the noise, but there was nothing there. *Stop wasting moonlight, and get inside.* After another steadying breath, he took his own advice.

Once inside, Caleb's body moved on instinct, passing through the kitchen and ascending the stairs. Exhaustion clung to his limbs, but even his tired mind knew better than to search for proof of Blythe's innocence in the home where, in her bravest moments, she had offered him a glimpse of her magic.

The same magic that now damned her.

At Blythe's bedroom door, Caleb paused. Though he was sure Blythe wouldn't mind, it felt odd to be here without her express invitation. Memories of previous visits to this room, her lips upon his, stirred something inside him as he opened the door and stepped through the threshold.

The walls were still covered in constellations, the desk covered in books. Everywhere he looked, Caleb found signs of Blythe's sharp mind and insatiable curiosity. A deep sadness clung to his heart as he perched on the edge of her bed. He needed sleep, but first, he wanted to review his meager list of suspects one more time.

There were plenty of men around town who stared at

his sister with a hunger Caleb hated to see, Mr. Eastey among them. The undertaker, too. Caleb shivered, thinking of his sister's body now under Mr. Upton's care. Unfortunately, his long walk hadn't helped him come up with anything more concrete.

Or, perhaps, Mrs. Bradbury orchestrated Bell's final moments to teach her daughter a lesson, to punish her for loving a minister's son.

But why was Mirabel in the woods at all? Mere moments before, Caleb had promised her a better future, had given her hope. Had he said something wrong? Had he unknowingly upset her in some way and sent her seeking solace among the trees?

Caleb shifted on the mattress, but something hard pressed against his leg. He stood and lifted the mattress, revealing a leather journal wrapped in rough twine. Caleb unwrapped the journal, his injured hands trembling, and found Blythe's sprawling cursive filling the pages.

"Blythe." His throat closed with the pain of missing her, and he ran his fingers along the soft pages.

Though he knew he shouldn't pry, he couldn't help but let his gaze flick across the pages. He found notes, mostly, about her studies of the stars, but when he turned the page, the dry parchment burst into flames. Caleb dropped the book and tore at the cloth on his hands. They had caught in the spark and now smoldered.

As the bandages fell to the floor and fire consumed the journal, Caleb stared at his hands.

The skin upon his palms was pristine.

Caleb stretched his hands, and the sudden absence of pain brought tears to his eyes. He wished he could show *this* magic to the court, wished he could trust the magistrate to see the beauty in the things Blythe could do. Yet he knew he couldn't. It would only confirm their suspicions of witchcraft. Caleb had already hurt her case enough on that account.

Downstairs, glass shattered, cutting off Caleb's thoughts. He stepped softly toward the open door and listened. More glass broke. A window? Had townsfolk come to pilfer the Bradburys' abandoned belongings? Did they come to destroy what was left of their home? Caleb closed the bedroom door to block himself from view.

A chorus of angry voices rose beneath him. People were shouting. A *lot* of people. He glanced out the window where the citizens of Brekham had gathered, dozens and dozens of them. Many he couldn't recognize, faces masked by the dark of night, but others carried torches.

Mr. Pratchett.

Isaac's father.

The Redds.

Even Mrs. Putnam watched from behind her short garden fence, lit candle in hand, a delirious smile stretching her wrinkled face.

A booming voice rose above the rest, and Caleb recognized it immediately.

"If we can't yet burn the witch, we can burn this twice cursed building!" Pastor Walcott's words were met by a cheer, and the crowd surged forward.

"No, no, no." Caleb rushed to the stairs, but his voice didn't carry over the shouting outside. The townsfolk tossed burning torches through broken windows. The rugs caught fire first, and the room filled quickly with smoke.

Caleb hesitated on the bottom step. If he ran out the front door, there was no telling what his neighbors would do to him. He couldn't save Blythe if he was injured or in a cell alongside her. More glass broke behind him, and torches crashed into the kitchen.

There was no way out.

Except up.

Caleb turned and raced up the stairs, heading for the room at the back of the house. He burst in and found another bedroom—probably Mrs. Bradbury's—but he didn't have time for details. He threw himself at the window and fought with the latch. "Come on. Come on!"

The crackling below grew into a roar, and smoke spilled through the open bedroom door.

Caleb tugged at the window, profanity spilling from his lips, but it was painted shut. He paced the room, coughing as the smoke thickened. Sweat trickled down his brow. He cursed again and picked up the small table beside Mrs. Bradbury's bed. With everything he had inside, he heaved the table through the window.

Glass shattered and cold air rushed into the room as flames crawled down the hallway.

With a final glance back at the encroaching fire, Caleb eased through the shattered window. Bits of glass caught in his cloak and tore into his arm. He gripped the edge of the sill, lowered himself down as far as he could, and dropped.

The cold earth rose quickly to greet him, and he collapsed in a heap on the grass. But Caleb couldn't delay As the fire grew, more and more light cast around him. The people of Brekham cheered at the destruction, oblivious as Caleb slipped away, keeping to the cover of darkness. Each step brought him pain, his ankle protesting even the smallest pressure, but he had to get away. Had to find someplace safe to weather the elements and the town's rage.

But even if *he* survived the night, the old Sanderson house—Blythe's *home*—would be ash by morning.

In the two weeks since Father had almost shattered her fingers, Mirabel hadn't touched an instrument outside of church services. She itched to play, but whenever she approached the piano, all she could see was the rage on her father's face and his fist poised to strike her. Mirabel had tried to forget, but after what she'd read the night before in Caleb's private journal, she couldn't think of anything else.

Mirabel pulled the final tray of cakes from the brick oven and set them on the windowsill to cool. Without music to busy her fingers, she'd spent the entire day baking. She had made all of Caleb's favorites, hoping enough sweets would loosen his tongue. She needed to know how much was true, if Caleb believed their father was capable of such horrors.

Based on the shouting coming from Father's bedroom and study, it might take more than a few sweets to win her brother's good mood. Father's voice rose through a rapid crescendo and culminated in the shattering of glass.

Mirabel flinched at the sound. She could guess at Father's expression. Caleb's, too.

She didn't have to guess for long. A moment later, a door slammed and Caleb stormed into the kitchen. He pulled the towel from her shoulder and uttered a defeated sounding, "Hi, Bells." Caleb wiped droplets of red wine from his face and shirt, and Mirabel thought of the entry in his journal.

B believes the pastor's violent outbursts started far sooner than I remember, that I was not the first target of his wrath. I didn't want to believe, but after what he tried to do to Bells…

"Wait," Mirabel said, shoving the memory away and grabbing a bottle of vinegar from beneath the sink. "Use this. It'll help with the stain."

Her brother accepted the bottle with a forced smile and scrubbed at his shirt. After a minute, he gave up and sank into a chair.

"What was it this time?" Mirabel didn't want to upset her brother further, but she couldn't very well dive into her questions without preamble. She retrieved the towel and vinegar from Caleb and worked on a stain on the back of his shoulder. "Is it because you fell asleep in church yesterday?"

"No. Actually, I think he missed that, and I'd appreciate it if you didn't tell him." Caleb ran his hands through his red hair, flinching when he came upon a bit of glass. He sighed and set it on the table. "At this rate, we won't have enough glassware to make it through the winter."

Mirabel finished with the stain on Caleb's shoulder and tossed the towel on the counter. "What was it, then?" she asked, packing a tray of cooled cakes in a wicker basket.

"You know how he gets when he's drinking. The minister will always find a reason to be upset." Caleb accepted a lemon pastry and bit into it. While he chewed, Mirabel glared at him until he finally sighed. "He doesn't think I carved enough sun charms for the church last week." Caleb took another bite and spoke with his mouth half-full. "This is incredible, Bells. Almost as good as Mother's."

Though her brother had clearly meant to compliment her, a rush of tangled emotions tore through her with lightning speed. She reached for her mother's necklace to steady herself as grief and fear and anger burned inside her. Mirabel had almost no memories of their mother, and now, Caleb thought their only remaining parent might have had something to do with her death.

"Bells? Do you feel well?"

"Was he always like this?" Her voice came out smaller than she intended, so she cleared her throat. "What I mean is… Do you think Father was this cruel when Mother was alive?"

Caleb froze, the pastry paused halfway to his lips. He glanced up to meet her gaze, and she saw the moment he chose to lock away the truth. The shift in his features before he set the pastry on the table. "His anger isn't our fault, Bells."

That wasn't what she meant, and Caleb knew it. He understood what she was trying to ask, and yet he still deflected. Did he think her a fool? And if he didn't understand, then *he* was the bigger fool. But Mirabel didn't need him for answers. She could go to the source.

She could go to *B.*

Mirabel grabbed the wicker basket packed with pastries and tucked it in the crook of her arm. "Try not to antagonize him while I'm gone. You ought to change out of that shirt and give it a proper wash while you're at it, too."

"And just where are you going on the cusp of evening?" Caleb asked, following her to the front door.

"I'm bringing these to a friend."

"Miss Fredrick," Caleb guessed. "She's been gracious to host you so much the last few weeks."

"Indeed, she has been." Guilt tugged at Mirabel's chest. She hadn't technically lied—Sally had truly been gracious—but that wasn't where she was headed.

And Mirabel was fairly sure the One God didn't condone *technicalities*.

"Do you need an escort?" Caleb opened the door for her and reached for his cloak.

She nearly confessed her true intentions, but Mirabel reminded herself of her brother's lie. She only wanted the truth. "No need. It's not a great distance, and I won't stay long." She paused when something crashed in the rear of the house. "Maybe you should visit Mr. Carrier until I return."

Caleb shook his head. "I'll be fine. I should finish those carvings before the minister asks after them again."

"If you're sure…"

"Go, Bells."

So, she swallowed her guilt and disappeared out the door. Outside, the One God's sun slipped down the horizon, the sky shot through with vivid reds and oranges. As she made her way across town, the small hairs at the back of her neck stood at attention. For a moment, she worried someone followed. Perhaps Mr. Eastey or the creepy undertake Mr. Upton. But after several glances over her shoulder revealed no one, she blamed it on the cold and continued past her father's church.

By the time she reached the Bradbury house—Blythe Bradbury being her best and only guess for the identity of the initial *B* in Caleb's journal—Mirabel's nerves had risen to new heights. Even as she forced herself to knock upon the door, panicked thoughts berated her for thinking this was a good idea. If her own brother wouldn't share his theories with her, why would a veritable stranger?

The house sat quiet and still for a few moments after Mirabel finished knocking, long enough for worry to speed her heart. Finally, the door swung open, revealing Blythe's mother.

Mirabel had never seen Mrs. Bradbury up close before, but it wasn't the similarities to her daughter that unsettled her most. It was the disdain written all over the older woman's face. Deep lines furrowed her brow as she scowled, and her lips pressed into an impossibly thin line.

"Forgive me for arriving unannounced, Mrs. Bradbury," Mirabel said, stumbling over her words. "We haven't officially met yet, but my father is the minister at the church across the street. I was hoping to speak with your daughter, and I brought cakes to—"

"I know who you are, Miss Walcott." Mrs. Bradbury crossed her arms as if to ward off the chill of the night air. "I'm afraid you wasted a trip. You are not welcome here."

"But I—"

"Good day." Mrs. Bradbury reached for the door as footsteps approached from within.

"Mother, what are you doing?"

The door paused halfway closed, and through the slim opening, Mirabel saw Blythe. Miss Bradbury looked so much like her mother—dark hair, freckled skin, eyes a blue that seemed almost gray—but instead of disdain, there was worry written across the daughter's face.

Mirabel's throat tightened as Blythe approached and pushed open the door. This girl held the answers she was too afraid to ask her brother outright. Mirabel didn't know why, but already it felt more possible to ask such horrendous things of this near stranger than her own brother.

The Bradbury women glared at each other, an unspoken challenge passing between them, Finally, the mother sighed and turned away. "Speak with her if you must, Blythe, but if you insist on making mistakes, you alone shall own the consequences." Mrs. Bradbury turned and disappeared into the back of the house, leaving Mirabel standing on the front porch, her cheeks burning with shame.

"Maybe this was a bad idea…" Mirabel stumbled back a step.

"No. Wait." Blythe followed her onto the porch and closed the front door. "Don't take anything my mother says personally. We move so frequently, she's forgotten how to trust others." She pointed to the basket of treats in Mirabel's hands. "Is that why you came?"

"Yes. I mean, no. I— Here." Mirabel thrust the basket toward Blythe, nerves stealing her ability to form a coherent sentence. When Blythe took the basket from her, Mirabel squeezed her hands into fists, stared at the wooden planks beneath her feet, and forced out the words. "It's about my family. My father and Caleb and… And my mother."

Without glancing up, Mirabel could sense the shift in Blythe's energy. The sudden tension between them, the way her narrow fingers clutched tighter at the basket.

"Did something happen?" Blythe asked, her words pitched with fear. "Is Caleb hurt?"

Hearing her brother's first name from another woman's lips should have embarrassed Mirabel. Instead, it tolled like a bell of truth, validating everything she had read in her brother's journal. Anger and grief assaulted her senses, spilling tears down her cheeks.

"It's true, then, isn't it?" Mirabel wiped the tears away and looked up to hold Blythe's shocked gaze. "You really think Father is responsible for my mother's death."

"I don't—"

"Caleb isn't hurt," Mirabel continued, the words flowing like a rushing river freed from a dam. "But you're right to be worried. Father is cruel, and he drinks and swings his fist with abandon, and I can't tell anyone because who would believe me? And even if they did, what would become of our family? The church is all we have. *Father* is all we have, but you think it's his fault that Mother is gone, and Caleb won't talk to me and I didn't know where else to go and I—"

"Breathe, Miss Walcott. Breathe." Blythe set down the basket and rested her hands on Mirabel's shoulders. Together, the women took three slow breaths. "Now, one more time. What did your brother say to you?"

"Nothing! That's the problem." Mirabel pulled away from Blythe's touch and paced the length of the porch. "I had to read about his theories—*your* theories—in his journal. I tried to ask him about it, but he acted like he had no idea what I was talking about. I'm not a child anymore. He doesn't need to protect me."

When Mirabel turned back to face Blythe, she found the other woman unusually still. Her face, normally pale, looked nearly as white as snow.

"What—" Blythe lost her voice. She cleared her throat and tried again. "What exactly did your brother write about me?"

Mirabel felt herself soften, seeing Blythe so clearly nervous to know what Caleb thought of her. If she wasn't so upset with her brother, she'd be excited for them. There was clearly a spark of something there.

"Nothing untoward or damaging, I assure you. He

never writes your name, only the letter *B*, but I've seen how tongue-tied he gets around you, so it was easy enough to guess." Mirabel walked back toward where Blythe stood. "It's clear he trusts you, and I hope I can do the same. I only want to know what you've discovered about my parents. Caleb wrote that he believes you, but he included no details."

Blythe studied Mirabel for several heartbeats before sighing and shaking her head. "I have no proof, Miss Walcott, only theories. I've seen the damage the pastor has done to his son, and I... I heard what he tried to do to you."

As the wind whispered between them, Blythe shared her theories in hushed tones. She talked about medical complications that Mirabel didn't fully comprehend, but she understood enough to know why Caleb believed in Blythe's ideas. Mirabel had seen her brother's skin torn open by their father's hand enough times that she couldn't outright dismiss Blythe's claims.

But none of that made her heart hurt any less.

Fresh tears spilled down her cheeks, and she shivered as the wind tore through her clothes. "What happens now? What am I supposed to do?"

"I wish I had answers for you." Blythe reached out and brushed the tears from Mirabel's cheeks. "I wish I could save you both from the minister's wrath."

Mirabel leaned into Blythe's touch, and her heart did a funny little jolt. "He's not always angry. And Caleb protects me."

"I know." Blythe dropped her hand. "You owe me nothing, but if I could request a favor?" She waited for Mirabel to nod. "Your brother will never ask for it, but he needs someone to watch out for him, too. Could you tell me if things escalate at home?"

"You really care for him, don't you?" Mirabel asked. Blythe merely shrugged, but her rosy cheeks spoke of her true feelings. "Don't be embarrassed, Miss Bradbury. He cares about you, too."

Blythe chuckled. "You really shouldn't read other people's diaries, Miss Walcott."

"Do brothers truly count as 'other people' though?" Mirabel teased, her heart giving another leap when Blythe smiled at her. "Thank you, for speaking with me. You didn't have to do that."

"It was my pleasure." Blythe stepped forward and wrapped Mirabel in a tight hug. "I only wish I could do more for you both."

Mirabel returned the embrace, feeling dizzy from a racing heart, her senses flooded with the warmth of Blythe's skin and the scent of lavender in her hair. She wasn't sure what else the other woman could possibly do to help, but she was glad for the sentiment all the same.

Reluctantly, Mirabel pulled away and bid Blythe Bradbury goodnight.

She only hoped she'd return home to find her brother still in one piece.

TESTIMONY OF THE EASTEYS

"$\mathcal{I}$ call Mrs. Prudence Eastey back to the stand."

Pastor Lewis stared out at the afternoon assembly. Day three of the trial had garnered a smaller audience than previous sessions, perhaps because the townsfolk had gotten their fill of excitement the night before as they burned the witch's home to ash. Or maybe the return of a previous witness was not interesting enough to pull them from their duties.

There were crops to harvest and wares to sell, after all. The townsfolk could only neglect their duties for so long.

In the middle of the courtroom, two people rose from their chairs. Mrs. Eastey and her husband, Thomas. Mr. Eastey held his wife's arm and led her toward the front of the room. Though she did not protest his grip, she angled herself away from him. The pair settled together at the witness stand.

The minister studied the unexpected pair of witnesses. "Thank you for returning today, Mrs. Eastey. I know it must take great courage to speak out against the witch." Lionel Lewis adjusted his spectacles and tugged at his vest.

"Mr. Eastey, you I did not expect. Have you come to support your wife in her testimony?"

Mr. Eastey scowled. "I have come to speak for her." He turned his glare on his wife, who fussed with the handkerchief in her hands.

"Why? Mrs. Eastey provided compelling testimony last we spoke."

"And that was the last time she spoke at all!" Mr. Eastey pointed an accusing finger at Blythe. He looked as though he might scale the railing and wrap his hands around her slender neck. "The witch stole her voice."

The small crowd in the courtroom gasped. Those closest to the accused eased from their seats to find places farther away to sit. Even the prosecutor paled.

But hidden at the back of the room, Caleb Walcott did not flinch. Instead, he burned a secret hope in his heart that his father would be the next to lose his voice. He imagined the peace of such quiet. The possibility.

"How did she curse your wife? When?" Pastor Lewis stood close to the jury, retreating as far as possible from the witch without outright fleeing the room.

Mr. Eastey gestured toward his wife, making her flinch. She only relaxed when his hand paused before reaching her. "Do I look like the sort of man who studies the details of witchery?" Anger flashed in his eyes. "All I know is that my wife hasn't spoken in two days. The witch cursed her!"

"And you are very brave to stand before the court after such ill has befallen your family." The minister brushed the front of his vest. "Have faith in the One God. He will restore your wife's voice once the court has properly dealt with the witch. Will your wife still testify today?"

"Yes," Mr. Eastey said. Prudence trembled as she bowed her head.

Pastor Lewis approached the witness stand. "I understand that by virtue of your proximity to the Bradbury home, you have knowledge of their visitors?"

Prudence nodded. She gestured toward the young woman taking notes of the trial and mimicked writing her answers. The prosecutor gathered extra parchment, quill, and ink from his table and set them before Mrs. Eastey. With a quick glance at her husband, Prudence scribbled something across the parchment.

Thomas Eastey squinted as he tried to make out his wife's writing. "She says... the witch did not take many guests this fall." He paused while she wrote further. "But there were some."

"Who were these guests?" Pastor Lewis turned away from his witnesses, speaking more to the jury. His voice soft, calming. "Who called upon the witch?"

Mrs. Eastey scrawled across the parchment. When she was done, she pushed the note toward her husband. He scowled as he read. "Why didn't you say something? You should have told me the moment you saw!"

Prudence shrank from her husband, but the minister approached before anything transpired between the couple. "Who did she see? Who visited the Bradbury house?"

"A man called upon her while the mother was out of the house." Thomas shook his head. "Seems the woman is a witch *and* a harlot."

Hidden in the back of the room, Caleb Walcott stared at the floor. He pulled the cloak tight over his head to hide his red hair, but he couldn't stop the blush that spread across his fair skin at the memory.

"Did she see his face? Does she know who it was?"

Mr. Eastey screwed up his face like he tasted something foul. "Caleb Walcott."

If the thought of *any* man calling upon the witch was

cause for scandal, to hear it was the dead girl's brother sent the audience into a frenzy. Pastor Walcott's face burned red with rage. Though all had seen the strange protectiveness the minister's son had developed for the witch, knowing he had been ensnared for so long and without his father's knowledge... It was an unthinkable embarrassment.

Bang!

Magistrate Hawthorne brought his gavel down upon his bench. *Bang, bang, bang!* "Everyone, back to your seats. Now. Or I'll have all save the jury removed."

The oldest Walcott dropped his head into his hands, and Caleb shrank farther from the crowd, tucked into the shadows at the back of the room.

Pastor Lewis waited for the small crowd to settle before returning to his witnesses. Tears hung heavy in Mrs. Eastey's eyes. Her husband kept a tight grip on her hand, though it was unclear whether he sought to provide comfort or pain.

The minister softened his voice and spoke as if to a scared child. "Did anyone else call upon the witch, Mrs. Eastey? Have you seen anything that proves more than corrupted morals?"

Tears fell from her eyes and left a trail down her cheeks. She nodded and tugged her hand from her husband's to grasp the parchment and quill. She scrawled a quick name and passed it to the minister instead of Thomas.

The prosecutor read the parchment three times before looking up at his witness. "Really?"

Prudence nodded.

"Gentlemen of the jury, Mrs. Eastey is perhaps the bravest of us all. Even after the witch cursed her, she risks herself to bring us evidence for our second charge against Miss Bradbury. She gives us proof of a connection between the accused and her victim. Proof that the witch knew and sought to corrupt young Miss Walcott."

Pastor Lewis read again the name on the parchment and held it up for all to see. "Mirabel Walcott visited the home of the witch." He paused, surveying his audience, savoring their rapt attention. "Alone in the Bradbury house, the witch had every opportunity to poison the younger girl's mind. Perhaps she sought to turn Miss Walcott into a witch herself."

The sparsely-filled court erupted. They wondered at their good fortune for attending despite the repeat witness. Their neighbors would be filled with regret for missing the afternoon.

Blythe's shoulders quivered. She clenched her bound hands into fists.

The coarse ropes bit into her flesh and smeared blood into the wooden amulet she wore at her wrist.

No one noticed the grief that pulled at her features.

No one could have guessed at its cause.

Caleb was running out of time.

He and Mirabel were at the church again, him carving the last of the minister's required sun charms while her fingers plucked out a tentative melody on the piano, never straying from church-approved songs. But it wasn't his sister's presence that worried Caleb. Their father had stayed later than expected, holed up in his office to prepare for the morning's sermon. If the minister was still around when Blythe arrived... Caleb could hardly stomach the thought.

It had been days since he'd seen her last, since he'd felt the tender press of her kiss. If his family didn't return home soon, Caleb wasn't sure when he could slip away next.

"It's getting late," Caleb said, raising his voice over Mirabel's quiet playing. "You should take the minister home for dinner."

Mirabel's fingers stilled on the keys. "Why can't you do it?"

"I—"

"Wait." Mirabel slipped off the stool and hurried down the aisle toward him, a knowing smile on her lips. "You're planning to see her tonight, aren't you?"

"I don't know who—"

"Miss Bradbury," Mirabel said, voice reverent. "Don't bother denying it, brother. I spoke with her last week. Besides, your face is redder than a sunset."

"Quiet, Bells, please. Father can't find out. You've seen how he gets whenever he notices her across the street." Caleb glanced out the window. The last rays of daylight were slipping away. "He can't be here when she arrives."

"So, she *is* coming to call upon you."

"Mirabel. I'm begging you."

His sister rolled her eyes. "I'm only teasing, Caleb. I quite like Miss Bradbury. She cares for you." Mirabel turned and walked back down the aisle, toward the minister's study. "I'll see if I can lure him home. You'd best figure out an excuse to stay."

A sudden warmth filled Caleb's chest. It was good to see his sister in bright spirits again. She hadn't been fully herself since the incident with their father, and she had been asking dangerous questions of late. He didn't know what to say when she questioned their family's past. Caleb wanted irrefutable proof of their mother's death before sharing the discovery with his sister.

He didn't dare break her heart over conjecture.

As Mirabel slipped out of view, someone knocked on the front door. Caleb's heart plummeted. *She's too soon.*

Caleb spun and raced to the front door, pulling it open just wide enough to peer through. Blythe stood before him, beautiful in the light of the rising moon. She smiled at the sight of him, and for a moment, all his fears fell away. She reached for him, trailing the tips of her fingers across his cheek.

"I've missed you," she said, her voice carrying through the small church.

Behind Caleb, another door creaked open and slammed shut. Worry soured his gut. "You have to go. The minister is still here."

Blythe's dark eyes grew wide. "You said he never stays this late."

"He normally doesn't." Caleb glanced over his shoulder and felt the blood drain from his face. His father was stumbling down the aisle, a flustered Mirabel trailing in his wake. "My sister was trying to get him to leave, but — He's coming. He's—"

"It will be all right, Caleb. Breathe." Blythe dropped her hand and stepped back several paces, putting a more respectable space between them.

Only a breath later, the minister grabbed the door and hauled it fully open, striking the edge of the wood against Caleb's chest. Caleb resisted the urge to rub the spot while his wine-soaked father glared down at Blythe.

"What are you doing here?" the minister growled, looking Blythe up and down. "What are you doing with our basket?"

Blythe merely smiled, raising a basket Caleb hadn't noticed before. It was filled with muffins and small cakes. "Your daughter was gracious enough to bring my family a gift last week. It didn't feel right to return an empty basket."

"That's very kind of you," Mirabel said softly as she tried to inch past the minister, but Pastor Walcott grabbed hold of her arm. Mirabel hissed in a pained breath.

"What did I tell you about consorting with these

women," he slurred, pulling Mirabel close before Caleb could intervene. "I told you not to speak to them until they attended services!"

"Father," Mirabel said, voice pinched with pain.

Caleb stepped toward his father. "Let her go."

"Useless. The both of you." The minister shoved Mirabel away as Caleb raised his hands against him. Mirabel stumbled back, her shoe catching in her skirts. She fell, crying out as her elbow hit the wooden floor.

"Mirabel." Caleb rushed to his sister's side and knelt before her. "Are you injured?"

"She's fine," the minister snapped.

"No thanks to you," Blythe cut in, an edge to her voice. Caleb glanced over his shoulder as Blythe pushed her way into the church. "She nearly struck her head on the pew."

"You are not welcome in here, wretch." Pastor Walcott reached for Blythe, but he caught the woven handle of the basket instead, upending the desserts. Muffins and cakes tumbled across the floor. "Those who shun the One God do not belong in Brekham."

As Caleb helped his sister to her feet, Blythe held her ground. "Any god that allows a father to abuse his children is unworthy of my devotion."

The minister lunged, howling with rage, and shoved Blythe against the wall. "Vile, loathsome creature. You dare speak ill of the One God? You dare challenge *me* within these walls?"

"Someone ought to." Blythe held her chin high.

"Father, please," Mirabel cut in, but the minister only shook his head. Pastor Walcott spared a repulsed glance at his children before curling his hand into a fist and spinning toward Blythe.

"No!" Caleb lunged forward, reaching for his father.

He pulled the older man back, but he wasn't fast enough. The minister's fist still caught the edge of Blythe's jaw, and her head whipped to one side. Caleb struggled to draw his father further back, but all he could see was Blythe. The blooming red on her skin where she'd been struck. The glittering tears in her eyes.

The pain he'd been too slow to prevent.

Blythe's fingers trembled as she raised her hand to her face, but her gaze was hard as iron as she watched the pastor struggle in Caleb's grasp.

"You will pay for this insolence," the minister said, twisting out of Caleb's grip. "I know how to handle women like you. You and your mother will not last long in this town."

For the first time, fear flashed across Blythe's features. She spared Caleb only a glance before she stumbled toward the still-open door and fled into the night.

Caleb pushed past his father. "Blythe, wait!" He made it to the doorway, but a large hand gripped his upper arm.

"If you chase after her now, boy, I'll name a different heir. I'll cast you out. I'll—"

Glass shattered, and the minister collapsed to the floor. In his place stood Mirabel, the neck of a broken wine bottle still clutched in her grip. She let the final bit of glass fall to the ground where the wine was soaking into the floor and their father's clothes.

"Bells, I..."

"With any luck, he won't remember anything when he wakes." Mirabel studied the minister's prone position a moment before glancing up the stairs, where they kept the cleaning supplies. "I can take care of things here, convince him he simply had too much to drink and imagined the rest."

"Mirabel."

His sister shook her head and rubbed the elbow that had hit the floor. "I'll be fine. Go after her."

Worry and gratitude warred within him, but Caleb nodded. "Thank you." He slipped out of the church and ran after Blythe.

The forest was more than happy to swallow them both.

Caleb left the courthouse, his mind buzzing with questions. When had Bells visited Blythe? Why hadn't either of them said something? What other secrets had the women in his life kept from him?

He couldn't go on like this, chasing after the flimsiest clues in his search for the truth. He needed something more, something solid to start from. Caleb hurried down the stone steps, his body protesting each movement. He'd barely slept the night before, tucked up against the trunk of a tree. With any luck, the doctor's offer the day before would hold. Caleb couldn't stomach the thought of another night in the cold, and there was nothing in this world that would have him begging for help from his father.

But first, Caleb needed answers. He rounded the side of the courthouse, toward the back door that led to Blythe's cell. He pulled up short when he turned the corner. Two guards stood stationed before the door. Caleb cursed and turned back the way he'd come, emerging into the town square.

He paused a moment at the fountain. Water trickled over stone, and the mist felt like flecks of ice against his skin.

If Caleb couldn't get answers from Blythe, perhaps he could find a way forward with Mirabel.

Though Caleb hadn't gone to the undertaker's house when his mother died, he knew where it stood. With a final bracing breath of misty air, he turned and left the square.

On the edge of town, Mr. Upton's home sat back from the road, the stone walk lined with dried roses. Caleb's shoes clicked against the cold stone as he approached the small wooden house, and he paused at the threshold. His sister lay somewhere inside. What was left of her, at least.

Not bothering to knock—it seemed wrong, somehow—Caleb eased open the door. "Hello?" he called as he stepped inside. The warmth surprised him. He expected the building to be cold, like death.

"Good afternoon, sir." Mr. Upton, a rail thin man with a hooked nose and pallid skin, stepped into the foyer. He raised his voice. "What brings you here, Mr. Walcott?"

"I've come to visit my sister." Caleb stepped farther into the room. "Is she beyond that door?"

The hawkish man scuttled forward, blocking his path. "You don't want to see your sister like this, Mr. Walcott. Trust me." The man was practically shouting. "Preserve your fonder memories."

"I must see her," Caleb shouted back, concerned the man might be hard of hearing. When Mr. Upton didn't move, Caleb hurried around him. The undertaker wasn't quick enough to stop him, and Caleb swung open the door. "You can't keep me from—"

Caleb stopped dead in his tracks.

His sister's coffin lay on a table. Open.

And Isaac Carrier stood beside her.

"You." Caleb curled his hands into fists. "Step away from my sister."

"Caleb." Isaac stepped back from the casket and raised his hands in surrender. "You were supposed to be at the courthouse."

"I was." Caleb advanced into the room. He kept his eyes averted from Bells, focusing instead on his former best friend. "What are you doing here?"

Isaac glanced at the undertaker and leveled a shrug. "Paying my respects?"

"You seem unsure about that, Carrier."

"I was. I swear it." Isaac retreated until his back hit another table.

"Then why do I find it so hard to believe you?" Caleb closed the gap between them. "What cause do you have to visit Mirabel?" He fisted his hands in Isaac's shirt.

"She was like a sister to me." Isaac squirmed under Caleb's grip.

Caleb barked a laugh. "Don't lie. I know you hated Bells, always complaining when I had to keep an eye on her." Caleb gripped Isaac's shirt tighter, mostly to prevent himself from hitting his old friend.

But there was a reason Caleb had never fought with Isaac before. Isaac knocked his hands away and shoved Caleb in the chest. "Believe what you want, Walcott. I was leaving anyway." Isaac stormed toward the door.

"One day."

Isaac pulled up short.

"One day, Carrier, or they'll all know."

Isaac's shoulders tensed, but he stormed out the door, past the undertaker. Caleb's anger stretched wide inside him, and he latched quickly onto another target.

"And you," he said, thrusting a finger at Mr. Upton.

"You're supposed to protect her privacy. What was he doing here? Why did you let him in?"

"The minister approved it," Mr. Upton said quickly, cowering away from Caleb. "Many people have come to pay their respects."

"I need a list."

"But Mr. Walcott, it's been nearly half the—"

"I want a list, and I want a moment alone with my sister." Caleb held the undertaker's gaze until the older man nodded and slunk away.

Finally alone, Caleb released a breath. His lungs ached, and his eyes stung. He stepped up to the table that held his sister's coffin. After a few moments, he found the strength to glance inside.

"Mirabel—" His voice caught, and then he was choking, struggling for each breath. He squeezed his eyes shut and gripped the edge of the table for support. "I'm so sorry, Bells. If I had just paid closer attention to you that night…"

Caleb lost his voice, each breath a struggle. He prayed his father was right about the One God, that He had welcomed Mirabel into a better place, had granted her a place in the warmth of His light.

For several minutes, Caleb stood alone, fighting to make his lungs work, desperate to keep himself upright. When he managed to collect himself, he was still alone. If he didn't manage to save Blythe, he'd spend the rest of his miserable days on his own.

"Bells, how will I ever survive without you?" He pressed his palms to the side of her coffin. He couldn't bear to look into her too-still face. He stared at her shoes instead. "The world is turned upside down in your absence."

Wind trailed through the open window, and Caleb

could almost hear the last melody Mirabel translated to the piano. An unexpected smile pulled at his lips. Yet still his chest ached. The wound was still there, it would *always* be there, but—for now—it no longer bled.

"This never should have happened." His voice grew hard, and he wiped the tears from his face. "I'll find whoever did this to you, Bells. I swear on my life I will find them, and they will be punished."

Caleb forced himself to look at his sister, to *really* look at her, but something was wrong. Something more than just the wrongness of her skin and the stillness of her chest. Something was missing. Something was—

Mother's necklace.

Mirabel never took it off, was never parted from the One God's sun with the amber stone at the center.

"Where is it?" he asked, voice soft but then rising with panic. "Where is it?"

"Where is what, Mr. Walcott?" Mr. Upton asked softly behind him.

Caleb whirled around, his heart smashing against his ribs. He couldn't let Mirabel be buried without it. She would be devastated if she knew. "My sister's necklace. Where is it?"

Mr. Upton shook his head. "There was no necklace, Mr. Walcott, but I have the names you requested." He held up a bit of parchment.

"But there must be! She never goes anywhere without it. She—" Caleb cleared the emotion from his throat. "If you lost it, if you *took* it, I swear—"

"Mr. Walcott, please. I know seeing a loved one like this is an impossible challenge, but I've served Brekham faithfully for years. I do not pilfer from the dead."

"No, you simply stare after women far too young to warrant such looks." Caleb hated that Bells was stuck here with the undertaker until her burial. She had never liked the strange man.

"I—"

"Mirabel will be buried with our mother's necklace." Caleb snatched the bit of parchment from Mr. Upton's hand and shoved past him toward the exit. "I suggest you double check every inch of your home and ensure it hasn't been misplaced."

Caleb slammed the door behind him when he left and glanced at the parchment. As Mr. Upton had warned, there were dozens of names. Caleb would look into every single one if he must, but first, there was one place he had to search. One other place Mirabel may have lost her necklace.

The place she died.

"*B*lythe! Wait!"

Twigs snapped at his face. Overhead, the interwoven branches blocked the moonlight, casting the world into shades of gray. Caleb had no choice but to slow his stride as he picked his way through the trees. Blythe was little more than a flash of fabric and a bend of branches before she disappeared again.

"Blythe, please. Wait." His eyes adjusted to the dimness of the forest, and Caleb quickened his chase through the maze of trees and bushes.

"It's too late," she said. Ahead, to his left. "I've ruined everything. It's over." Her voice broke, breaking his heart in turn.

Caleb emerged through a row of trees and nearly toppled over Blythe. She stood on the edge of a clearing, her face buried in her hands as silent tears trembled through her entire body.

"What do you mean?" Caleb's chest tightened to the point of pain, pain that had nothing to do with the door that had struck him. "You've done nothing wrong. This was my fault. I should have been faster. I should have protected you."

Blythe didn't answer.

Caleb slowed his breathing to a more normal pace, though his heart still raced. He stepped closer and placed his hand gently on her shoulder. "Blythe, please. Look at me."

She shrugged away from his touch. "Mother was right. I was a fool to let myself fall for a minister's son. She knew the risks. Warned of the dangers of religious men in places like this."

"I don't—"

"He knows what I am!" Blythe whirled around to face Caleb, her expression full of grief and fear and regret. "You heard him. He'll accuse Mother and me of witchery and run us out of town. Or worse, drag us to the gallows himself."

"That's not possible." Caleb shook his head. "He was drunk. He was trying to frighten you. My father can't possibly know the truth. If he did, he would have said so, not leveled generic threats."

"It doesn't matter." Blythe wiped a stray tear from her cheeks. "Once Mother finds out, she'll make us leave. She won't risk our safety."

"But you *can't* leave. We've only just found each other." A terrible pain closed Caleb's throat. It couldn't end like this. He wouldn't let his father destroy the one good thing he'd found for himself. "Is there anything you could do? Is there a tea or a… a spell that could make him forget?"

A sad smile pulled at the corner of Blythe's lips. "I don't think magic is the best way to avoid accusations of witchery, Caleb."

"I suppose not." He let out a deep sigh, feeling the weight of his future laying heavy on his shoulders. "My sister thinks the minister drank enough to destroy his memory of the night. Can't we at least wait until we know for sure?"

"Caleb."

"Please?"

Blythe sighed and stepped forward into his arms, the tension in her shoulders relaxing as Caleb ran his hands along her back. "I don't want to leave," she whispered into his chest.

"Then stay. At least long enough to see if he forgets." The tightness returned to his throat, and Caleb pulled away enough to look at Blythe. Her face glowed in the sparse moonlight, and he brushed a section of loose hair behind her ear. The skin was pink where the minister had struck her. He sucked in a breath.

"What is it?"

"I hate that he hurt you." He reached forward and trailed his fingers along the side of her face, hoping to soothe her pain. "I should have stopped him."

She leaned into his touch. "I'll be all right."

Caleb nodded, but in his mind, all he saw was his father striking her over and over on a loop. He felt the weight of his failure and would give anything to go back to that moment. To be faster. To strike his father down before he could lay a hand on either of the women he loved—his sister *and* Blythe.

The thought rattled through his ribcage, and the rightness of it burned within him. He wanted to pull Blythe close, to protect her from everyone who might wish her ill.

"We have to do something. It was one thing when he only hit me, but now Mirabel and you? I can't let him do this. Something has to be done. People need to know."

"People will inevitably disappoint you, Caleb. He's their pastor. I'm a strange woman with no father and no husband. No one will believe us. No one will care what happens to me."

"I care. I will always care." Caleb reached for Blythe's hands, trailing his thumbs along her wrists. "If the choice is between you and my father, I'll choose you every time."

Blythe's fingers trembled against his. "But he's your family."

"If family is who we love, that man is no family of mine." Caleb pressed a kiss to Blythe's forehead. "He's not, but you, Blythe Bradbury, you most certainly are."

"What are you saying?" she asked, but the way she glanced up at him, hope softening every worry, said she knew.

"I love you." He pressed another kiss to her temple. "I choose you." A kiss to the hollow of her throat. "All I need is a little time." Caleb held her glittering gaze. "Please don't follow the Traveler's stars without me."

Blythe rested her hands over Caleb's heart. "I'll give you every second I can spare." Her hands slid up the planes of his chest, coming to rest at the back of his neck. Then she drew him near, rising onto her toes to kiss him like they'd never kissed before. Her touch was desperate and rough, her fingers coiled in his hair, pulling him ever closer.

Caleb wrapped his arms around her waist, pulling their bodies flush, kissing her deeper. She was warm against him, a burning fire against the chill of night.

Desire flared somewhere deep inside Caleb. Somewhere low. It pulsed through him with an urgency he'd never before experienced. His body grew tight with need, his longing obvious, but Blythe never shrank away from him. If anything, she pulled him closer, pressed their bodies tighter. When that wasn't enough to satisfy either of them, she stood on her toes and wrapped her arms behind his neck, hands gripping tight to his bare skin.

Their world was an explosion of touch and taste and heat. Blythe captured Caleb's lower lip in her teeth, and a deep, urgent sound caught in his throat. He felt her smile as she kissed him again, and Caleb traced his tongue along her lips. She tasted of honey and cinnamon.

Caleb broke the connection only long enough to press his lips along her jaw, kissing her neck, kissing every bit of exposed flesh he could reach. Her skin was smooth and soft and warm against his lips. He pressed a kiss to the hollow behind her ear. Blythe's breath caught in her throat, and she pulled him higher so that she might capture his lips once more. He never wanted to stop kissing her. Never wanted to return to the coldness of the church. To the emptiness of his life without her.

As if sensing the shift in his focus, Blythe pulled away, just enough to keep their lips apart. Her eyes searched his. There was a warmth—a fire—in her gaze Caleb had never seen before. "Do you need to return?"

"Not tonight."

"Good."

Caleb leaned in and kissed her again.

*C*aleb had meant to go straight to the place where he'd found Mirabel that night, but when he passed the empty church, something pulled him toward his mother's grave. Whether it was memory or grief or fear that kept him out of the forest, Caleb wasn't sure. The effect was the same regardless.

The sun headed toward the horizon, but it still cast enough light over the small cemetery behind the church. All the flowers were long dead, and since Caleb hadn't intended to come, he arrived empty-handed at his mother's grave. He sank to his knees. The cold, damp earth soaked his pants in seconds, and though he shivered, he didn't mind the chill.

"Mother…" Caleb traced the carving of her headstone with his fingers. *Isabella Marie Walcott. Beloved Wife. Cherished Mother.* She was the original *Bells* in the Walcott family.

The minister never called Mirabel that after their mother's death.

Caleb glanced back at the church. It still appeared empty, but there was no telling how long until his father returned. He could never go too long without a glass full of wine.

A breeze picked up, blowing cold air across his face. A realization made him shiver. The Walcott women had lost their lives far too young, and his father blamed both deaths on women he claimed were witches. Though Blythe had a power Caleb couldn't fully understand, she was not evil. She would never hurt Mirabel. The minister was wrong about Blythe, which meant he was probably wrong about the Sandersons, too. Caleb hadn't wanted to believe it before, even after the information Blythe uncovered in the medical texts, but he remembered how easily his father had hurt Bells. How little remorse he had for his actions.

Had Tobias Walcott stolen them both and cried witch to shift the blame?

In the distance, leaves rustled loud in the trees, drawing Caleb's gaze. He stared at the forest, and the forest seemed to stare back.

The flash of a memory, bloody leaves clinging to a torn body, gripped him. Caleb fought the urge to be sick, fought the crushing weight pressing on his lungs.

"Please take good care of her, Mother. She missed you so much." He pressed his hand to the headstone, swallowed down the still-rising bile, and rose to his feet. He had somewhere to be.

Caleb bid his mother goodbye and forced himself to enter the forest. He picked his way through the trees, led by muscle memory more than his own decisions. He'd been to the clearing many times in the weeks before. The place had once been sacred to him. It was *their* place. The place he first told Blythe how he felt. Where they did so many things for the first time.

As he neared the clearing, flecks and small pools of dried brown liquid littered the ground. Caleb crept forward, his stomach in knots. He knew what had left those marks, knew what horrors awaited him once he made it through the last line of trees.

Caleb stepped into the clearing, his vision assault by the blood-soaked earth. A ring of short, stubby candles remained on the ground, so close to where Caleb had once kissed Blythe until their lips went numb. He shoved the memories aside and tried to search the clearing. Someone must have removed the knife when they carried Mirabel back to town that night, but if she lost Mother's necklace anywhere, it had to be here.

He searched the trampled grass, tried to avoid the pool of blood, but eventually, he had to search even that. The blood-soaked blades of grass were brittle against his skin, and the prickling stirred the sick in his stomach. Caleb tried to shove it down, but when his fingers grazed something that wasn't grass, something cold and mushy. Something that smelled of rot and—

Bile burned at the back of his throat, and this time, Caleb couldn't swallow it down. He turned and fled from the clearing, breaking through the first row of trees just as his body gave out. His stomach heaved, and he expelled what little he had eaten until his insides were empty and his mouth tasted bitter.

When it was over, a large hand clapped him on the back. "Are you all right?"

The husky voice, eerily familiar yet not easily placed, startled Caleb. He stood and wiped his shirtsleeve across his lips before turning to face the intruder. He couldn't place the man at first, not until he saw the reflection of the man's father—Mayor Eliot. Which made this man, younger than his voice suggested, the young widower, Amos Eliot. The mayor's son was only eight years Caleb's senior, but the lines around his eyes made him look far older. Mr. Eliot wore his brown hair longer than customary in the town, and his beard was thick.

Amos stepped closer. "Mr. Walcott? Are you ill?"

Caleb fell back. He didn't know Amos well, but he remembered the rumors. His young bride died while she carried their child, when the pair was not yet twenty. Amos had been an outsider ever since, despite his family's attempts to find him another suitable match.

"What are you doing here?" Caleb asked.

"I could ask you the same thing."

Caleb clenched his fists. "I have every right to be here."

"I never said—"

"My sister *died* in this clearing." Caleb swung his arm toward the break in the trees. "So, I will ask you again, *Eliot*, what are you doing here?"

Amos narrowed his eyes but otherwise ignored the slight. He lifted his shovel and set it against his shoulder. His other hand raised in surrender. "The mayor keeps me busy with the town upkeep. He wanted me to clean…" Amos stopped himself and merely gestured forward.

"No." Caleb placed himself between Mr. Eliot and the clearing. "You cannot erase her." *Not while there might still be clues to discover. Not while there is still a chance to save Blythe and catch the real killer.*

"I'm sorry, Mr. Walcott. I understand how this must feel, but I—"

"Have you been here before?" Caleb asked, mind racing. "Have you already taken items from the clearing?"

"I don't—"

"My sister had a necklace," Caleb said, interrupting the mayor's son. "It was our mother's, the One God's sun, made from gold, with an amber stone set at the center. Have you seen it?"

Amos shook his head. "This is the first I've come to tend to the area."

"But then why isn't it here?" Grief overtook Caleb's anger. "Mirabel *must* be buried with it. She never took it off. She never—"

"I'm sorry, Mr. Walcott. I will keep a watchful eye while I work." Amos Eliot lifted the shovel again. "If I find anything, I'll make sure I give it to the minister."

"No." The word whipped between them, harsher than the coming winter wind. "Not my father. Me. It has to be me."

Though he looked unsure, Amos Eliot nodded. "I'll take care with the space. You have my word." He rested the shovel across his shoulders and stepped past Caleb. "Where can I find you, if I come across anything?"

"I… I don't know." Caleb shivered in the cold. "I thought perhaps I could stay with the doctor tonight."

Mr. Eliot gave a brief smile, though Caleb could only tell from the way the man's beard quirked up on one side. "Oliver is always taking in strays. I'm sure he'll be happy to help."

The clearing became *their* place.

It was where Caleb first admitted the depths of his feelings. The place they came whenever they needed a moment together, where they didn't have to wait for parents to be otherwise occupied. Though the minister often raged when Caleb returned home with no proper accounting of his time, he didn't care. Caleb could handle the threats and the occasional bruise. All of that faded away when he was with her.

Every unaccompanied trip to the church became an opportunity to disappear into the forest. To find her waiting for him, as if she *knew* when he might come. He had asked once, if predicting his arrival was one of her gifts, but Blythe merely shrugged and kissed him until he forgot he ever asked.

The afternoon was sunny and warm, a welcome reprieve from the recent spell of unseasonably cold weather. Caleb and Blythe lay on a blanket taken from her home, nestled together near the center of the clearing. He smiled as she shifted closer to him, curling her body tightly against his, her head resting along his chest. He held her close and pressed a kiss to her forehead, but when he looked down, worried lines furrowed her brow.

"Is something wrong?"

A dusting of pink settled in her cheeks as she shifted to lean over him. "Everything's fine." She bent and pressed her lips to his, kissing him fully. The world spun, and Caleb brushed a hand along her face. Her hair tumbled over his arm like silk.

Caleb was the first to pull away. "I'm serious, Blythe. You seem unsettled." He brushed a light kiss against her lips. "And I am not so easily distracted."

"It's nothing." Blythe nestled back into Caleb's side, resting her head on his shoulder. "You needn't worry." Her tone said otherwise.

"Asking me not to worry is a recipe to ensure I do. Please, Blythe. I want to know what troubles you." Caleb rubbed her back, and she shivered beneath his hand. She fell silent for a long time, and he didn't press. Her touch warmed him, and he longed to pull her closer. Longed to cover her body with his, to press tight against her while she wrapped her arms around him. To feel her every curve beneath him…

Get it together, Caleb. Now isn't the time for such thoughts.

But in his distraction, in his silence, Blythe found her voice again. "I can't stop thinking about the first night we spent here."

Caleb thought often of that night, of the way she'd kissed him before he had the chance. The way their breath had become shallow and fast. The taste of her lips. The urgency of it all. His heart skipped at the memory.

As if sensing where his thoughts had gone, Blythe pulled away and sat upright. "Not that part." She blushed as he sat opposite her, their knees brushing. "Well, perhaps

I do think of *that part* often, too, but it's not the memory that troubles me."

"The minister," Caleb said. It wasn't a question.

She nodded.

Caleb scowled.

"The minister remembers nothing of your visit, I promise. You're still safe here. There's no need to flee Brekham." Caleb wanted so desperately to pull her close and protect her from every darkness in the world. But he could see the doubt in her eyes, so he merely held her hands.

And waited.

"Blythe, please. I can't help if I don't know what troubles you."

She paused for several heartbeats more, then finally nodded. "I love you, Caleb. With all my heart." She paused, letting her declaration hang in the air between them. It was the first time she'd spoken those words since Caleb uttered them two weeks prior. He wanted to remind her that those feelings were returned, that her admission would never scare him away, but he kept quiet.

After a moment, Blythe shook her head and continued. "But every time I remember the things your father said to me… I'm overcome with this gnawing sense of foreboding. If he discovered me once, it's only a matter of time before he comes to the same conclusion again. This town will never be safe for Mother and me." Her voice broke, but she pushed through the tears gathering in her eyes. "I have to tell her."

A bone-deep chill spread through Caleb's body. "Your mother?" he asked, and Blythe gave a shallow nod. "But she'll make you leave! There has to be another way. I can't lose you."

"Then come with us. We can follow the Traveler

together, journey east across the seas." Blythe leaned forward and kissed him. "You could study medicine properly instead of reading an old doctor's cast away texts. You could save lives."

"And you?"

"I will study the workings of the world. I'll make new discoveries. Chart the stars unlike anyone before." Blythe punctuated each dream with a kiss until Caleb was dizzy with imaginings. They could get a small home, be together always.

But reality finally broke through. "What of my sister? I can't leave her behind with the minister."

"Then she'll come with us. If she wants." Blythe settled more fully into Caleb's lap, the hem of her dress inching up to her knees.

Caleb traced her exposed skin with the tips of his fingers. "When do we leave?"

Blythe shivered against him. "Mother hates to travel during the winter months, but I don't know if we can remain safe that long."

"We'll figure something out. I know we will." He kissed her again. Deeply. Fully. She sighed into him, setting that inner fire ablaze.

After a moment, he pulled away and offered a bright smile. "Actually, I made you something that might help." He dug in his pocket and curled his fingers around the smooth pendant of wood attached to braided leather ties, pulling it out to show Blythe.

She arched away from him, raising one brow. "A sun charm? I appreciate the gesture, but I will not wear a symbol of your god in hopes of fitting in. That's not who I am."

Caleb grinned, undeterred. "Remember what you taught me? About the sun simply being a star close enough to share its warmth?" He waited for Blythe to nod. "This is how I imagine the Eastern Star, if it were as close as the One God's sun."

Blythe sucked in a startled breath, tears sparkling in her eyes.

"And on the back," Caleb continued, turning over the smooth disc of wood to reveal a series of indentations.

"The Traveler," Blythe said, her words more breath than substance. Her face shone with awe and gratitude and something Caleb saw as a mirror of the love he felt for her.

"The people of Brekham will make assumptions that keep you safe." Caleb traced his fingers over the pattern of stars that he'd so carefully carved. "But we will know the truth. May I?" He pointed to her wrist.

Blythe nodded and offered her hand.

Caleb placed the charm along the back of her wrist, the Traveler hidden against her skin, and he tied the two ends of the leather together. When he was done, Caleb let his hands fall, his fingers brushing Blythe's bare leg. "Do you like it?"

"I will cherish it always." Blythe leaned forward and captured his lips. Her kiss was fierce and full of longing, full of an intensity he'd never felt before. Caleb's fingers trailed up her leg, slipping beneath the hem of her dress to brush her upper thigh. Blythe tugged his shirt free from his trousers and pressed her fingers against the bare flesh of his stomach.

Her touch sent a pulse of desire to intimate places. He sighed into her kisses, drawing her closer.

As if she'd plucked his earlier thoughts from his mind, Blythe eased onto the blanket, pulling him to lay on top of her. Caleb settled his weight against her slowly, but Blythe traveled her hands beneath his shirt until they rested on his bare lower back. She pressed him tighter to her. Under his weight, he could feel every curve of her flesh. His body was on fire, his breathing rapid and shallow.

Blythe's hands continued their exploration, shifting to travel over the front of his trousers. She pressed firm against the tightness in his groin, and the sensation drew a deep moan from his chest.

But then she was reaching beneath the fabric, her fingers curling over hot, bare skin, and Caleb pulled away. His heart wanted this—his body, too—but still his mind pushed the words to his lips. "We're not married. We can't—"

Blythe pulled her hand free and stared up at him. There was no judgement in her eyes as she searched his gaze. "My gods celebrate all acts of love. They do not require vows in a church to bless our union."

She kissed him then, her lips light on his. A question, not a demand. When she pulled away, she let her hands rest on his hips. "I offer all of myself to you, Caleb. If you'll have me."

Caleb rested his forehead against hers, his body braced above. His whole life, he'd been taught to follow the One God's laws, to uphold them. Yet he had never truly believed, never saw the point in such rules except to have reasons to shame those who stepped out of line.

"What of children? We can't—"

"I have ways to prevent such things." Another gentle kiss. "One of my small gifts."

Caleb's body and heart begged him to continue. "If you're sure you're ready."

"I am," she said, tilting her face to kiss him again. "I choose you, Caleb. Until my dying breath."

"Until my dying breath," he echoed, pressing his body back into hers, kissing her with all the fierce love in his heart. This time, when her hands found their way beneath his clothes, he kissed the hollow of her neck. When she raised her skirts, he kissed lower and lower, until she was crying out his name.

And when she pushed Caleb onto his back and settled herself over him, he feared his heart would give out if they delayed a moment longer.

"Until my dying breath," she promised again as she joined their bodies together. She angled herself to kiss him, and they moved as one, delighting in the physicality of their love. Savoring every touch. Every breath. Until finally, their joy filled the world around them.

TESTIMONY OF GRACE PRATCHETT

Isaac Carrier and Grace Pratchett were out of time.

The pair sat together at the courthouse, a row away from Grace's twin, Verity. Isaac and Grace bent forward in prayer, their foreheads so close they nearly touched. But their eyes did not close, and the whispers on their lips did not plea to the One God for strength. Grace touched a hand to her stomach, for only a moment, before clasping her hands again.

At the back of the courtroom, Caleb Walcott watched. Waited. Agonized. Though he had known Isaac all his life, Caleb would do anything to save Blythe from the gallows. Even if that meant destroying his friend's reputation.

No, he hadn't destroyed anything. Isaac had made his choices.

Isaac had lied to hurt Blythe.

The One God couldn't fault Caleb for telling the truth. That is, if the One God cared at all for the people of Brekham, if He even existed. But the town believed. And if neither Isaac nor Grace would rescind their lies and speak true, Caleb would share *their* truth with all of Brekham.

At the front of the courtroom, Pastor Lewis stood and faced the crowd. "A witness has asked to return to the stand this morning." The prosecutor pushed his spectacles up his nose. "Miss Pratchett, if you please."

Grace straightened in her seat and stood. She cast a lingering glance at Isaac, who nodded encouragingly. After she was seated at the witness stand, she looked again into the crowd. A soft smile lit her face when she saw Isaac, but as she looked further into the crowd and caught sight of Caleb, she scowled.

The prosecuting minister paced before the court. His brows rose, deepening the lines of his face. "Miss Pratchett, your father contacted me late last night. He said you were insistent that you appear before the court again. What new evidence do you bring?"

"After my previous testimony, I have thought of little else." Grace shifted in her seat, fidgeting with the edges of her long sleeves. "I'm worried I failed to share the whole story."

"Do you have more information about the relationship between Miss Bradbury and Miss Walcott?"

"Yes, sir. I saw them often around the town square. Wherever they went, men followed, eager to talk to Miss Bradbury. It was as if she had ensnared their minds."

Caleb stepped forward out of the shadows. The movement caught the witness's eye, and she paled. "It's possible the men were simply intrigued by Miss Bradbury, by virtue of her being new in town," Grace rushed to add.

The prosecutor turned back to this witness. "What are you saying, Miss Pratchett? Which is it?"

Grace worried at her lip and sought out Isaac in the crowd. After a nod from her beloved, she took a deep breath. "I'm sorry. Being so near the witch has me flustered. What I mean to say, is that I may have thought the interest in Miss Bradbury was normal at first, but I was wrong." She tilted her chin up and stared straight at Caleb. "But when Miss Bradbury ensnared my betrothed, my Isaac, I knew there must be wicked magic at work."

This was not the deal Caleb had struck. Betrayal burned through him, and he stormed down the center aisle toward Isaac. "What are you doing, Carrier?" he asked when he reached the seated man. "Tell the truth or I shall tell yours." Caleb spun on the witness stand. "And you. Why would you risk everything for more lies?"

The magistrate banged his gavel. "Sit down, Mr. Walcott. If you continue to harass the witness, I shall have you removed."

A guard blocked Caleb's path, ready to restrain and remove him if necessary.

Caleb stepped back, but when his gaze fell over Blythe, his retreat faltered. Resolve hardened his heart. "I will tell them, Miss Pratchett." The guard gripped his arm, and Caleb tried to pull away. "Set things right, or I will tell them."

"Miss Pratchett, what is the meaning of Mr. Walcott's outburst?" Pastor Lewis asked.

"Actually, Minister, I am no longer Miss Pratchett." A crooked smile lit her face as the guard dragged Caleb toward the rear of the courtroom. She raised her left hand, a gold ring set with a honey-colored stone glinted in the light. "As of dawn this morning, I am Mrs. Carrier."

The courtroom froze. Even the guard paused Weddings weren't supposed to take place at the crest of winter. Marriages begun during the darker months brought ill fortune. No one would agree to such a thing. It wasn't the proper way of things.

"How?" Caleb pulled away from the guard but did not advance on the witness. "It's not possible."

The witness smiled. "Your father married us this morning, under the first light of the One God's sun. It's unusual, but these are unpredictable times." Grace lowered her hand and admired her ring. "I wouldn't risk the danger of testifying if I couldn't greet the One God as my true love's wife." She looked up and caught Caleb's eye. "Pastor Walcott shared our fears and agreed it was worth the break in tradition."

"But that's——" Under the watchful eye of the guard, Caleb sank into the last row of benches and stared, unseeing, at the floor. With his reputation destroyed and no physical proof that her pregnancy came before the wedding… he had no leverage. He had nothing to save his love.

Nothing except finding a different truth.

Grace continued to weave lies before the court, keeping the men of the jury—her father among them—on the edge of their seats. She spoke of Mirabel's obsession with the witch. Her desire to share in that dark power. Caleb barely heard any of it, his mind busy with more important matters.

There was still a way to save Blythe.

He had to find Mirabel's true killer.

He had to find irrefutable proof.

The air inside Blythe's cell threatened to suffocate her. Dust clung to the moisture in the air until it felt like breathing in mud. Each day in this place, blocked from the earth and the moon, she felt herself withering away. She feared she wouldn't survive long enough to face the gallows. Sitting alone on the cold stone, every bit of her body bruised and numb, Blythe counted the minutes between her and a noose.

Footsteps echoed in the halls. Soft. Near silent save for the crunch of dead leaves and dirt beneath boots.

Someone approached, someone other than the guards who roamed the underground cells. The guards stomped through the maze of hallways, never concealing their presence, never arriving alone. Only one pair of footsteps came now, someone who wished to go unnoticed, who wished to decide when the witch would know they were near.

Blythe struggled to her feet, clothes rustling against the stone floor. She staggered forward and knocked into the metal tray that held her half-eaten meal. It clattered against the floor. The bread, too hard to chew, tumbled off and rolled to the back wall.

Blythe flinched. Silence fell. The footsteps stopped.

She brushed the dust from her clothes, though it did little good. The dirt had woven into the fabric of her dress. It would never truly be clean again, but that didn't stop her from trying.

The footsteps drew closer again, and Blythe stepped toward the bars of her cell. Her broken heart fluttered against her ribs, hoping beyond hope that someone special had come to visit.

There was only one person in Brekham she longed to see. One person to whom she owed answers and explanations. One person who did not wish for her death.

And that was *not* who stepped around the corner.

Blythe stumbled away from the bars, but she held herself tall. She would not yield to this man. She would not yield to *any* man. Her brows pulled together, and she crossed her arms beneath her breast.

Pastor Tobias Walcott stopped before her cell, reeking of wine and sweat. Blythe wondered whether he had bribed the guards to let him pass or if they were happy enough to let a man of the One God visit a wretch like her. The minister said nothing for a long while, but he made no move to leave. He watched Blythe, and she held his stare. The corners of the minister's lips twitched down, deepening his usual scowl. "With what lies did you poison my daughter, *witch*?"

Blythe let silence speak for her, let it hum with violent energy. The air crackled as if an oncoming storm bore down upon them. Her gray eyes tracked his movement when he stepped closer to her cell. She pressed her lips into a thin line. She owed this man nothing, not even her voice.

"You *will* answer me. I have ways to make you talk."

He laid a hand to his pocket but did not reach inside. "Did you corrupt her? Did you turn my daughter into a witch? Is that why she's gone from me?" Pastor Walcott stood mere inches from the bars.

Close enough to touch.

Close enough to hurt.

A wicked feeling, angry and hot and bitter, tore through Blythe's veins. She stepped forward, chin tilted high so she might better meet the minister's eye. "You do not *make* a witch, old man. A witch is or she is not. From birth."

"And you?" the minister pressed. "Were you born a witch?"

"Hasn't your god told you?"

Quicker than a serpent's strike, the minister's hands shot through the bars and gripped the front of her tattered dress. He dragged her forward until she was pressed against the cold metal bars. "I should kill you where you stand. No one would mourn your loss." His fingers traveled higher until they closed around her throat, until he squeezed the breath from her body. The minister's face burned red, and his breaths came in sharp gasps.

But Blythe? Though she stood on tiptoe to lessen the pressure, she seemed impassive to the hands at her throat, as if she welcomed death. She watched the man who sought to end her life and didn't even gasp for air. Until finally, her voice fighting around the hands at her throat, she spoke.

"Caleb would care."

Pastor Walcott flinched. He squeezed tight, so tight he might snap her neck, but then he shoved her away. Blythe stumbled back in a fit of coughing as air rushed too fast to her lungs.

"You will not take both of my children from me. I

won't allow it. Remove your poison from his mind, witch, or I swear—"

"I have done nothing to your children but soothe pain *you* have caused." Blythe righted herself, the grip of his hands leaving a lingering ache. "What do you care of Caleb's wellbeing? You've done nothing but berate and abuse him for all the months I've—"

"I am a good man. A holy man!" Spittle flew from his lips.

"Are you? Caleb no longer sits beside you in court." She tilted her head to one side. Her eyes flashed. "Precisely whose fault is that?"

"Bite your tongue. Or I'll—"

"Or you'll what? I already march closer to the gallows each day. There's nothing you can do but hasten my arrival there." Her lips rose to bare her teeth. "You hold no power over me."

The minister stumbled over his words, rolling insults around on his tongue. Then finally, "I will not offer you spiritual closure. You'll go to your death condemned, damned to a fiery afterlife."

Blythe laughed. The mirthless sound echoed and fractured upon the uneven stones. "As if I need *you* to appeal to my gods."

"There is only the One God!"

She shrugged, her bony shoulders visible through the thin fabric of her dress. "Believe what you must to sleep at night, Minister."

"You insolent, thrice-damned woman. Demons have their claws buried in you, and you cannot see it."

Far off voices echoed back to them. Hard boots clacked against the stone floor.

The guards were coming.

Blythe glanced out her slit of a window. Night had come. Time for another meal of inedible bread.

Pastor Walcott cast a final glare upon the witch. "This isn't over."

He turned and fled, so he did not hear Blythe's final words.

"Yes. It is."

~

The guards slid the metal tray into her cell with hardly a glance at their prisoner. They did not notice the red marks upon her neck, nor did they pause long enough to see the especially ashy pallor of her skin. The guards simply deposited the food and continued their sweep of the damp cells. The door thudded against its frame as they pulled it closed.

Blythe was alone.

Again.

She swallowed another breath, more mud in her lungs. Her fingers danced across her neck, pressing against the aching places where the minister had held her. She pressed deeper into the marks until tears pooled in her eyes. Squeezed harder. As if the pain was all that tethered her to this world, all that reminded her that this was *real*.

Blythe hissed when the pain grew too great and dropped her hands. She wondered how often the minister had laid hands upon her love in the years before her arrival. How often since she'd been locked away. Her heart ached at the thought of him hurt, of the possibility that the minister was going after him as she sat upon the hard floor.

Sitting beneath the tiny, barred window, Blythe leaned against the coolness of the stone wall. Tears pooled in her eyes and grew too heavy to hold. They fell, carving a path down her cheek. She didn't bother wiping them away. They cut through the dust on her face, a trail of fresh skin, a mark that meant she was alive. For still, she lived. Despite the minister's wishes.

There had to be a way to warn Caleb. To ensure he was safe.

Blythe pushed away from the wall and pulled herself upright. She paced the small cell, a fluttering feeling coming to life inside her chest. She searched the cramped space, her movement growing manic. A thin blanket lay on the hard stone, too thin to protect her from either the cold or the hardness of the floor. She tossed it aside, ignoring the spilled tray of half-eaten food beside her feet and the fresh one near the bars. But behind the metal door, something caught her eye.

Blythe stumbled and fell before the edge of the cell. Her knees protested the impact, aching and sore. When she reached through the bars, she wrapped her too-thin fingers around the tools she needed.

Guards had brought the items to her the night before the trial began. *After* the magistrate had deemed her civilized enough to wield a quill. A stack of blank parchment sat there, untouched, the edges damp and dirty from the cell floor. The magistrate had meant for her to write her confession, but Blythe had nothing to confess. At least, nothing she could remember.

In the days since her mother had abandoned her, since she had last spoken to Caleb—last felt the sweet press of his kiss, only flashes of memory had surfaced. Humming in the kitchen while she kneaded bread. The scent of rosemary and garlic in the air. A knock upon her door. Then nothing but darkness and fear and pain.

Still, she could make use of the magistrate's unintentional gift. She pulled the pages close and scrawled curling ink upon the parchment.

It took three false starts, three crumpled beginnings that burned in the hallway torches, before Blythe found her words. She sat upon the dirty stone floor, using the ground as a desk. The flickering torches cast barely enough light to write by, but Blythe managed, though the missive would win no awards for penmanship. The shape of her words mattered much less than their meaning.

When she was done, Blythe read the letter three times, her lips forming the silent words. Satisfied, she folded the parchment in half and kissed its back. She carried the letter, hands shaking until the parchment quivered and crackled in the silent cell, back to her tiny window. Tears streamed from her eyes, but she brushed them away.

Her fingers, wet with tears, moved with nimble grace, folding the parchment again and again until a bird took shape from her folds. A smile touched her features, and she cradled the parchment bird in cupped hands and brought it close to her lips. That fluttering in her chest stretched and grew until it filled the whole of her with warmth.

"Find my love," she whispered.

Blythe leaned against the cold wall and rose onto her toes. She reached as high as she could, her fingers grazing the bottom of the window. She offered the bird to the world.

She stood there. Frozen. Waiting.

Until—

The bird birthed of parchment fluttered its wings. Slow at first, the creases still stiff, then faster. It raised an inch from her hand, hovering above her flesh.

"Fly to him."

Wings rustled faster. The bird slipped through the small window and shot into the cold night.

Blythe collapsed into a heap on the floor, the fluttering inside having gone with the bird. She wrapped her arms around her legs and pressed her forehead to her knees. The tears came stronger, stealing her breath. She should be saving her strength, should be preparing, but she couldn't leave Caleb unprotected.

"Please find him," she whispered into the silent night. "Keep him safe."

The cell echoed with her muffled sobs, but there was no one there to hear them.

The darkness of night enveloped Caleb as fully as the blanket around his shoulders. He sat at a desk, a candle burning low beside him, as he made notes about everything he knew.

The undertaker's list of visitors was long and varied, but as far as Caleb was concerned, every person on it was a suspect. Everyone who testified, too, except perhaps Mrs. Putnam. The old woman couldn't have maneuvered through the forest on her own. One name surprised Caleb with its appearance—Amos Eliot.

Had the mayor's son been in the woods that night? Had he been the one to hurt Bells? It would explain how Amos found the right location in the woods the day before. Perhaps the mayor hadn't asked him to clean up. Perhaps Amos was covering his own tracks.

Still, another part of Caleb wondered if his father was responsible. The minister got to Bells first, and Caleb knew well the violence the minister could bestow. Was it an accident? An act of anger that went beyond bruises and sore ribs?

Perhaps he should focus on the townsfolk who visited Mirabel's body *and* were part of the mob that burned down the Sanderson home. Except... Caleb hadn't seen everyone there that night. Too many faces were cast in shadow.

Caleb sighed. His life was so full of tragedy, it sometimes felt hard to breathe. His best friend had betrayed him. His father had tossed him from his home and his church, forcing him to take refuge with Dr. Hale. His mother and sister had died far too young, and the woman he loved was doomed to follow in their fate. Caleb felt destined to walk the earth alone, longing for all he had lost.

Tink.

Caleb looked up, but silence descended again. Until—

Tink. Tink.

He stood, the book falling from his lap. *Tink.* Caleb turned. *Tink. Tink.* The sound came from the window.

For a moment, Caleb wondered if someone meant to disturb him, but none besides Dr. Hale and Mr. Eliot knew he was there. Whatever it was, it hit the window again, harder this time. The sound dulled to a *thunk*.

With steady hands that belied the thundering of his heart, Caleb reached for the latch and swung the window wide. He ducked, expecting a rock to strike him through the open window, but nothing came through. He straightened to look out into the dark night. A flash of white darted past. Caleb spun. A piece of parchment, folded into the shape of a bird, lay still on the floor.

"Blythe..." Already he could feel the warmth he'd come to associate with her power. Caleb grasped a corner of the parchment and carried it to the small table. He unfolded the wings and smoothed out the damaged beak, flattening it along the wooden surface. Scrawling script covered the inside of the bird. Handwriting he recognized from the notes she wrote in the library.

He reached for his candle and pulled it near. Some of the ink, still damp, shined bright under the candle's warm glow. Caleb smoothed the parchment open, again and again, rubbing his hands against the creases until it lay flat upon the table. Then finally, he began to read.

Dearest Caleb,

I know this isn't what you want to hear, but please trust the wisdom of my words. You must stop defending me. I cherish your efforts, but nothing will sway the mind of this court. Nothing. Already, I imagine your arguments. Well-reasoned though they may be, I've spent the whole of my life studying the ways of these men—men who claim piety but want nothing more than to watch women like me hang or burn or drown. They do not care for facts or evidence. They crave only my death, at any cost.

What's happening here will have echoes far beyond my demise. You must understand that the town will shun you if you continue to align yourself with me. You must claim that I bewitched you and denounce any allegiance to me. You must find a way to make a life for yourself when I'm gone. Denying my guilt will only turn the town against you.

Please, Caleb, trust me on this. I have lived in places where none would meet my eye, and I do not wish that for you. It was a cold and lonely existence, and I was there for mere months. I shudder to think what a lifetime of that would be like. It hurts me to think you might face such a fate when I'm gone.

It's too late to save me, Caleb. I know you don't want to hear this, but it's true. Do not put yourself in harm's way for a cause you cannot hope to win.

Please stop. Please be safe.

All my love,

Blythe

Caleb stared at the letter. He read it again. He read it a

third time, looking for clues to Blythe's true meaning. She couldn't possibly mean for him to take these words at face value. She wouldn't tell him to give up, not when giving up meant watching her die.

Anger flared deep in his chest. How could she expect him to live his life knowing he'd done nothing to protect her? He didn't give a damn what the people of Brekham thought of him. He would gladly let small-minded bigots spurn his name.

He couldn't let this letter be the final word between them. Caleb folded the parchment and shoved it to the bottom of his pocket, along with his suspect list. He would go to the courthouse. Even if a hundred guards patrolled the perimeter, he'd find a way inside.

He'd find a way to Blythe.

And he would save her.

~

Dr. Hale's house was dark as Caleb picked his way around carefully arranged furniture. Light flickered from within the doctor's bedroom, but the lights in the rest of the house were long since extinguished. At the front door, he grabbed his cloak where it hung on a hook and pulled the door—

Caleb froze, startled by the presence of a large man on the other side of the door, his hand poised to knock. The man's long hair was tied neatly at the nape of his neck, and a hat shielded most of his face save for the neatly-trimmed beard.

"Oh, I'm sorry." Caleb pulled the door wider when he remembered whose home he was leaving. "Are you injured? Do you need me to fetch the doctor?"

The man shook his head and removed the hat. "Don't

trouble yourself, Mr. Walcott. Oliver knows I'm coming. I can manage on my own."

"Mr. Eliot?" Caleb stared at Amos, a strange feeling itching at his brain. "What are you doing here?"

"I'd wager that's my business, not yours." Amos stepped aside and motioned for Caleb to pass. "As you were. It seems you're on your way out?"

Caleb stepped out onto the porch, yet he barely felt the cold. Something wasn't sitting right with him. He'd rarely seen Amos around Brekham before, but now they'd spoken twice in as many days? Caleb brushed his hand against his pocket, against the suspect list there.

"I know you visited my sister's body." Caleb stepped closer to Amos, and the taller man fell back, maintaining the distance between them. "Why? You've never been close with my family."

Amos backed down the stairs until he stood on solid ground. "I had no reason to avoid the visit, either, Mr. Walcott. When my father asked me to join him, I went."

"But you were also at the clearing," Caleb said, mind whirring as he tried to shove together disparate pieces of a colorless puzzle. "And now you're *here*. Are you following me? Do you mean to kill me like you did my sister?"

"What possible reason could I have for targeting your family?" Amos glanced past Caleb to stare upon the doctor's house. Yet he didn't seem ill. He didn't seem injured.

"Then what are you doing here?" Caleb followed Amos down the stairs. "You're the only one who knew I intended to stay here."

This time, Amos did not shrink back from Caleb's advance. He held his ground, hands curling into fists. "Leave it alone, Mr. Walcott. It has nothing to do with you."

Caleb knocked Amos back a step. "I'm not going anywhere until you explain yourself."

"Step aside. I will not ask again."

"Fine. Perhaps it's best I bring my concerns to the magistrate." Caleb shoved past Amos, but the man grabbed his arm.

"You will keep my affairs out of your mouth. Do you understand?"

"Just admit it. You're the one who hurt my sister." Caleb rushed Amos, throwing the older man off balance. "Admit it!" Caleb shoved again, and they both went down. Hard.

On the ground, they were a flurry of fists. Caleb's knuckles glanced off something hard. A nose? A collarbone? A fist hit him in the mouth. He tasted blood. Another blow glanced across his face. Lights danced before his eyes. Caleb swung again. Rage and grief and pain fueled him. Finally, he had an outlet for the fury boiling him alive. A fury that he'd felt ever since he had seen Mirabel's lifeless body.

Ever since he'd seen Blythe covered in his sister's blood.

Caleb couldn't stomach those images, but he had strength enough for the ache in his hands. He could understand the pain in his lips and the blood on his tongue.

Those were easy.

Caleb landed another punch. His fist came away sticky and red.

But then there were new hands on him, dragging him to his feet, dragging him away from the focus of his rage. "Let me go! He's hiding something. I know he is!" Tears flooded Caleb's eyes that had nothing to do with the bruises that would surely cover his face by morning.

"Grief has addled his mind," Amos wheezed as he

rolled to all fours, coughing and spitting blood onto the ground.

Caleb struggled against the hands that bound him. Mr. Pratchett and Mr. Eastey each held one of his arms. He tried to pull from their grip, but they held firm. "If you didn't kill my sister, who did? Who?"

"Such a disappointment." Pastor Lewis stepped into view and adjusted his spectacles. "Your father will be so ashamed when he hears of the trouble his only son has caused."

Dr. Hale appeared in Caleb's periphery and pushed past the minister. He kneeled beside Amos, gripping his arm. The doctor glanced from Amos to Caleb and back again, and Caleb swore he saw betrayal beneath the worry. When Mr. Eliot made it to his feet, he merely glared at Caleb, wiped blood from his lips, and followed Dr. Hale into his home.

The visiting minister watched the men leave, then settled his attention on Caleb, where he still struggled under the grip of Mr. Pratchett and Mr. Eastey. "It's taken us far too long to find you, Mr. Walcott. I think it's best that you spend the remainder of the evening at the courthouse. We don't want you running off before your presence is required."

Panic fluttered in Caleb's chest. Would he be thrown in jail for the fight with Amos? Mayor Eliot was sure to be furious. He couldn't let that happen, not until he cleared Blythe's name.

"Why?" Caleb tried, and failed, to keep his voice steady. "What do you want from me?"

Pastor Lewis grinned. "At dawn, you'll testify against the witch."

TESTIMONY OF CALEB WALCOTT

*P*astor Lewis arranged for only one witness that day. The energy in the packed courtroom pulsed and shifted. A new current ran through the crowd. The tides had changed.

Brekham no longer feared its witch.

The villagers gossiped in the space around Blythe, doing nothing to disguise their words. Their voices rose to a dull roar, but that day, the magistrate didn't seem to mind the noise.

Magistrate Hawthorne leaned over his bench to speak with the thin, angular prosecutor. The men had smiles in their eyes as they glanced, more than once, at the accused. With this next witness, the second phase of their trial would reach its conclusion.

Blythe seemed for all the world indifferent to the noise around her. But beneath the table, her fingers worried together, her thumbs tracing erratic patterns on her hands. Her gaze, though it didn't rise above the table before her, was restless.

Pastor Lewis nodded to the magistrate and stepped

away. He turned to the crowd and asked for quiet. The room fell to a hush and then to silence.

It was time to begin.

"Ladies and gentlemen of the gallery, welcome. Gentlemen of the jury, I thank you for your continued service." Pastor Lewis pivoted on his heel and paced before the magistrate's bench. "Today we have a most important witness. He is perhaps the person in Brekham who knows the witch best, and whether he wish it or not, he *will* tell us the truth of her."

The prosecutor lifted his head so he looked to the back of the room. He raised his voice. "Bring him in."

The courthouse's heavy doors creaked open. The flash of red hair was all it took for the townsfolk to identify Caleb Walcott. The guard shoved him down the aisle, and people watched, transfixed, as he stumbled past. His whispered name worked its way forward and landed upon the witch's ears. Her gaze left the table, and she turned in her chair to see for herself if the whispers were true.

Blythe's eyebrows arched high when she caught sight of her beloved. The skin around his eyes and temples was a patchwork of purple and blue and angry red. His lip was swollen and split. There was panic in his eyes, and he struggled against the guard who pushed him toward the witness stand.

The prosecutor grinned when the guard shoved Caleb into the seat and took his place behind the reluctant witness.

"Thank you for joining us this morning, Mr. Walcott."

Caleb scowled. "As if I had a choice."

Pastor Lewis ignored him and looked to his notes. "You and the accused struck up a fast friendship this summer when she moved to town. Is that correct?"

Caleb pressed his lips together and merely glared at the angular man.

"We can do this easily or painfully, Mr. Walcott. It makes no difference to me. We'll get our answers either way." The prosecutor waited a moment, but when Caleb still didn't answer, he sighed. "Permission to treat Mr. Walcott as a hostile witness?"

The magistrate nodded. "Permission so granted." He gestured to the guard.

The guard pulled a leather instrument from his belt and struck the back of Caleb's hand where it rested against the witness stand. The *snap* echoed through the court, and Caleb couldn't bite back the cry of pain. He swallowed the sound a moment later, but already the town had heard the effects.

None seemed to flinch harder than the witch.

She stared at Caleb, eyes pleading. She'd warned him not to protect her. He needn't suffer for her.

"Let's try this again, Mr. Walcott. You know the accused well, correct?"

Caleb cradled his hand to his chest, but he nodded. "Yes."

"Furthermore, you are the brother of the victim, Miss Walcott." The minister paused. "Or rather, you *were*."

"If you have a question, ask it," Caleb snapped.

The men of the jury shared long glances, their brows rising high into their wrinkled foreheads. The witness would do well to remember his place, lest he earn another rebuke from the guard.

"What was the nature of the relationship between Misses Walcott and Bradbury?"

Caleb glanced at the accused, and his gaze softened. The tension in his shoulders relaxed, if only a fraction. "I know of no ill will between them. Neither spoke poorly of the other, but they were rarely together for more than a few minutes. Miss Bradbury was more my friend than my sister's, and I was closer to Mirabel than anyone."

Pastor Lewis dropped his notes on the table. The parchment scattered along the wooden surface. He rounded on the witness stand. "Were you only friends? Rumor suggests you know Miss Bradbury rather…*intimately*."

The crowd snickered. The men of the jury tried to conceal their grins, but even they couldn't hide their amusement. Pastor Walcott fumed, glaring at his son, his face growing redder with each breath.

A blush spread across Caleb's bruised face. He might as well have admitted the charge for all the good his silence did.

The magistrate banged his gavel, hushing the crowd. "Move along, Minister."

Pastor Lewis cleared his throat. "Why did you attack the mayor's son last night?"

Caleb furrowed his brow. "Excuse me?"

"The fight with Mr. Eliot. Why did you attack him?" The minister closed in on the witness stand. His dark, beady eyes narrowed.

Caleb swallowed, his pulse hammering visibly in his throat. He swung his gaze toward the back of the room, where Mayor Eliot's son stood with a bandage over his nose and a swollen, black eye. "I had reason to believe he was involved with my sister's death."

"And what possessed you to think such a thing?"

Sweat prickled at Caleb's brow. "I caught him at the clearing where Mirabel… where she was killed."

"You found your sister the night of her death, correct?"

"I… I found my way there." Caleb's voice was strained, and he closed his eyes. His whole body tensed as if he could see the scene unfurling before him. "But my father reached her first. Mr. Eastey, too. I think. It all happened so fast."

The minister nodded. "So very tragic. Truly, the court is sorry for your loss." He paused and adjusted his spectacles, any sympathy tossed aside. "How did you know where to find her?"

"I didn't. I had to search like all the rest."

"But you found your way, as you said. The woods are vast. How did you find her?"

Caleb closed his eyes, but it was too late to hide the tear that slid down his bruised cheek. "There was screaming."

"But you must have been close, to be able to follow the sound."

"Not close enough to save her," Caleb said, his voice broken and his face filled with rage. "Is that what you want to hear? That I was too slow to protect my sister?"

Pastor Lewis tilted his head to the side, hawklike. "Were you aware she needed protection from Miss Bradbury?"

"There's no proof she did it!" Caleb leaned forward like he meant to leap from the witness stand, but the guard grabbed hold of his shoulder, shoving him back in the chair. Stuck in place, Caleb raised his hand to point at his father. "The minister is a cruel and violent man. A drunk who talks more with his fists than with any sort of piety. He's hurt Mirabel before. He reached the clearing first."

"You expect us to believe a minister of the One God killed his own daughter?" Pastor Lewis scoffed. "What proof could you possibly have?"

The witness sank back into the chair, silent for breath after breath. Then finally— "Dr. Hale. He's seen my father's violence directed at me. He can speak to the rage."

In the crowd, Pastor Walcott sprang to his feet. "Only

after your wretched whore killed my daughter! Only because you'd already forsaken this family!"

The crowd erupted, and Magistrate Hawthorn banged his gavel against the bench, calling for order. As the room quieted, the prosecutor shook his head. "In all the witch trials I've conducted, Mr. Walcott, never has a man so thoroughly disgraced and abandoned his family. Miss Bradbury has buried her claws in deep, hasn't she?"

"You—"

"I wager there's proof enough that you've served as an accomplice for the witch. Perhaps you should stand trial alongside her, Mr. Walcott."

Blythe bolted from her seat. "No!"

Her voice rang out, loud and full of force. It was the first word she'd uttered in the courtroom, and those sitting closest to her scrambled away. Pastor Walcott went pale, even as he glared at his bruised son on the witness stand.

"Caleb knows nothing, has *done* nothing." Blythe stared at Caleb, pale eyes wide and pleading. "Release him, and I'll tell you all you wish to know."

The guard shoved the witch back into her seat.

Pastor Lewis grinned. "Does the witch mean to confess?"

Caleb shook his head, his swollen eyes widening with fear and pain and panic. "Blythe, no. Don't confess to crimes to which you're innocent. I can still fix this."

Blythe dropped her gaze to the charm resting against her wrist, to the star hidden as a sun. She thought of the constellation—the promise—carved on its back. Her silence was the only defiance she could risk.

The prosecutor shrugged. "No matter. By week's end, we will know the truth. And you, witch, shall hang."

Mirabel worried for weeks that her father would remember the night she attacked him. She didn't regret her actions, not fully, but her nerves made it hard to sleep at night. Whenever Father called her name, she feared his memories had returned. Panicked that he might strike her or devise some other punishment —like marrying her off to someone awful.

Unlike Mirabel, Caleb seemed unbothered by the horrors of that night, his mood buoyed and light, especially the past two weeks. The siblings had spent the entire day at the church, their father shuttered in his private office. Normally, Caleb would spend the day complaining, but instead he hummed as he worked. When they'd finished cleaning and Father still wasn't ready to return home, Caleb had retired upstairs, Mirabel trailing after him.

She watched him from across the table, scribbling in a journal. He pretended it was full of notes for future sermons, but she knew it held secrets about their father's past and Caleb's growing devotion to their neighbor.

Mirabel hadn't read any of it since Miss Bradbury asked her not to, but she could guess the things her brother might write. She'd never seen him so fully distracted.

Her fingers itched to play the old harpsichord in the corner, her nails tapping out the patterns on the small table. Yet that was another thing Father had stolen from her. Music used to be her escape, but playing felt more dangerous than ever.

Mirabel sighed and wished her brother would put down his pen long enough to see how miserable she was. How *bored* she was now that she had nothing to do.

She leaned forward and made increasingly strange faces at her brother, trying to distract him. When that didn't work, she settled back in her chair. "Caleb." No answer. "*Caleb.*" Still nothing. She stood and reached across the table to flick his ear. "*Caleb!*"

He jumped, dropping his pen. "*What*, Mirabel, what?"

Sitting back in her chair, arms folded across her chest, Mirabel stuck out her bottom lip in a pout. "I called your name three times."

Caleb bent and picked up his pen. Instead of returning to his entry, he closed the book and studied his sister. "What is it?"

Mirabel fidgeted in her seat, words drying up on her tongue. She didn't know how to explain the unease inside her, not without souring his good mood.

"Come now, Bells." He reached across the table and captured her hands in his. He gave them a gentle squeeze. "What's bouncing around that head of yours?"

"I'm worried about Father," she admitted at last.

"What of him?"

"Do you think he'll remember what happened? What I did?" Mirabel dropped her hands to her lap, all her fears bubbling up. "I'm scared, Caleb, all the time. How have you survived so long, not knowing what will inspire his rage? How am I supposed to spend the rest of my life like this?"

"Bells…" Caleb glanced toward the stairs, as if making sure they were still alone. "You won't have to grow old with him."

"As if I have a choice!" Mirabel flinched at the volume of her voice and tried to swallow the panic. She couldn't let Father overhear. "He won't let me leave unless I'm married, and the men in this town are vile. They stare after me like I'm some rare cut of meat. It's disgusting."

She watched as her words landed, the shock widening her brother's eyes. He tapped the edge of his pen against the table and checked the stairs once more. "What if there was another way?" Caleb whispered, voice barely audible in the quiet church.

Hope fluttered in Mirabel's chest like flimsy butterfly wings. "What do you mean?"

"I can't say much yet." Caleb leaned farther over the table. "But I'm working on a way to get us out of here."

"How?" Mirabel failed to come up with any viable options. "When?"

"We're still figuring out the logistics, but we'll have to wait for spring."

Hope sharpened into wariness. "We?" She watched her brother's expression shift from excitement to embarrassment to apology, and she sighed. "You mean you and Miss Bradbury. Caleb, I don't want to be a bother."

"And I will not leave you here. Not with him." Caleb reached for her hand again, squeezing tight. "If we can get through the snowy season, we'll be free. Trust me, Bells." Caleb tilted his head in a way that most women found charming. She found it irritating.

"Please don't make me wait months for answers." She pulled her hand away. "Promise you'll explain once the plan is set."

Caleb smiled and cracked open his journal again. "I promise, Bells."

Mirabel watched her brother work, but she couldn't shake this sense of worry. She hated being left out of things, hated leaving her future up to someone else's plans. When her nervous energy became too much to bear, she shoved away from the table and crossed the room, pressing her warm face against the cool glass. Winter would come soon. Already the dew was crisp with frost each morning, so it made sense to wait. But could they survive the season? How long did Caleb expect her to endure this fear without knowing his plans for escape?

Something fluttered at the edge of her vision, and Mirabel pulled away from the window to get a proper look. A cloak rustled in the breeze. A figure passed below, heading for the forest.

Blythe Bradbury.

Mirabel glanced at Caleb. When he'd denied her the truth before, Blythe had filled in the gaps. She charted her path. Behind him, the stairs. At the door below, her cloak. She hesitated, fresh worry twisting her insides into knots.

Oh, just go, Mirabel.

With a final fortifying breath, she swept past her brother, down the stairs, and swung the cloak over her shoulders.

Moments later, Mirabel emerged from the church. She shivered and tugged the cloak tighter around her shoulders. She glanced toward the forest where she'd seen Blythe slip between the trees.

Mirabel gave chase.

Her footsteps were quiet against the soft earth. Though

it was cold, the ground had not yet frozen, and it muffled her sounds. She didn't want to sneak up on Blythe—not really—but she didn't want Blythe to send her away. It would be hard to argue her continued presence if Blythe could simply point to the visible church and tell her to leave.

And she refused to depart without answers.

Mirabel picked her way through the dense trees, looking for any sign of Miss Bradbury. For several unsettling minutes, she followed little more than instincts and a vague memory of the last time she'd followed Blythe into the woods. Then finally, a trace of smoke crossed her senses. She followed the smell until she saw the flickering of candles.

Mirabel approached the clearing with care. Blythe was there, surrounded by a circle of tiny flames. Light and shadow danced across Blythe's face, and she moved through the circle with confidence and delicate grace. A knife in one hand, Blythe paused at the four corners of the clearing and raised the blade to the sky. Mirabel couldn't hear the words that fell from her lips, but everything inside warned her of danger as an impossible truth echoed in her head.

Blythe Bradbury was a witch.

In a rush, Mirabel remembered the first time she had seen Blythe acting strangely in the woods. Caleb had explained it away, but she knew, deep in her bones, what she was seeing.

Her brother had lied, and she was so tired of being kept in the dark.

Mirabel abandoned her hiding spot behind the tree and stepped forward.

She walked past the line of candles.

Blythe tensed. Her arms dropped to her sides. She spun, eyes wide with alarm. "Miss Walcott," she whispered. "You can't be here."

WRITTEN TESTIMONY OF BLYTHE BRADBURY

*I*n parts of the world, women like Mother and me are treated as guides. As healers. Mother tells stories of places where we're respected instead of feared. Places out east. Places where you and I dreamed of living and learning, bound together for the rest of our days.

Your sister's killer did not come to me for healing.

I told you once, that I had… ways to tend to my own body, that I had knowledge that allowed us to be together without fear of a child coming before we were ready. Though it is a skill not often used, a spell I had never woven for anyone before, there are ways to terminate that which isn't prevented.

Perhaps if this town wasn't so obsessed with rules and prohibitions, if it wasn't so afraid of natural, physical expressions of love…

I'm sorry. I do not mean to shift blame. It's my fault that I didn't say no. It's my fault that I gave in instead of telling my mother and escaping Brekham in the dark of night.

I didn't want to lose you, so I didn't run.

And for my selfishness, you lost everything.

MOMENTS BEFORE THE MURDER

"*M*iss Walcott… You can't be here." Blythe's words cut like a knife, but she dropped the blade in her hand. The silver flashed in the firelight as it fell to the earth. "You need to leave. Now."

"I'm not going anywhere without an explanation." Mirabel stepped closer.

Blythe retreated, a panicked look in her eye.

"How are *you* afraid of *me?*" Mirabel scowled and grabbed her mother's necklace, holding tight to the amber stone in the center of the One God's sun. "I'm not the one flouncing around under the watchful eye of the One God's enemies."

Confusion creased the witch's brow. "What?"

Mirabel pointed overhead. "The night sky. The darkness that blocks His light." Mirabel tugged at the end of her braid as a breeze blew the witch's loose hair into her face. "I should have known the moment you moved into the Sanderson house. At least guessed when you didn't come to church that first week."

"Miss Walcott, please. You must go."

"What have you done to my brother? Did you spell your way into his heart? Have you bewitched his mind?" Mirabel's voice rose as her heart—and the hope for her own future, her own escape—plummeted. "I demand to know what wickedness you intend to conjure tonight."

"Mirabel, *please*." Blythe reached out and grasped Mirabel's wrist. "I will answer anything you ask, but not tonight. Not here. Please, go back to the church."

"No." Mirabel pulled away from Blythe's touch and held her ground. "I'm not leaving until you *talk to me*."

The candles around them flared a few inches higher.

Then died.

"No. No, no, no, no." Blythe scrambled around the circle, relighting the candles as quickly as she could. She moved so fast Mirabel didn't see her light the match. But she must have. "They're coming," she said as she moved past Mirabel to light another candle. "You have to go."

"What are you talking about?" Mirabel asked, less sure now. "Who's coming?"

"What is *she* doing here?"

Mirabel froze, a sudden sickness swirling in her stomach. She knew that voice.

"Nothing." Blythe grabbed Mirabel's shoulders and tried to lead her to the edge of the clearing. "She's leaving. She doesn't know anything."

"She already knows too much," a second voice said, deeper than the first but even more familiar.

Mirabel couldn't help it. She craned her head to look.

The pair stood together, fury and fear flickering across their faces. A hand grazed a belly before resting over a heart. The other bent and retrieved Blythe's discarded blade.

"No one can know."

"It has to be done."

Mirabel backed away as the blade glinted in the moonlight. "I won't tell. I promise, I won't."

There was an exchange of glances. A determined nod.

Fear coursed through Mirabel's body, and she turned to run. The wind raced against her skin, and people shouted behind her.

"Do it!"

"Stop her!"

"No!"

Pain exploded across Mirabel's back, throwing her off her feet. She crumpled to the ground, a scream tearing from her lips. Large, rough hands turned her to her back. Then the pressure of knees against her ribs. The impact of the blade being driven again and again and again into her flesh.

She couldn't draw air.

Couldn't scream.

A new voice picked up where hers left off. Panic and rage and fear filling the night as Mirabel's vision went dark.

As the light went out.

As her life slipped away.

PART III
DEATH

None pose a greater danger to the One God's children than witches.
Born of shadow and beholden to the tides of the moon,
these creatures will stop at nothing in their quest to obliterate His
light.
The only proper remedy is death.

-*The Book of Light*

WRITTEN TESTIMONY OF BLYTHE BRADBURY

*S*o many things went wrong that night.

I went into the forest ahead of the others to prepare the ritual space. I set the candles, cast the usual protections. I took every precaution I knew to take. I gathered the necessary herbs and imbued my blade with power and intent.

Everything was ready, all that was left was the subject of my spell, but then your sister stepped into my circle. I don't know how she found me, but once she did— She was angry. So very angry. I tried to turn her away, but she was a lot like you, that first night you found me in the forest. Mirabel demanded answers. She saw what I had prepared and thought the worst of me. She wouldn't leave. She wouldn't—

And then they arrived.

For so long, their images were nothing more than hazy shadows, and no matter how hard I tried, I could not bring their faces into focus. I could not piece together the fragments of memory. I think… Did something happen that night? I thought at first my mind was protecting me from the guilt of my actions, but I think it's more than that.

It's like someone knocked the memories out of me.

I thought I might never remember, until I saw the wink of gold,
and everything fell into place.

TESTIMONY OF PASTOR WALCOTT

*D*espite the howling winds, the courthouse pulsed with heat. Bodies packed the courtroom, pressed shoulder to shoulder, waiting for their minister to reveal the word of the One God. Children as old as thirteen sat on their parents' laps to better fill the seats. More people stood at the back and spilled into the hall.

Pastor Lewis stood before the town and straightened his vest. The corner of his lips twitched as if he suppressed a smile. Never before had such a captive audience attended his sermons, never before had so many people clamored for his every word. After the trial, he may never have this chance again.

Guards led the accused to her seat, but the gallery barely spared her a glance. She looked the same as the days before, though perhaps dirtier from the time spent in her cell. Purple shadows hung heavy under her eyes

With the witch seated at her table, the minister cleared his throat. The room fell silent, eerily so for a space packed to bursting with people.

"Today, we begin our third and final line of witnesses.

Thus far, this court has proven that Miss Bradbury possesses magic that defies the One God. We have proven that she was acquainted with the Walcott family, including the deceased. Brave neighbors and peers have testified that Miss Bradbury intended to remake Miss Walcott in her wicked image." He paused, watching his words work through the crowd.

"Starting today," the minister continued, "our final witnesses will prove that the Bradbury witch *killed* young Mirabel Walcott." He gestured to the empty chair beside the magistrate. "I invite the victim's father, Pastor Tobias Walcott, back to the stand."

In the row behind the accused, the broken minister stood and made his way to the witness stand. Caleb watched his father from under the hood of his cloak, his swollen lips pressed together. His bruised face burned red.

"Pastor Walcott." The prosecutor approached the witness stand. "Please share with the court your proof of the witch's guilt."

Mirabel's father ran a hand over his face, like he could block out the memory of his daughter's lifeless body, but finally, he nodded. He looked tired and drawn, like a piece of clothing worn thin over time. "The moment I met the Bradbury women, I knew something was not right with them. At first, it was only a feeling in my chest, but I am a faithful servant of the One God, sir, and I did what any minister would do. I prayed."

The witness exhaled a long sigh and faced the men of the jury. "The One God speaks to me, gentlemen. He has all my life, and His voice has only grown louder in the eight years since Magistrate Hawthorne made me Brekham's minister."

As his words hung in the courtroom, Blythe looked up from her table. She studied the minister with narrowed eyes. Each of his lies grated against her skin like coarse gravel. Even her gods didn't speak in clear words. They didn't answer demands.

"What has He said?" prompted the prosecutor.

"The One God warned me to keep the girl away from my children. I did my best, but the witch ensnared their attention, especially that of my son." The minister's eyes flashed as he searched the crowd for his firstborn.

Caleb shifted at the back of the church. He pulled his hood further over his hair and fidgeted with the sleeves of his shirt. Caleb glanced at Blythe, but she didn't turn to meet his gaze. They had not spoken, not since the letter. Not since she had claimed his innocence in court.

"As soon as I saw my daughter in the forest, I knew." Pastor Walcott rubbed his hands over his eyes. His voice broke.

When the prosecutor approached the witness stand, he kept his voice low. Reverent. "And has the One God confirmed your fears. Has He told you of the witch's guilt?"

The witness's eyes fluttered shut, and his chin tipped toward the heavens, as if he sought those answers from the One God that very moment. If anyone in the courtroom cared at all for the truth, they might find it strange that the minister acted as if their deity would answer to his every beck and call. That the minister expected the people of Brekham to believe he had such a direct line to the divine.

They might have even noticed the stale whisper of wine on his breath when he'd first walked past.

Alone at her table, the witch's gaze grew dark. She glared upon the witness, her hands pressed tight together. A chill crept through the room. Frost crawled in spiraling patterns along the fogged windows and across her wooden table. She was done hiding herself, but she couldn't afford to expend too much.

There was so much more left to do before she left this place.

In the back of the courthouse, Caleb Walcott watched his father. A shiver worked through the youngest remaining Walcott, his breath visible in the cooling air. When his father opened his eyes, Caleb scowled to see the smile upon his father's face.

"Yes, Minister, He does. The One God confirms her guilt." Pastor Walcott watched as his words incited gasps and hushed conversations in the crowd. He drank in their surprise and delight, and it warmed him almost as much as his alcohol.

Pastor Walcott continued. "The witch killed my daughter. She poisoned my son against me." He paused, his words heavy in the air.

"Is there anything more?" Pastor Lewis asked, but there was a glimmer in his eye, like he already knew. It seemed as if the pair of ministers had already discussed this very moment. Had known it would come.

The witness nodded, a false solemnity written into the corners of his eyes. "We must cleanse the witch from our town."

He smiled at Blythe, a look of willful cruelty.

"The One God wills it so."

NOW

She poisoned my son against me.

Caleb did not hear anything more. The prosecutor paced before the court, his mouth moving, but Caleb couldn't hear the words. His pulse pounded so loud in his ears he heard nothing but his father's voice. *She poisoned my son against me.* Though he knew his father would lie on the witness stand, to hear it so blatantly, to hear lies woven about *himself*, broke something inside Caleb.

How many times had his father used religion to send innocent women to the gallows? How many families did he destroy before the Sandersons, before Caleb was old enough to remember?

It was all Caleb could do to wait until the court recessed to stumble outside and let loose the scream in his throat. The empty streets bore witness to his outburst. Most of the onlookers stayed behind to share in their gossip, but they didn't delay long. Before Caleb could fully collect himself, the doors to the courthouse slammed open.

He slipped out of sight, disappearing into the alcoves

and shadows of the building. He watched, his pulse throbbing behind his eyes, as the townsfolk filed out of the courthouse. They skipped down the stairs, heads bent together in conversation, too quiet for Caleb to hear.

And then they were gone, returned to their lives. The testimony an amusing bit of entertainment before they returned to their whole and happy families, returned to their jobs and hobbies and loved ones.

Caleb couldn't go back. He had nothing left to go back *to*. His sister was gone. His father had betrayed him and cast him out. There was nothing for him in this world. Nothing but pain and anger and the mind-numbing rage.

Why wouldn't Blythe defend herself? He understood her reluctance. Clearly the court wouldn't believe her, but even in her letter, she didn't deny the charges levied against her. And before, the one time he managed to visit Blythe in her cell, she wouldn't deny it then, either. She claimed her memory was gone. Claimed it *could* have been her.

A terrible panic grabbed Caleb's chest and stole the breath from his lungs. He needed to hear her say it, needed to hear her explain what happened that night. But would she? *Could* she? Had she remembered anything more of that night? Doubts crept inside his mind, like a weed growing through a crack to split apart a hard stone.

Caleb's heart already struggled to keep beating. He didn't know if he could handle another crack.

He might shatter.

He might—

Behind him, the doors to the courthouse banged loud against the stone exterior. Caleb turned in time to see the minister emerge, stumbling and red about the face. Before he realized what he was doing, Caleb was stalking after the old man. By the time his father reached the town center, Caleb had closed the gap between them.

"Take it back."

Pastor Walcott paused before the fountain but did not turn. "No." He resumed his journey home without looking at his son.

"No?" Caleb grabbed the minister's elbow and tugged, spinning the older man to face him. "That isn't an option. Fix this. Take it back."

"There is nothing to recant, boy. I spoke only the truth." Pastor Walcott pulled from Caleb's grip and adjusted his cloak.

"The truth? You know nothing of truth. You invent stories to suit your needs and invoke the One God's name to pass off your lies as divine. You—"

An open hand struck his face.

Caleb tasted blood where his cut lip reopened.

"How *dare* you speak to me—speak of the One God— like that! I was there in the forest. I saw your sister's body. I saw the blood on your witch's clothes." Another strike across his face. "You were there, Caleb, you saw what I saw." A closed fist hit his temple. Caleb fell to the cobblestone street.

"If you can see that and have any doubt... The witch has surely poisoned your mind. I hope her death will release your addled brain." The minister spat at him.

Everything hurt. Memories flooded Caleb. Blood. The coppery smell of it on the air. Mirabel's crumpled body. *No.* Tears stung in Caleb's eyes. He was so tired of being the focus of his father's abuse. He was tired of taking it. Tired of being the good son who didn't flinch. Tired of letting his father place blame wherever he liked.

Caleb pulled himself to his hands and knees and spit blood onto the ground. He wiped a hand over his mouth, but he didn't see the boot until it was too late. The minister kicked him in the ribs, sending him sprawling.

A groan rose to his lips, and Caleb couldn't catch his breath. "Enough," he wheezed and spit again. He was done with his father's abuse. Tired of everyone telling him he was wrong when he knew he was right. Caleb pulled himself to his feet before the minister could land a second kick. His father took a swing, but Caleb was ready this time. He ducked and hurled his fist forward, striking his father across the temple. Once. Twice.

His father went down. Hard.

It was then Caleb noticed the crowd that had formed around them. Mr. Pratchett peeled away and approached the fallen minister.

"He doesn't deserve your compassion," Caleb said, holding his ground against a town that had already so clearly turned against him. "The minister hurt me for the first time when I was eleven. The same day you declared him your minister. I still have scars from the bits of broken wine glass that cut my face."

A dozen familiar faces stared at him, but they held no compassion. Not even any pity. Mr. Pratchett helped the minister to his feet, and Mrs. Eastey silently dabbed at his bleeding brow with a handkerchief.

Caleb felt suddenly cold and so thoroughly alone. The only bit of warmth he felt was the ember of anger burning in his gut.

"Don't act as if none of you have ever done wrong. Protecting my father won't protect your secrets." This time, his words seem to penetrate. A few of the townsfolk dropped worried gazes to the stone beneath their feet.

"You've done enough to embarrass yourself, Mr. Walcott," Mr. Pratchett said. He handed the minister off to Mr. Eastey and gripped Caleb's shoulder. "There's no point making things worse for yourself. It won't bring your sister back."

"That's not what this is about." Caleb shrugged away from the touch. A hundred memories, snippets of conversations Caleb overhead these people having with his father, swam to the surface of his mind. "My father isn't the only one in this town who's less pious than he seems. None of you are without fault."

When the crowd shook their heads and began to turn away, the minister still cradled among them, Caleb kindled the furious fire in his heart. If the town already hated him, he might as well burn it all down. Caleb lunged for the fountain, climbing to stand on the edge so he was a head taller than everyone else.

"Mr. Eastey beds other women when he travels without his wife. He asked my father for advice, but he still lusts after other women. Even some in town."

A low murmur worked through the crowd, and Mr. Eastey froze. Pastor Walcott pulled himself away from the now-sullied man.

"He's far from the only one. Mrs. Kasur destroyed her neighbor's garden. Mr. Demarche sabotaged *his* neighbor's fencing and set his horses free." Caleb watched as the crowd shifted, as townsfolk started to regard those around them with suspicion. Near the back, he spotted his former friend.

"None of you are without fault. Not even the witnesses. Not Isaac Carrier nor his bride." Caleb pointed to where Isaac stood, Grace clinging to his arm. Even from the distance, her large ring—no doubt one of Isaac's own designs—winked at him in the sun, the stone at the center shining like bright honey.

"Don't you dare, Caleb," Isaac called, extracting himself from his wife.

"Isaac never feared Miss Bradbury. Neither did Miss

Pratchett. They couldn't wait until summer to marry without—"

A feral scream drowned out Caleb's words, and Isaac charged him, throwing all his weight against Caleb. A second later, the frigid water of the fountain consumed both young men. Hands circled Caleb's throat, and though he tried to surface, Isaac held him firmly under.

Caleb thrashed against Isaac's hold, but the cold water constricted his lungs. He didn't have the strength to fight off his friend, even when he could breathe. As he continued to struggle, his vision went dark. No one was coming to his aid. No one in Brekham cared if he lived or died. No one—

Isaac's hands ripped away from his throat, and a moment later, new hands fisted in his shirt. Someone dragged Caleb to the surface, and he gasped for breath, swiping water from his eyes.

Two men stood in front of him, but he could still see Isaac and the crowd just past them.

"No one believes the word of a witch's pawn, Caleb." Isaac tried to rush him again, but the larger of the two men blocked his path. "No one." Isaac turned and pushed his way through the crowd.

And the small crowd? They parted for Isaac while Caleb's teeth chattered and his fingers grew numb. The people of Brekham turned their backs on Caleb, and it was as if he hadn't said anything at all. Like his accusations had been proven false by the simple reminder that he believed in Blythe's innocence.

They entire town shunned him. They wouldn't even look at him.

All of them, except the men standing guard before the fountain.

The shorter one turned first, and Dr. Hale reached to help Caleb from the water. When Caleb ignored him, the young doctor sighed. "Take the help, son."

Caleb studied the man before him, but the cold made his decision. He gripped the doctor's hand and heaved himself out of the fountain. His entire body convulsed with cold when a gust of wind tore through the square, and he braced his hands on his knees, still gasping for breath.

"We should get out of the cold before the minister decides he isn't finished with his son," the taller man said, finally turning to face Caleb. Amos Eliot's face was a patchwork of bruises—injuries that were Caleb's doing—but he still looked kindly at the town's newest pariah.

Dr. Hale offered a hand to Caleb again. "Come on, let's get you dry before you freeze to death."

"Why are you helping me?" Caleb stared at the offered hand, too numb and confused to access the offered kindness.

Amos Eliot held out a hand as well. "Because Oliver's heart is too big, and he has a soft spot for hopeless causes."

The doctor rolled his eyes. "I do not."

"You do."

Something about their banter, the warmth between them, thawed Caleb's concern. He reached for their hands and pulled himself to his feet. "I'm not under some kind of spell. I don't need to be fixed."

"No," Dr. Hale agreed. "You need fresh clothes and a warm meal. And unless something has changed, last I checked, you had nowhere else to go."

Caleb nodded and risked a glance at Mr. Eliot's bruised face. "I'm sorry about that, by the way."

Amos nodded for Caleb to follow him. "We can talk over dinner."

~

A chill lingered on his skin, despite the fire's warmth. Caleb sat in the doctor's sitting room, dressed in dry clothes and wrapped in a thick quilt. The doctor had tended to his injuries before leaving him to change, and already Caleb's body ached fiercely. The doctor had disappeared into the kitchen with Mr. Eliot, and slowly the small home had filled with the sounds and smells of cooking.

By the time Dr. Hale entered with two steaming bowls, Caleb was ravenous. He eagerly accepted the offered bowl as Amos entered with soup of his own. The two older men sat close together on the couch, across from where Caleb sat in the armchair.

Caleb inhaled the spicy, herbal scents of the stew, letting the steam warm him from the inside out. "Thank you," he said at last. "And I'm sorry, again, about all the trouble I've caused."

Silence fell over the room as the three of them dug into their meal. It was a warm silence, though, so different than the tension of the courtroom. After a few moments, the doctor let his spoon rest in the bowl. "Can I ask you something, Mr. Walcott?"

"Of course. And you've more than earned the right to my first name. 'Caleb' is fine."

"Thank you, Caleb. I was wondering..." The doctor paused, as if to choose his words with more care, and rested a hand on Mr. Eliot's knee. "Why exactly did you attack Amos the other night? He said you blamed him for your sister's death, but I don't understand why you'd think so."

Caleb rubbed the back of his neck. He'd made such a mess of things. He was lucky the doctor hadn't thrown him out. Clearly, he and Amos were friends. "*Someone* killed my sister, Dr. Hale, and with the town so convinced it was Miss Bradbury, no one is looking for the real culprit."

Amos took another bite of his stew. "Please believe me, Caleb, when I say I had nothing to do with your sister's death."

"I want to believe you," Caleb said carefully, "but it's impossible to know who to trust. I don't understand why you're being so nice to me after everything I've done. Why don't you hate me like the rest of Brekham?"

The two men shared a look, and eventually Amos inclined his head. Oliver returned his focus to Caleb. "Amos and I... we know a thing or two about losing a town's good graces." He reached for Amos's hand and intertwined their fingers. "I can promise you that Amos had nothing to do with your sister's death. He was here that night. With me."

Caleb stared at the men for one moment. Then two. Until—

"Oh." Heat burned Caleb's face. It seemed so obvious, now that he'd opened his mind, what the doctor was implying.

"I trust that's not a problem." There was a thread of warning and worry in Oliver's tone.

"Of course not."

Caleb had read stories of men who found companionship with other men, and of women who did the same. He had even read, once, of a traveler who fell in love with all sorts of people during the course of their adventures. Sure, the stories were fiction—and his father claimed the One God didn't approve of such couplings—but Caleb had always figured there was a bit of truth to them.

He wondered if Amos Eliot was like that adventurer. If

he'd loved his wife before her passing, or if that match had been of the mayor's design. Caleb had a feeling he shouldn't ask, though. After attacking Amos, Caleb didn't think he had the right to such intimate confidences.

"And you won't go shouting our secrets in the square like you did today?" Amos prompted.

Heat rose to Caleb's cheeks. "I've really made a mess of things, haven't I?"

"You have indeed." Amos released the doctor's hand and resumed his supper, only to notice Oliver glaring at him a moment later. "What?"

Dr. Hale sighed. "What Amos means to say, is that we understand. Love does funny things to us all. I can't imagine what I might do if I found myself in your situation. I see how this trial breaks you, and no one should bear that much hurt on their own." A shadow passed over his face. "I also know a little something about disapproving fathers."

Caleb had no words. Not at first. He'd held so long to anger to avoid his hurt, he couldn't yet unbury the sting of his father's abandonment. He couldn't even think about what the future might hold. Everything he was supposed to inherit—the church, especially—was no longer an option. "Thank you. For taking me in."

His thanks were met with a nod, and the three of them finished their meals in comfortable silence, the crackle of the fire and the scrape of spoons against their bowls the only sounds in the house. When they were done, Amos took their bowls back to the kitchen, and Oliver added another log to the fire.

"You're welcome to stay in the guest room as long as you need. I do suggest you try to get a good night's sleep." Dr. Hale turned his back on the fire, and the light left his face in shadow. "Tomorrow is likely to be a trying day."

A tremor of worry upset Caleb's full stomach. "Why?"

Dr. Hale passed Caleb and paused at the bedroom door. Amos joined him a moment later, a hand on the doctor's back.

"The magistrate has summoned me to testify."

TESTIMONY OF DR. OLIVER HALE

*R*umor spread through Brekham that Pastor Lewis was calling his final witness, an expert whose testimony was full and real and true. An expert who even the most cynical of men—like the witch's most fervent defender, Caleb Walcott—would have to believe.

Magistrate Hawthorne sat behind his bench, wrinkled skin sagging like melted wax, and kept a watchful eye on the over-packed gallery. The men of the jury settled into their seats, straight-backed and formal, their eyes on the still-empty witness stand. Pastor Lewis, true to form, paced the front of the room. His shoes clacked against the floor like an ill-timed metronome.

At her small table, Blythe Bradbury tugged at the ropes that bound her wrists. The bruises that peeked out from her collar had paled to a greenish yellow, yet no one bothered to make note of them. She bowed her head, as if in prayer, but to which gods she prayed, no one knew.

The door swung open, and a bitter breeze tore through the room. In the wake of the violent wind came Caleb Walcott and Dr. Hale. The men settled together in the row of seats kept vacant behind the minister. Caleb tensed, shoulders bunching tight around his ears as they sat so near his father, but Dr. Hale placed a hand on his arm. Though Caleb seemed to relax, his arms remained steadily crossed against his chest. He kept his gaze averted from his father, letting it settle instead on the accused.

The magistrate banged his gavel and called for the day's session to begin.

Pastor Lewis turned to the crowd. "For my final witness, I call Brekham's esteemed medical expert, Dr. Oliver Hale."

Caleb shifted to let the doctor pass into the aisle. Dr. Hale patted the younger man's shoulder before straightening his jacket and turning toward the witness stand. It seemed as though the crowd held its collective breath as the doctor walked to the stand, the exhale coming, finally, as the witness took his seat.

"Dr. Hale, you examined Miss Walcott's body after she was brought back into town, correct?"

"Yes." The doctor looked to Caleb, a silent apology written in the lines of his brow. His gaze shifted forward to settle on the witch. "I did."

"And you examined the witch here at the courthouse a few days after?" Pastor Lewis spoke calmly, as if he discussed the weather with a colleague.

Dr. Hale nodded, causing his dark curls to fall forward into his face. "I examined Miss Bradbury, looking for injuries or evidence."

"Please, Doctor, tell us what you found over the course of your examinations." Pastor Lewis settled himself near the jury and leaned against one of the columns, crossing his ankles.

The silence that followed was laced with fervent anticipation. This was it. Everyone knew it. This was the definitive proof they hadn't known they wanted but suddenly needed.

A long sigh passed the witness's lips, but he straightened and seemed almost to become someone else. Someone older. "The victim arrived at my home late that night. I examined the young woman and found several deep lacerations that punctured internal organs. The origins of these wounds came from both the posterior and anterior axis."

Pastor Lewis cleared his throat and resumed a more formal posture. "In common terms, doctor?"

"Someone had stabbed Miss Walcott. There were several injuries to her back, presumably while she tried to get away, and several more on her chest and abdomen. Those were considerably deeper, and at a more perpendicular angle, so I suspect she was no longer standing at that point."

Dr. Hale swallowed hard, his eyes glazing over as if seeing the carnage again as fresh and vivid as that first night. A collective shudder worked through the crowd, through the jury, even through the prosecutor.

Still sitting behind his father, Caleb paled considerably, a tinge of green working into his fair skin. Tears sparkled in his eyes, but he brushed them away. No one could fault him for the show of grief.

Pastor Lewis pushed his spectacles higher on his nose with trembling hands. "When men searched the forest, they found the witch's dagger amid the bloody field. Were you able to examine its shape and compare that against the wounds?"

"I was."

"Is this that blade?" Pastor Lewis approached his table, the one he so rarely used except to hold his notes. The minister plucked a coarse bag from the pile and withdrew a bloodied blade wrapped in fine cloth. He handed it to the witness.

As Dr. Hale grasped the blade, the witch stiffened. The pulse in her neck beat faster, harder. Her lower lip trembled. The pupils of her eyes blacked out the gray.

"Yes, this is the blade I examined." The doctor handed the knife back to the minister, shuddering. "To the best of my knowledge, it is also likely the same blade that ended Miss Walcott's young life."

"And what of our accused?" Pastor Lewis turned to pace closer to Blythe, but before he got halfway, he seemed to think better of it, coming to a stop in front of the magistrate. "What did your examination reveal?"

Before he answered, Dr. Hale looked again to Caleb, as if seeking his approval or, perhaps, his forgiveness. "There was significant blood on Miss Bradbury's clothes, more than could have come from her own wounds. She had suffered a head wound, and there were several other, smaller, injuries. She developed significant bruising along her arms in the first couple days after the incident, just prior to the start of the trial."

The prosecutor nodded. "And given all of your examinations, what conclusion have you come to?"

Dr. Hale let out a slow breath and stared at his hands. "It's hard to know for certain what happened that night. Without having been there, we may never know for certain *exactly* what transpired."

"But you *can* offer an educated assumption. Right, doctor?"

"Based on my examinations…" The doctor forced his gaze up and let it settle on the jury. "Given only the evidence available to me, I can find no other explanation."

Behind the accused, Caleb bowed forward to put his head between his knees. Rapid breaths shook his back as he fell apart before the court. Silent in his breaking, in his grieving, in his shattered beliefs.

Dr. Hale cleared his throat.

"I will not wade into speculations as to whether the accused possesses any sort of magic, but she is almost certainly the one who stole Miss Walcott's life."

MOMENTS BEFORE THE MURDER

Caleb sat hunched over his journal, listing all the things that needed to be done before he escaped Brekham. He hoped to stay long enough to attend Isaac's wedding, and though eager to leave his father, Caleb wanted to ensure the old man could survive on his own. He also needed a way to earn money on the road. Caleb wouldn't rely on Blythe's mother. He wanted to sustain his family himself.

Somehow.

A slap to the back of his head jolted Caleb back to the present. He looked up and found the minister standing over him, a scowl on his face and a wine stain on his shirt.

"Was that necessary?"

The minister glared at him. "I called for you three times, boy. Where's your sister?"

Caleb's heart settled to its normal speed, and he closed his journal, hiding away his plans. "She's right here." He gestured toward the window where he'd seen his sister watching the outside world. She wasn't there. "Bells?"

Caleb stood and searched the small attic living space. "Mirabel, this isn't funny. Where—"

As Caleb passed his father, the minister gripped him by the ear and twisted hard. "You were supposed to watch her. What was so important that you lost track of your sister?"

An automatic apology rose to Caleb's lips, but he shoved it down along with a painful wince as his father twisted hard. "She must be downstairs. You could have missed each other when you came up."

The minister only glared, and Caleb pulled away and hurried downstairs to search the rest of the church.

Mirabel was nowhere to be found.

Wood creaked as Pastor Walcott stumbled down the stairs. "Mirabel!" he yelled, searching the offices at the back of the church. "Show yourself at once." When the minister caught sight of Caleb again, he swung an open palm, but Caleb ducked out of the way. "If she's lost or hurt, I'll have your hide."

Caleb ignored the threat, but an uneasiness settled through him. Mirabel should *be* there. It was late. And dark. And cold outside.

"Bells, where are you?" He grabbed his cloak and called out to the minister. "I'll check the cemetery. Perhaps she's visiting Mother." Caleb fled the church without waiting for a response. The cemetery came quickly into view, but it was empty. "Bells!" he called into the crisp night. "Mirabel!"

Silence.

Then a new sound. The quick puffing of breath. Relieved, Caleb turned, but it was only the minister. Caleb parted his lips, ready to rattle off another explanation, anything to keep the minister's violent hands away until he could solve this, when a sound pierced the night.

A scream.

Mirabel's scream.

The blood rushed from his face. His heart tripled in speed. "No…" Caleb turned toward the sound. Mirabel was somewhere in the forest.

Another scream, louder than the first.

Caleb ran.

~

*I*nside the forest, the darkness was absolute. Caleb raced through the trees, moving more by memory and instinct than sight. Mirabel's scream echoed in his head, louder than his frantic heartbeat. Branches snapped in his face. Thorns tore at his skin as he slipped past. Caleb's foot caught on an exposed root, and he crashed to the earth, biting his lip. Blood filled his mouth, bitter and salty, but then he was up again, racing through the forest.

"Mirabel!" Caleb paused to listen for a response. "Bells, where are you?" The silent night greeted him. Bird and beast and insect quiet as death around him. Still he ran, ran until panic closed his throat and he couldn't breathe. Until he had to stop. Caleb braced his hands on his knees and fought for air, sucking in one constricted lungful after another.

Then he was off again, searching every place he and his sister had ever been together. The spot they had once picnicked. The small clearing where Bells liked to pick flowers in the spring. The tree a young Mirabel used to climb.

Nothing.

Caleb called her name again and again, but his sister never replied. There was nothing but the whisper of wind through the trees and familiar voices—his father and Mr. Eastey and maybe others—also calling for his sister.

The men in this town are vile.

His stomach clenched with the memory of Mirabel's words.

They stare after me like I'm some rare cut of meat.

It's disgusting.

For a moment, Caleb hoped Mr. Eastey or one of the other men would find his sister. She would be properly embarrassed, and it would serve her right for wandering off and scaring him half to death. But a breath later, he remembered the look on her face when she spoke those words, the revulsion and dreaded acceptance, like she had no hope for a better future.

He had to find her first. He had to protect her until spring came and they could escape east with the Bradbury women.

Caleb quicken his steps, his feet leading him to the clearing where he spent most of his recent afternoons, delirious with love. He was still a hundred steps from the break in the tree line when fresh screams split the night. The sound burrowed into his marrow, leaving him frozen in place.

Then more shouting. Branches snapping. Deep, angry voices and his father's shock giving way to a violent rage Caleb knew all too well.

That sound unstuck Caleb's feet from the ground. He had to protect his sister. He wouldn't let the minister lay hands on her again. Caleb pushed every last bit of energy into his legs and ran, but breaking through the trees into the clearing nearly broke his mind.

A circle of candles framed the center of the field.

Two figures lay unmoving on the ground.

The scent of blood on the air.

Pastor Walcott ran past Caleb, a thick branch clutched like a weapon, wordless screams tearing from his throat. Mr. Eastey was fast on the minister's heels, screaming of magic. Of devils. Of witchcraft.

Blythe…

Wind whipped at Caleb's face as he charged forward. He wasn't going to be fast enough. The minister was too far ahead. Caleb let loose a feral scream as his father swung the branch at the first still figure. A horrible sound split through the night as the branch connected, and seconds later, Caleb crashed into his father, throwing him to the ground.

Sobs erupted from the minister's throat when they hit the firm earth, but Caleb didn't have time for that. He spun and crawled to Blythe's side. Instinct had warned the body was hers, but to finally see her lying there, her dress covered in blood, a fresh bead of red falling from her temple.

Even as he noted the steady rise and fall of her chest, rage tunneled his vision until Caleb could see nothing but the blood on his love's face. His father had done that. Caleb had seen it. He'd been too slow to stop it.

"What have you done?" Caleb demanded, whirling on the minister. The old man was a sobbing mess, Mr. Eastey kneeling to help him. "What kind of man strikes an unconscious woman!"

"Mr. Walcott, the witch—"

"I wasn't talking to you." Caleb cut off Mr. Eastey, ignoring his accusation. These men knew nothing of witchcraft. If Blythe was responsible for the circle of candles, she had a good reason.

"But your sister." Mr. Eastey pointed away from Blythe, and Caleb suddenly remembered the second form he'd seen in the grass.

He didn't want to look. Couldn't bear the thought of his sister and his love both hurt, both bleeding. How did this happen? How—

"This is all your fault." Pastor Walcott appeared in front of Caleb and struck him across the temple. "She would still be alive if not for you. You stupid, careless, insolent boy." The minister grabbed Caleb by his hair and dragged him across the muddy field. "Look at what your witch has done!"

The minister released Caleb, and he slid into something wet and warm and thick. Carefully, he reached for his sister. She looked much like Blythe had, still and covered in blood.

But Mirabel's chest did not rise.

It did not fall.

"Mirabel, please." He shook his sister, but her body moved wrong. Her skin was too cold. He wanted to comfort her, to do *something*, but every inch of Mirabel was bloody and broken and torn.

Caleb was vaguely aware of his father shouting. Of Mr. Eastey calling out into the woods for others to find them. None of this was supposed to be happening. There had to be a way to fix this. There had to be—

Blythe.

It had been a small thing, but she'd healed him once. Maybe she could do it again. Maybe she could save his sister.

In a blink, he was on his feet, stumbling toward Blythe's still form. His sister's blood on his hands. Her blood staining his clothes.

"Stay back, Mr. Walcott." Mr. Eastey appeared in front of him, arms outstretched. "It isn't safe. There's no telling what the witch could do."

"But she could save her!" Caleb shoved the older man

out of the way. Or at least, he tried to. The minister gripped his arms, and their neighbor pushed him farther away. Caleb whirled on his father. "If you hadn't hit her, she could have stopped this. She could have saved Bells."

Pastor Walcott slapped him with an open palm. He grabbed Caleb's chin and forced him to stare at Mirabel's broken body. "This is what the witch has done. She brings only destruction."

"No…" But Caleb's voice was less sure now. His heart breaking into a thousand tiny pieces. It cut him up inside like shattered glass. *You're wrong. She wouldn't do this.* But he couldn't voice the words. The tears were coming too fast now. His stomach sick.

Mr. Eastey stood behind them, a sentry over Blythe. "Help is coming," he promised, but the words were little assurance. "Prudence will have sent the others by now. They're coming."

But it was too late.

His sister was gone.

The woman he loved, the only one who could have possibly saved his sister's life, was injured and unconscious and blamed for the death.

Everything they had planned, the future Caleb had imagined for all of them, crumbled to dust.

TESTIMONY OF A WITCH

On the final day of the trial, the sun rose in an unblemished sky. The air was crisp in the way late autumn can be, before the arctic chill of winter creeps in. A beautiful day by all accounts, the sun warm on the skin despite the cool air. Had this been any other year, the people of Brekham might have gathered around bonfires to eat roasted pumpkin seeds and drink mulled apple cider. A final celebration before the snow barreled down upon them.

But this was not any year.

And this was not an ordinary day.

It was the day Blythe Bradbury took the stand.

Inside the courtroom, everything was bright. The light streaming through the windows seemed especially strong after the week of thick clouds. Yet despite the sun and relative warmth, those in attendance were on edge. The minister sat in his usual place, his faced bruised from the altercation with his son. A thin cut over his eye had scabbed over. Behind him, hovering at the very edge of his seat, sat Caleb Walcott. His bruises had faded and his split lip was healing, but the haunted look in his eyes aged him.

Dr. Hale sat near the middle of the courtroom. His shoulders slumped forward, and he massaged his temples. A hand squeezed his knee. A hint of a smile crossed the doctor's features. He covered the hand with his own and glanced up at the man sitting beside him.

Amos Eliot risked a smile. But his warmth also faded, leaving a heaviness lingering around his eyes. Though he had found common ground with the victim's brother, the bruises on his face still ached. There would be no forgetting. For any of them.

The men faced forward as the guard shoved Blythe toward the witness stand. She was unsteady on her feet, her face gaunt with hunger. The guard attached the ropes binding her wrists to a hook on the table to keep her in place. To protect those who must sit near her: the magistrate, the prosecutor, the jury.

When the witch was bound, Pastor Lewis approached, but he did not get near enough to reach out and touch her. "Is your name Blythe Bradbury?"

She turned her gray eyes on him but remained silent for several seconds. Finally, her lips parted. "It is." Her voice was rough from days of disuse.

Pastor Lewis stumbled over his next words, as if surprised she'd answered him at all. "Are you a witch?"

Her eyes narrowed. "No."

"It does you no good to lie to the court, Miss Bradbury. We have already proven your guilt on that count." He cleared his throat and forced himself to meet her eye. "I ask again. Are you a witch, Miss Bradbury?"

Blythe tilted her head to one side. Something flashed in her eyes. "I am no more a witch than you are, Minister. No more a witch than your wife."

Pastor Lewis fumbled and stopped dead. His face drained of color. He swallowed one breath, then another. "What did you say?" His voice came out a whisper, one that did not reach beyond the first row of the gallery.

The witch smiled. "You heard me, Minister."

"How... How can you possibly know of that?" The minister stumbled to the witness stand, keeping his voice low. "It's not possible... Only with witchery could you know that."

Blythe leaned forward. "So, tell them. Tell them I used magic to learn that your first wife burned as a witch. And your second." She spoke so softly, none save the prosecutor could hear.

The magistrate cleared his throat. "What delays you, Minister? Please, proceed with your questioning."

Pastor Lewis stepped away and shook his head. "Lie all you like, Miss Bradbury. The court knows you are the lone witch in our midst." He turned and walked toward the jury, his steps careful even as his hands trembled. "Did you know Mirabel Walcott?"

A long pause. "I did."

The minister pulled a handkerchief from his pocket and dabbed at his brow. "And how did you get along with the deceased?"

Blythe sliced him a look. "We were not overly close, nor did we have any disagreements."

"So, you weren't jealous of Miss Walcott's closeness to her brother? She didn't disapprove of your illicit relationship?"

Her gaze flickered to where Caleb sat behind his father. "I don't know what she thought." Blythe returned her attention to the prosecutor. "Not that my relationships are any concern of yours."

The thin man shook his head. "There's no point

denying the relationship. Mr. Walcott has made his feelings plain enough through his attempts to clear your name." Pastor Lewis turned away from the witch when she refused to blink, her gaze bearing down upon him. "Let's talk about the night you murdered Miss Walcott."

"I didn't murder—"

"You were in the forest that night," he said, cutting off her objection.

She glowered at him. "I went in alone. She was not meant to be there."

"Why?"

Blythe shrugged. "I don't know why she came."

"Lies!"

The shout came from somewhere near the back of the courtroom. It broke the dam that held the onlookers' opinions at bay. The room erupted.

"She went to become a witch!"

"The young girl wished to dance with demons!"

The accusations came from every corner, growing in volume, drowning out the magistrate's gavel. When no one would listen, he stood from his bench. "ENOUGH!" The shouts died off. Townsfolk returned to their seats. Isaac and his bride sat close together, hands clasped and shoulders tense.

"The next person who speaks out of turn will be expelled from this courtroom." In the wake of the magistrate's words, a fragile calm settled over the room. "Right then, Minister. If you please."

Pastor Lewis straightened his vest. "You misunderstand, Miss Bradbury. I didn't mean for you to divulge your victim's motives. I want to know why *you* were there."

Blythe said nothing. Instead, she stared at the town that had come to watch her demise. She studied each one.

"Miss Bradbury?"

She counted the people she knew, watched them whisper, studied their smiles. Memorized their faces.

"Miss Bradbury!" Pastor Lewis snapped his fingers in front of her face. "Why were you in the forest that night?"

The accused blinked and looked at the tall, thin man before her. She tugged on her wrists. The rope bit into her skin and pressed Caleb's charm tighter against her flesh. Blythe glanced toward Caleb, and for the first time since taking the stand, there was panic in her eyes.

"Answer the question, Miss Bradbury." The magistrate's voice broke whatever connection had formed between the lovers. Caleb glanced away, leaving Blythe lost in a sea of accusations with no life raft and no way to swim. His absence hung like weights around her neck as she was thrown overboard.

She dropped her gaze to her lap. "I needed to clear my head. I used to find the forest calming," Blythe said at last.

Pastor Lewis considered her and pushed his spectacles back up his long nose. "Why were there candles? What purpose could you have for them save unholy rites?"

"Do they not use candles in your church?" Blythe looked up. The sickly-sweet smile was back. "I find their flicker calming. You would not ask a young lady to stand alone in the dark, would you?"

"Then what of the knife?" the prosecutor snapped.

"Protection from animals." Her voice grew rough. Hard. Bitter.

"But it wasn't an animal you slaughtered that night. It was Pastor Walcott's daughter. Why? Why did you murder her?"

She found Caleb in the crowd and willed him to meet her eye. "I did not harm her. I tried to get her to leave."

"Leave what? What wickedness were you working

under the cover of dark? What was important enough to hide that you killed an innocent woman?"

"I—"

"Don't bother denying it. This court has *proven* your guilt. It was your knife. Your hands. All we ask of you is why!"

"I didn't do it!"

The hand swung through the air before anyone could react. The prosecutor's palm left the witch's cheek flaming red. "Her father was there that night," he growled. "He saw you covered in his daughter's blood. You will not sit there and deny the truth."

The air in the room lost all its warmth. Frost crackled along the wooden rail before her. When Blythe spoke, her breath was visible in the air, a white cloud in the chill of the room. "I have no answer to give you, but I do offer a question. You who wish so strongly to see a woman hang, ask yourselves: who is the true monster here?"

She looked past the minister at the crowd gathered to watch her confession. "For it is not me."

Caleb flinched when Pastor Lewis struck Blythe. He rose to defend her, but the gleam in Blythe's eyes stopped him. There was something cold there. Something dark. It pushed a shiver down his spine that forced him back into his seat.

The prosecutor growled accusations, reminders of all the blood and violence. The words transported Caleb back to that cold night. His hands shook in his lap. His stomach churned and threatened to expel what was left of the breakfast Dr. Hale had provided.

Inside his mind, all he could see was blood. Everywhere.

It had covered his sister's ruined body. The redness slick under his hands. His knees cold where they pressed into the near-frozen earth. Blythe's face had been so pale, so drained of color. Except for the blood, the dark red splattered against her face.

His heart struggled in his chest, and it was near impossible to breathe around the lump in his throat. He was here. In the courthouse. Not in the forest. Blythe sat at the witness stand, her face clean of blood.

Blythe did not kill his sister.

But she must have. Who else?

No. It wasn't her. There must have been someone else in the forest that night. Or perhaps it was indeed his father. Or maybe a dark spirit had taken over her body. Was that a possibility?

There was still so much of her magic that he didn't understand.

Why was Blythe even in the forest that night? He should have asked her before, the one time he'd managed to sneak down to her cell. Now it was too late. He might never know.

Caleb forced his attention back to the front of the room. Blythe sat at the witness stand, tilting her head to one side. She had once turned her head like that for him. It was cute then. Endearing. On this new Blythe, the expression looked almost mad. Crazed. Her voice dripped honey, but it was laced with poison.

"You who wish so strongly to see a woman hang, ask yourselves: who is the true monster here?" Her gaze swept the room. "For it is not me."

The prosecutor raised his hand again to strike her, but the magistrate banged his gavel on the bench. The noise startled the thin man and much of the crowd. Pastor Lewis dropped his hand.

"Have you any more questions for the accused?" Magistrate Hawthorne spoke with measured calm, his voice low and deep.

"None, Your Honor."

Blythe tilted her head to the other side, watching the thin minister with the feral hunger of a wild animal. It was as if she sought to take him apart, piece by piece. As if she could peel back the layers of his mind and find all the thoughts buried in his head.

Caleb shivered, wondering if he ever knew Blythe as well as he'd thought.

He couldn't get the doctor's testimony out of his head. *She is almost certainly the one who stole Miss Walcott's life.* Caleb had clung so tightly to that word—that *almost*—but was he nothing but a fool?

The magistrate gestured toward the jury box. "Gentlemen, please adjourn to the discussion room. Take as long as you need. You must decide unanimously the fate of Miss Bradbury on the charges of witchcraft and murder."

Chairs scraped against the wooden floor as the men stood. The noise jostled Blythe, and she shook her head. The disturbed smile slipped from her face, and she once again donned the indifferent expression she'd worn for most of the trial.

Giving the witness box a wide berth, the men of the jury filed out through the door at the back of the room. Caleb watched them go, his heart in his throat. These men would decide the fate of the woman he loved.

No. The fate of his sister's murderer.

No. No, no, no.

Caleb hung his head and stared at his hands. Hands that once caressed Blythe's bare skin, hands that had held her close as their bodies came together as one. The same hands that were smeared with his sister's blood. He didn't know what to think. He couldn't believe that Blythe would hurt his sister. And yet—

And yet—

Dr. Hale was a man of science, a *doctor*. He had examined the wounds. He saw in Mirabel's mangled body the truth of what had happened that night. Dr. Hale said Blythe had done it. Who was Caleb to say otherwise?

The guard unhooked Blythe's ropes from the witness stand and shoved her toward her normal chair. She sat, her back to Caleb. Blythe's shoulders slumped forward, and her head dipped. A rush of warmth washed through Caleb's chest. He wanted so desperately to rush forward, to throw his arms around her and hold his love in the final moments before the jury returned.

He wanted so desperately to hear the words *I'm innocent,* spoken only for him. Not denials made before a court that wanted to see her death. If he heard those words… He would crush his lips over hers and damn the consequences. If only she would say those words, he would kiss her until their lips were numb, even in front of his wine-addled father.

He would do anything for those words, anything for the jury to return with the verdict *not guilty*.

Anything.

Caleb didn't have to wait long to hear Blythe's fate. Less than five minutes after she returned to her usual place, the door at the back of the room swung open.

And the jury filed back into the room.

NOW

*E*very soul in the room grew very, very still. No one breathed. The townsfolk had given up all their afternoons to hear the news the jury now carried. The quick decision left little doubt as to what conclusion the men had reached, yet no one dared miss it.

Least of all Caleb.

Magistrate Hawthorne sat taller in his chair and turned to face the jury. "Gentlemen, on the charge of witchcraft, how do you find Miss Bradbury?"

The eldest man on the jury stood. He cleared his throat, but still his words came out like wheels against loose gravel. "Guilty."

"And regarding the murder of Miss Mirabel Walcott, how do you find?"

The room tensed. Caleb couldn't breathe. His mind screamed, *Innocent, innocent, innocent.* He glanced toward the heavens, sending frantic pleas to the One God, even as his faith shriveled to nothing. *Please. Please, let them say that she's innocent.*

Not that it would matter. They would hang her as a

witch, whether or not anyone had died.

The elder paused, as if savoring the thick anticipation in the air.

"We find her… guilty."

The final word echoed through the room, but it was not the wooden walls that bounced the verdict. Around the courtroom, onlookers whispered to each other.

Guilty,

guilty,

guilty,

guilty.

They seemed to revel in the verdict.

Caleb swallowed. His stomach felt hot and sick and twisted. Tears stung his eyes, yet a sense of calm blanketed the rage in his heart.

Every moment, ever since the Bradbury family moved to Brekham, since they made the fatal mistaking of moving into the abandoned Sanderson house, had led to this verdict. It had gone just as Blythe warned Caleb it would.

And though he'd sought other suspects, he hadn't come close to another truth. He didn't have the skill to save his love from a town of fearful men who were filled with prejudice. Blythe didn't kill his sister. She did *not.*

And still she'd pay the final price.

Behind him, the crowd stood in a roar of celebration. A thunderous applause filled the room. In the back, someone shouted, "Burn her!"

To his right, another voice rose over the swell of cheers. "Hang her!"

"Press her!"

Those voices meant nothing to Caleb. Idiot people in a town of fools. He saw how quickly they had taken to tall tales, even when placed upon the witness stand. He didn't care what they thought. If the men of the jury had any brains at all, they must have seen through the fevered lies of bored townsfolk and scared widows. But Dr. Hale's testimony… they must have believed the doctor at least.

Doubt twisted in Caleb's gut like roots of a rotted tree.

Should *he* believe the doctor, too?

In front of him, the minister stood, adding his voice to the cries for vengeance. Caleb leaned farther back in his chair, feeling very small and so terribly alone in the crowded room. When Pastor Walcott turned and spotting Caleb sitting behind him, the older man smiled. A wicked, satisfied, smug grin. "Perhaps now you will return to your senses, boy."

Caleb rose to his feet. He held his father's stare despite the pain consuming him.

"If not now, then perhaps in the morning, after the whore witch is dead."

Caleb's knuckles hurt before he realized he had struck his father. The impact of the punch, the scrape of chairs as the minister stumbled back, cut through the cheering of the crowd. Pastor Walcott surged toward Caleb, but was rewarded with another fist to the face.

Blythe turned to watch the scuffle, a deep sadness in her eyes.

Caleb drew back to throw another punch, but strong arms gripped him. He glanced over his shoulder. Dr. Hale held him back, a look of warning in his eyes.

But the distraction was all the minister needed to land a blow of his own. The fist slammed into Caleb's gut, doubling him over. Caleb gasped for air, holding the back of the bench for support. And then Dr. Hale's grip was gone. Caleb glanced up in time to see the doctor shove his father aside when the minister tried to hit Caleb again.

And then something in the air *snapped*.

The courtroom erupted. Hands and fists swung from

every direction as those closest to them joined the fray. Caleb tasted blood. Someone knocked Dr. Hale to the ground, and Amos Eliot hurried to help the doctor back to his feet. Before Caleb could see if the men could escape the crowd, a thick arm snaked around his throat and pressed tight against his neck.

"You should have kept your mouth shut." The familiar voice in his ear could only belong to one man.

Isaac.

His former friend squeezed tight, choking the life from his lungs. Caleb jabbed his elbow into Isaac's gut, and managed to get away, but Grace appeared suddenly before him. She raised her hand, the amber stone in her wedding ring winking in the light, and struck Caleb across the face.

The magistrate banged his gavel, again and again and again, but it held no power. Not anymore. Not as Isaac lunged for Caleb again, wrapping calloused fingers around his neck. Caleb struggled to breathe while Isaac's pregnant wife looked down her nose at him.

Then someone screamed, high and long, piercing through the rumble of fists and grunts.

Blythe? Caleb recognized her voice a moment later, his name falling from her lips. She screamed for someone to help. Shouted for the fighting to stop. "Leave him alone!" Blythe's voice carried strong to Caleb's ears, pierced straight into his mind. "Do what you will to me, but don't touch him."

Her words did nothing to still the fighting around him. Caleb struggled to breathe with Isaac's grip tightening around his neck. He reached for Isaac, clawing at his arms, but Isaac wouldn't let go.

The windows shattered—a high, clattering sound as bits of glass rained down upon them.

Isaac flinched, and Caleb managed to pull free from his

grip. Caleb turned to throw a punch, but he caught sight of Blythe.

And his heart stopped.

The blacks of her eyes had tripled in size. Yet still they grew until her gaze was a pit with no bottom. Wind whipped through the shattered windows and swirled around the room. The temperature dropped, lower and lower, until the men were shaking. Those closest to Blythe fled for the back of the room, stumbling over each other to escape.

Pastor Walcott backed into his son and shoved Caleb ahead of him, a shield against the witch. Caleb elbowed him away, and his father fled.

Parchment flew off the magistrate's desk as he, too, backed away from the witch. The wind swirled faster and faster, pushing people away from Caleb, who stood—with Blythe—at the center of the growing tornado.

The blackness in her eyes faded to their regular gray, almost silver in the flickering light of the room.

"Forgive me," she yelled over the roar of the wind.

Caleb had no words. Fear and awe in equal measure tore at his heart as he witnessed what he could only assume was the height of her power, something he had never seen before. Somewhere in the back of his mind, a voice whispered that power like this was enough to kill while the rest of him refused to believe her guilt. He wanted to tell her how much he loved her. To tell her that he still dreamed of following the Traveler east, across the vast seas, if only she could explain what really happened to his sister.

But he never got the chance.

The guard approached Blythe from behind. He hit her. Hard.

Blythe crumpled to the ground.

And the air in the courtroom fell still.

NOW

Caleb didn't speak for a long time after that. He watched, stunned and silent, as the guards dragged Blythe away. He stood frozen in place until both Dr. Hale and Mr. Eliot came to drag him out of the courthouse. Back at the doctor's house, Caleb said nothing while Oliver tended to his fresh wounds. He said nothing while Amos prepared them supper. The house was uncomfortably silent save the sizzling pans and bubbling water. As they ate, the doctor tried to apologize for his testimony, but Caleb didn't have the heart to hear it. The other witnesses he could write off as gossips and liars, but Oliver was a doctor. A man of science.

His testimony sowed the first *real* seeds of doubt. Already they grew roots and seemed impossible to shake.

After the older men retired to the bedroom, Caleb paced the small living area as a manic kind of energy overtook him. Two weeks ago, before his sister's death, before all of *this* happened, his life had so much potential. So much hope.

He had already given Blythe his heart, and he knew it

was only a matter of time before they wed. They had plans to travel east, to follow the Traveler and her Eastern Star. Together, they would attend university and explore whatever they fancied. Caleb could study medicine and discover a way to cure infections like the one that stole his mother. Blythe might spend her life studying the workings of the world, her curiosity insatiable.

They were even going to find a way to bring Mirabel with them, to help her escape the future their father had planned. The Walcott siblings would be free, and Caleb could make a life with the woman he loved. Mirabel could craft whatever future she desired. Perhaps she'd build a life as a musician, playing for the most important people across the sea. His sister was so full of talent, so full of *life*, before all this.

Now, everything was different. That future was gone.

Caleb shook his head. He would not—could not—give up so easily. He and Blythe would find a way to escape, immediately. Caleb grabbed his cloak and slipped out of the house.

He kept to the shadows, avoiding torchlight as best as he could. Near the center of town, he passed the tavern, full of laughter and flowing ale, even with the late hour. Caleb could hardly remember the last time he'd laughed. It was probably something Isaac had said or—

Fresh grief snuck up on Caleb, leaving him with stinging eyes and a swollen throat. There had been so much to grieve, he hadn't let himself feel the loss of his friend. Isaac claimed that Caleb was the one who changed, was the one who broke their friendship by falling in love with Blythe, but it felt bigger than that.

It wasn't as if Isaac simply ignored Caleb's pleas for help. He had actively made things worse. Caleb rubbed his tender throat.

Isaac had tried to kill him.

Was it all about the child growing in Miss Pratchett's—*Mrs. Carrier's*—womb? If Isaac hadn't lied about Blythe in court, Caleb would have held his friend's secret close to his heart. Isaac should have known that. He should have told Caleb the moment he knew there was a baby on the way.

Caleb reached the town center and paused at the fountain where Isaac had shoved him in and held him under. He shivered. His life had become a nightmare, completely unrecognizable as the one from before the Bradbury women came to town.

As he turned and headed for the courthouse, Caleb steeled himself for what lay ahead. He would break Blythe out of her cell if he had to tear up each brick with his fingers. He would beg Blythe to use her power to bend the metal wide enough to free herself. She didn't have to hide the depth of her magic from him. He would never run.

Caleb crept around the courthouse, but stopped short when he noticed a guard seated beside the building, leaning against the bricks. There was a time when Caleb might have been able to talk his way past the guard, when he could have claimed he was there to provide Blythe a chance to repent to the One God, but the whole town had seen his father cast him out. They all knew his feelings for Blythe, even if they could never understand the true depth of them.

He needed another way through.

Before Caleb could do anything more than curl his hands into fists—thinking that perhaps he could knock out the guard long enough to sneak inside—a loud sound tore through the night. The guard's head tipped back, and a second snore punctuated the quiet.

A strange feeling shot down Caleb's spine, but he hurried forward anyway. He wouldn't let himself think too hard about whether the guard being asleep was simple good fortune or if Blythe knew he was coming and used her magic to ease his passage.

The exterior door was locked, but the keys dangled from the guard's belt. Carefully, Caleb retrieved the metal ring, flinching as the keys clanged together. He held his breath, but the guard didn't stir. Moments later, Caleb was safely inside the courthouse basement.

Though he'd only been there once before, Caleb moved through the semi-darkness with more confidence than he ought to have. With each corner he turned, he expected to find a dozen other guards, but it seemed the magistrate felt secure in the cell's ability to hold Brekham's latest witch.

At the final turn, Caleb paused to steady his pounding heart, and then peered around the corner. His cracked heart shattered when he saw Blythe. She looked so small there inside her cell, fragile as she hugged her knees to her chest. The image was so different than the previous one in his mind, the powerful woman who spun the wind like it was nothing.

"Blythe."

Her named slipped past his lips, and it was enough to spur him forward again. He hurried to her cell, fingers curling around the bars.

She looked up to meet his gaze, dark circles under her eyes. "You shouldn't be here," she said, but there was no bite to her tone as she pulled herself to her feet.

"Don't ask me to leave. Not tonight." Caleb leaned his forehead against the bars and fought the rush of tears that stung his eyes. "I should have been here every day. I shouldn't have left you alone."

Blythe approached him slowly and rested trembling fingers over his. "It's not safe to be here."

"I don't care." Caleb tipped his chin up and found Blythe so very close. Then she was rising to meet him, and he captured her lips. Their kiss was desperate and full of grief, a goodbye neither of them wanted to admit. Blythe reached for him, her hands traveling up the planes of his chest, but then she pushed him away.

"We can't, Caleb. You have to go before someone sees you."

"I'm not leaving without you." Caleb's voice echoed off the rocky walls. He stepped back and raised the key he'd stolen from the guard. "One of these has to work. We'll disappear before dawn. We'll leave this wretched town behind."

"Caleb…"

But he didn't listen to whatever she said next. He shoved key after key into the lock, twisting and jiggling, begging one of them to turn.

None of them did.

"I tried to tell you," Blythe said after Caleb's frustrated scream dispersed between them. "Only the magistrate has a key."

The ring of keys fell from his grip and clanged against the floor. Her words were like a bucket of ice water, dousing what was left of the fire burning inside him. "I tried so hard to figure out who did it."

"I know you did."

Caleb brushed the moisture from his eyes, a strange feeling curling around his heart. "Do you still remember nothing of that night?"

The silence between them grew heavy. Blythe fidgeted but said nothing.

"If you know who did this—"

"It's *my* fault, Caleb."

"No." Caleb shook his head. He refused to believe it. "You would never do that. I *know* you."

The shadow of a smile crossed her face. "I shared a lot of myself with you, but you do not know everything. We've only known each other for a season."

"You did not kill my sister," he said again, as if declaring it would make it true. "She was supposed to escape with us in the spring."

The witch merely shook her head. "I didn't wield the knife, but the blade was mine. *I* agreed to go into the woods. *I* agreed to work magic I knew I shouldn't. *I* was the one who didn't send her home fast enough."

"But someone else was there," Caleb said, piecing together the thin trail of clues she laid before him. "Someone else killed my sister. It wasn't you."

"It might as well have been."

Caleb gripped tight to the bars. "Tell me who it was."

She lowered her gaze. "Knowing won't bring her back. Knowing will only hurt worse."

"That's not your decision to make!"

Blythe pressed her lips into a thin line and stepped away from the cell door. "The answer has been staring you in the face for *days*. If you aren't clever enough to find the truth, then you aren't ready to know."

"Why didn't you tell the court? They could—"

"They would do nothing different. They've decided to kill me, and nothing will stop them from trying to do just that."

"But—"

"Get out." Blythe was shaking now, her eyes dark but full of tears. "If you won't listen to me, then get out. Don't bother coming tomorrow. You won't be able to change a thing."

Caleb did not move.

"I said *go!*" The air grew static between them, and the cell door rattled against the bars. "Or Mirabel won't be the last Walcott to meet an early end."

Displays of her magic wouldn't frighten him, but a brittle anger picked at old wounds. If she wouldn't tell him what happened, if she wouldn't save herself, then why should he continue to put himself on the line?

"Fine." Caleb turned and walked toward the exit. Before he rounded the first corner, he glanced over his shoulder to deliver a final parting phrase.

"Enjoy the gallows."

aleb hardly slept that night. He tossed and turned and stared at an unfamiliar ceiling. The few moments he did succumb to unconsciousness, his dreams were filled with every man, woman, and child in Brekham twisted into monsters, attacking his sister.

The answer has been staring you in the face.

Blythe's words taunted him, but Caleb found no purchase in his memory. He found no answers.

In the morning, he picked at his food—eggs and day-old biscuits that Oliver made—unable to stomach more than a bite or two.

"Are you sure you don't want to come?" the doctor asked as he set his empty teacup in the sink. "I can hardly imagine how terrible this must be for you, but I don't want you to regret losing your final goodbye."

Caleb pushed the remnants of his eggs around the plate and stared at his reflection in a cup of black tea. He looked older than he remembered, dark shadows under his eyes and his face more gaunt than ever before. "Blythe doesn't want me there."

"Miss Bradbury needn't know you are there. I worry how *you* will feel if you do not come. There are no second chances with matters like this." Dr. Hale laid a hand on Caleb's shoulder. "It's your choice whether you attend. Just take care that you're sure about your decision."

Caleb nodded, but he had no way to be sure. Every option was awful. Each decision led only to misery and pain. Unless he could puzzle together Blythe's meager clues, his attendance would change nothing.

"I'll stay here."

"All right, then. We'll see you after." Dr. Hale patted him on the back, joining Amos by the front door. The two men left for the town square, where the old wooden gallows had been resurrected in the hours since the verdict. Caleb's heart ached as the front door thudded closed, but he refused to shed a tear.

He'd shed enough to last a lifetime, and if he had to lose more, he would save them for his sister's burial. She would be laid to rest after the town had dealt with the witch who stole her away. The fact that Caleb hadn't found their mother's necklace—that Bells would be buried without it—was yet another wound upon his heart.

I agreed to go into the woods.

I agreed to work magic I knew I shouldn't.

The answer has been staring you in the face.

Caleb shoved away from the table, the tea sloshing over the edge of his cup, and began to pace. Who would go to Blythe for help? What magic had she been asked to work? And *why* wouldn't she simply tell him the truth? What was she protecting him from?

His pacing brought Caleb into the living room, where the curtains were swung wide. The first gold rays of sunlight spilled into the room, making the space shine like honey or amber, just like the stone at the center of their mother's necklace.

Just like—

Caleb froze, his limbs feeling suddenly like stone even as his heart raced faster and faster.

It couldn't be.

It didn't make sense.

It was the *only* thing that made sense.

Without stopping to grab his cloak, Caleb ran from the house into the cold. The bright morning sky darkened, storm clouds gathering from every direction to converge upon the small town. Winds picked up and tossed his red hair into his eyes. But still, he ran.

If only he could get there in time, he could tell the town the truth. He could save Blythe.

Because she was right. It was there in front of his oblivious face. Many in town had damning secrets. Many would do anything to protect their reputations and their wealth. But there was only one man who had asked for Caleb's help. One man who Caleb had laughed off, not understanding the seriousness of the concern.

One man who had tried to kill Caleb to silence him.

A man who could melt down Mirabel's necklace and repurpose the rare, amber stone.

When Caleb reached the town center, he stumbled to a halt. The whole of Brekham had come to watch her hang. Every last soul was there. He found Dr. Hale and Amos near the back of the crowd and rushed toward them. They caught him by the shoulder as he tried to push further into the crowd.

"Easy now, Caleb." Dr. Hale placed a hand on his arm. "Don't do something you'll regret."

"But I know who did it." Caleb tried to pull away from the doctor, but he lost his strength when he caught his first sight of Blythe. Her skin was so pale she hardly looked alive. A noose hung around her neck. But she was calm, so very calm despite the storm building above the square.

Her lips parted to speak, and her words carried across the crowd. "I will not waste my final breaths to claim an innocence you're determined to ignore. But I do have words for you, Magistrate."

The sound of her voice nearly broke Caleb. How? How could she greet her death so willingly? How could she let them kill her when she knew who the real villains were?

"My gods hear my prayers, and they smile upon me," she continued. "Can you say the same of yours? Will your god punish the fools who speak in half-truths and spew forth damning falsehoods?" A rumble of thunder shook the ground. "If you do this, my gods will send you swiftly into the earth."

Lightning streaked across the sky and rain so cold it was almost snow soaked Caleb in an instant. He had to hurry. He had to reveal the truth. Caleb tried to push through the crowd, but Amos held him back.

Caleb spun on the other man, a suspect turned friend. "Please, let me go," he pleaded. "I need to get to the magistrate."

"Don't be foolish. They won't hesitate to hang you, too."

"Please." When Amos did not release him, Caleb ripped away from his hold and shoved through the crowd. He yelled for the magistrate, but more thunder stole his words.

Scared near out of their minds, the onlookers jumped aside to let him through. Blythe spoke to the magistrate, but Caleb was too focused on reaching her to register her words. Thunder rumbled overhead. Caleb flinched but kept moving. *I'm not going to be fast enough.* He shoved people out of the way, picking up speed.

Blythe stepped up to the dropping platform. The noose tightened around her neck.

"No!" Caleb kicked into a run, weaving through the crowd. It seemed, somehow, to rain harder. The cobblestone slick beneath his feet. He ran, faster and faster, heart racing. He glanced up.

Blythe caught his gaze and held it. Her gray eyes flashed with fear and pain and sorrow and regret.

He saw his name fall from her lips.

The executioner reached for the lever, and before Caleb could call out, the man pulled.

The floor fell out from beneath her.

Blythe dropped.

Her body hung midair, suspended by the noose. The sky shrieked again. A flurry of lightning flashed around them as thunder shook the earth. Everyone, Caleb included, flinched away from the searing light and terrible sound.

When he righted himself—

The gallows were engulfed in flames.

*B*rekham was burning.

Caleb stood, shocked into stillness as an inferno raged before him. Lightning had hit the square. The angry sky had obliterated the gallows, the ruined bits burning in earnest. Chunks of wood shattered from the structure, shooting out spears of rough-edged wood

Sweat stung his eyes. Flames danced before him.

"Blythe!"

Caleb rushed forward, pushing past his neighbors as they fled from the square. He had to reach her. He had to pull her from the fire. She wasn't going to die. Not like this. Not like—

But Caleb couldn't see her anymore. The beam that supported the noose had collapsed, the whole structure falling in on itself. Her body's shape was no longer discernible through the smoke and haze. And still, Caleb pushed forward.

He had to reach her. He *had to* pull her free.

When he passed the front rows, Caleb paused. The

blast had tossed those closest to the gallows like dolls, scattered across the ground, discarded by a celestial child. Some struggled to escape the heat, using their elbows to inch away from the blaze. Others lay still upon the earth. Too still. Chests did not rise.

Still others screamed.

A familiar voice caught Caleb's attention, and he turned in time to see Isaac falling to the ground. Fire caught the edge of his pants, and in a burst of light, the fire spread up and up and up until it consumed all of him. Isaac screamed, but Caleb turned away.

He hoped Mirabel was the one who had sent the sparks Isaac's way. He hoped Mirabel was the one who blew in the wind and rain and lightning.

She deserved revenge on the man who killed her.

Caleb tore his gaze from the blazing fire and screaming killer. He stepped past neighbors on the ground, noting the trail of injured witnesses, people bold enough to stand near the front. Mrs. Putnam's children fussing over her still body. Mr. Eastey's arm dangled awkwardly from his side, bent in a very wrong direction. Caleb didn't have time to worry about any of them, the injured or the dead.

He pressed forward until he stood alone before the blazing gallows. The heat licked at his skin, the flames reaching out to embrace him. A deadly lover. As deadly as his love for Blythe. The rain that bled from the sky did little to dampen the fire, but it soaked Caleb through to the bone. He shivered as his world burned.

Wind whipped through the square, teasing the flames higher. Screams sounded all around him, but Caleb couldn't piece together their words. He couldn't match the voices to the names he knew in his head. The only voice he cared to find was hers, but he had yet to hear her scream.

"Blythe!" A crash of rolling thunder hid his voice. He hadn't seen where the lightning struck. Had it missed her? Did she escape the fire? Screams pushed through Caleb's thoughts enough to pull him around. Behind him, flames licked at the roof of the courthouse.

Fresh panic stole the air from his lungs. Caleb turned back to the ruined gallows and hurried forward, heedless of the flames eager for his flesh. He pulled at the fallen wood in the places least occupied by fire. He would dig to the center of the earth if that would save her. Caleb pulled another crumbled beam from his path, but the fire flared, temporarily blinding him. He raised his hands to shield his face. Pain laced up his arms.

Caleb dropped to his knees. The smoke wormed into his lungs, choking him, *killing* him. His hands curled inward, shielding his palms. He didn't dare glance at the ruined flesh. Caleb couldn't stomach the sight if they looked half as bad as they felt.

He tried to see through the blackening smoke. If only he could catch a glimpse of her form. To know if she struggled to live or if her life had already passed. "Please," he begged, but to what god he didn't know, "Don't turn her to ash. I must have something to bury." Fierce coughs racked his body, cutting off any further prayer.

Strong arms wrapped around his chest. They heaved, dragging Caleb from the fire, pulling him away from the place where his love would surely die, if she was not already dead. Away from the smoke, Caleb could breathe again. He choked on the fresher air as it flooded his lungs.

When he glanced at his protector, it was not Dr. Hale as he expected.

It was Amos.

The man Caleb accused of killing his sister, still

sporting the black eye Caleb gave him, had pulled him back from the brink of death.

"Damned fool," Amos whispered. Soot and sweat covered his brow and slid down his face, carried by the unrelenting rain. "Are you trying to get yourself killed?" Amos coughed and wiped the ash from his face.

"Where's Dr. Hale? Is he—"

"Oliver's fine." Amos pointed to his right. "He's helping where he can."

Dr. Hale rushed between the fallen, pulling those with life in their eyes farther from the fire. Caleb glanced away, and his gaze flitted over his ruined hands. His stomach clenched. His palms were covered in blisters, some of the skin torn away. Everything oozed. Caleb thought he might be sick.

"Caleb!" Dr. Hale called from his left. Caleb turned and found the doctor kneeling beside a man dressed in black. "Come quickly!"

Caleb struggled to his feet, leaning into Amos for support. Together the two men stumbled to the doctor, buffeted by the roaring wind and soaking rain. The sky flashed, and thunder rumbled again. Brekham flinched.

When they reached Dr. Hale, Caleb couldn't understand why the doctor had called him over so urgently. Caleb saw the face, but with the features covered in blood and boasting lifeless eyes, it took a moment to recognize the man at his feet.

"Father…" Caleb crumpled to the ground. Through stinging tears, Caleb looked over the injuries one by one, feeling each upon his flesh as if they were his wounds to bear. A piece of splintered wood had pierced the minister's chest. The force must have knocked him back, for his head had cracked open upon the stone. A pool of blood dyed his dark hair almost black, the bits of gray at his temples gleaming red.

"Why are you standing there? Help him."

"It's too late." Dr. Hale bent and closed the minister's eyes. "He's gone."

WRITTEN TESTIMONY OF BLYTHE BRADBURY

They're coming. I hear their footfalls against the stone floor. There's still so much to tell you. Still so much—

But there isn't time, so I can only leave you with this. If you do not wish to know the name, this is your last chance to turn away.

Isaac Carrier killed your sister.

He came to me with Miss Pratchett at his side. They were expecting a child, and they were so very afraid of what their fathers would do if they found out. The fear in her eyes… that would have been enough to convince me to make a terrible mistake, but they threatened to cry witch if I didn't comply.

Helping them was my only option to stay. My only chance to keep from losing you.

In the end, I lost you anyway.

Though Isaac wielded the blade, Miss Pratchett did not try to stop him. Their fear is no excuse for their actions, but it was real.

No matter what happens this day, I can promise you this: they will be punished for taking Mirabel from you. They will be punished for stealing her future.

Whether I survive the gallows or not, I know I have strength enough for that.

The guards are close now. Too close. I hear the keys. I have mere moments left.

I love you, Caleb. Never forget the truth of that. Until my dying breath, I love you, and I will do everything in my power to breathe beyond this day.

Yours forever,
Blythe

NOW

The day was long and full of pain.

Dr. Hale tended to the burns on Caleb's hands, but then his home transformed into a temporary hospital, the people of Brekham filtering through for help, some going home while others instead were transferred into Mr. Upton's care.

Caleb had watched them come and go, had held his tongue when they cried witchcraft and shared their relief that the witch was finally gone. There was only one person —one *couple*—with which Caleb wanted to speak, and the doctor was finishing with them now.

Grace had bled for hours in the doctor's small medical room. A section of the gallows had struck her hard across the abdomen, and she'd lost the baby. Oliver wouldn't tell a soul, but the house was too busy with injured people, and the news of her pregnancy, too far along to have happened after the wedding, quickly spread.

If Isaac wasn't already dying, Grace's father would have surely killed him.

As it was, Mr. Pratchett came quickly to collect his

daughter. Her twin, Verity, had suffered tremendous burns, and Mr. Pratchett wanted to take his family away from the cursed town. They were taking their wealth and heading for safer pastures, places where no one had ever heard of Brekham or the Carrier family.

From his bedroom—for Oliver had agreed to let Caleb stay as long as he liked—Caleb overheard Mr. Pratchett railing at his daughters. Hurrying them out the door. They were to be on the road before the sun had set. They were never coming back.

Someone cried loudly, but he couldn't be sure which pain drove the woman to tears.

After the Pratchett family left, there came a knock upon Caleb's door. Amos Eliot entered a moment later. "She was happy enough to let it go." Amos held up Grace's wedding ring. "You're sure it's the same stone?" he asked as he passed the ring to Caleb.

The metal rested on thick bandages, and Caleb examined it carefully. The setting was wholly different, but he had spent his life looking at the amber stone where it had previously rested in the One God's sun. Caleb nodded. "This is it." A lump formed in his throat. Even still, he didn't want to believe it.

But he deserved answers.

"Is Dr. Hale done with him yet?"

Amos leaned against the doorframe and nodded. "There isn't much more Oliver can do but ease the pain until the boy passes."

"I'm not sure he deserves even that kindness." Caleb stood and dropped the ring in his pocket. He'd make sure Mirabel got their mother's stone before she was laid to rest in the coming days.

"Caleb…" Amos said, a warning tone in his voice.

"Don't worry," Caleb said, slipping past the other man,

"I won't hurt him."

Dr. Hale wasn't actually finished with Isaac yet, but Caleb didn't have to wait long for Isaac to be alone. Once the doctor left to tend to other patients, Caleb slipped into the small room and shut the door behind him.

Laid out on the table, Isaac was barely recognizable. Each shallow, wheezing breath rattled his lungs, and all of his skin was covered in angry red blisters, other areas burnt black. He barely had any hair left that wasn't singed or disappeared completely.

"I know it was you."

Isaac tried to turn his head toward Caleb's voice, but even the tiniest motion drew out a moan of pain.

Caleb stepped up to the table and stared down at his former friend. At the man who murdered his sister. The man who pointed the blame at Blythe and stole her from this world. Yet it wasn't anger that filled Caleb to bursting.

It was grief.

"Why, Isaac? Why did you destroy our lives?"

Isaac closed his eyes. "If you've come to kill me, get it over with. It can't hurt any worse than this."

"I don't want more death. I want answers." Caleb waited, but when Isaac continued to ignore him, he held a hand over one of Isaac's injuries. "I'm not above causing more pain to get what I want."

This time, Isaac flicked his gaze to Caleb's, and he must have seen the determination, because he let loose a shaky breath and gave the slightest of nods.

"I only wanted help," Isaac began, his voice hoarser than Caleb had ever heard. "You said yourself that your father wouldn't marry us before spring, and we couldn't let her father find out. There were rumors in town about Blythe. We asked her for help."

"And she agreed?" Caleb couldn't believe Blythe would do something so foolish.

"Not at first. But Grace can be persuasive when she wants to be." Isaac lost his voice to a fit of coughs, and the movement of his body tugged at his burnt flesh. Fresh bits began to ooze. "She's gone, isn't she?"

"Her father came for her, yes." Despite everything, he felt a pang of loss for his old friend. He had to stay focused. "So, after you forced Blythe to help you, why hurt my sister?"

"Mirabel wasn't supposed to be there, but she saw us in the woods. She saw Grace touch her belly, and I *knew* the terror would figure it out." Isaac closed his eyes, and tears slipped down his ruined cheeks. "If anyone found out, we'd be ruined."

"So, what then? My sister had to die because *you* made a mistake?" The anger rose, and Caleb had to pace the room to keep from strangling Isaac. "You ruined so many lives. You *killed* everyone I loved! Bells. Blythe. Even my father."

"You had no love for that old man," Isaac argued, as if that absolved him for all the rest.

"He was a violent drunk, but he was still *family*." Caleb spun back to face Isaac. "I hope you survive these burns, Carrier. May your days be long and lonely and full of pain."

"Caleb—"

Caleb didn't hear whatever Isaac said next. He had what he'd come for—answers, what was left of his mother's necklace—and now he never wished to see Isaac again.

He had a family to bury, and so very much to grieve.

he whole town came to say goodbye. At least, what was left of it.

They moved through the graveyard like spirits in the soft light of dawn. There was no one left in town unaffected by loss. No one to offer a comforting word.

Brekham grieved in silence.

The birds and beasts in the forest joined the town in mourning. Even their songs did not cut through the dead stillness of the cold dawn. Not even the wind dared whistle through the dying grass.

Soon, a line of carriages pulled around the church, the wheels creaking as they bounced over uneven ground. The air was cold, so very cold that morning. The earth had frozen over, which made the morning's work of digging harder than expected. Yet even the wind had perished in the storm of fire and wind and rain. The people of Brekham shivered, their breath—at times the only sign they still lived—blew white in the air.

The carriages stopped outside the graveyard. The drivers, men from the neighboring town of Rowley, opened the doors and reached in for the plain pine coffins.

They pulled Mrs. Putnam from the carriages first. The stress and commotion of the fires had stopped the old woman's heart. She died surrounded by her children, who had come to town for the hanging.

Instead, they would bury their mother.

Mrs. Putnam: widow, busybody, neighbor.

As the men from Rowley carried Mrs. Putnam's coffin to her grave, Caleb Walcott emerged from the church. A heavily packed bag in one hand, Caleb spared a glance for the funeral attendees before turning toward the front of the church, where his own carriage waited. He tossed the bag inside and patted the horses tethered there.

Footsteps behind him approached and fell still. "Are you ready?"

Caleb turned to find Dr. Hale, dressed in his funeral clothes. Like Caleb, he wore black from head to toe. He glanced behind the doctor and raised a brow when he did not see Amos standing there.

A sad smile pulled at Dr. Hale's lips. "Amos and I do not often arrive together." He sighed. "You understand."

Caleb nodded, and together they walked around the church to the graveyard, where men pulled a second coffin from the carriages.

Magistrate William Hawthorne. Faithful servant of Brekham. Follower of the One God, keeper of His light.

Survived by his wife, children, and grandchildren.

Caleb bowed his head as the magistrate's coffin passed. His red hair glinted in the growing sunlight. Yet the sun did little to steal the cold from the air. Perhaps nothing would ever steal the chill from Caleb's heart. Everything and everyone he had ever loved was gone.

The young man, now orphaned, pulled in a shuddered breath. He pressed a fist to his chest as if his heart ached too much to continue to beat. A hand on his shoulder kept Caleb moving. Though Caleb had only known the doctor for a short time, already Dr. Hale was a lifeline in this empty world. A beacon of hope in a time of grief. Caleb smiled at the older man.

Dr. Hale would not let the young man drown. Not that day. Not in his own grief.

The men of Rowley carried more coffins past them. Pastor Lionel Lewis, the prosecutor who worked relentlessly to prove Blythe's guilt. He had been too close to the gallows and was crushed under their collapse. The executioner's coffin followed next. His body badly burned and hardly recognizable save for the sheer size of him.

Blythe's body was not found.

Caleb had nothing of her to bury. No way to lay her to rest.

The men from Rowley approached the last carriage and pulled out two final coffins.

Pastor Tobias Walcott. Grieving father and spiritual leader.

Bastard. Abuser. Drunk.

Mirabel Walcott. Sister. Musician. Taken from them all far too young.

Caleb averted his eyes from both coffins as grief threatened to drown him. The last words the minister had spoken to Caleb had been born of a deep hurt. Caleb's last living memory of his father was the flash of violence in his eyes before the minister slammed a fist into Caleb's face.

It should not have been like this.

Any of it.

Caleb clenched his fists but hissed at the pain and released them. Two days after the fire, the injuries on his palms still ached and throbbed. A reminder of all he had lost if ever his heart forgot to hurt.

As Caleb and Dr. Hale worked through the crowd, Caleb kept his chin tilted toward the sun. It warmed his skin even as a chill shivered down his spine. The people around him met his eye. The horror of the fire had scorched away the hate in their gazes.

They were equals in their pain.

Finally.

Though Caleb had lost more than most, he took comfort in the vacant expressions, free of hate, free of derision. Caleb was no longer the wayward boy in love with a witch. He was the broken young man who had lost everything.

Their pity stung less than their sneers.

As the men laid the coffins in the earth, Caleb stepped forward and knelt beside his sister's resting place. He placed the ring on top of her coffin. Though he'd wanted to pry the stone loose from the setting, his injured hands wouldn't cooperate. But his sister deserved to be buried with the last remnant of their mother.

"I'm so sorry, Bells," he whispered, dropping the first handful of dirt over her coffin. "Play a song for me, wherever you are."

As he stood, the first snow of the season fell from the sky, blanketing the world in white.

NOW

Brown earth mixed with white snow as the last shovelful of dirt fell over the dead. Caleb had said his goodbyes so many times in that small graveyard that by the time the men lowered Pastor Walcott into the ground, Caleb didn't have any left. As a child, he'd said goodbye to his mother, the parent who loved him most. The parent who held him tight, who hugged him like she meant it.

Then Mirabel. His darling sister. Bells. The world was too quiet without her. The piano left untouched. Unplayed.

Lastly, he laid his father to rest in the freezing earth.

That goodbye was the easiest and the hardest.

Caleb and his father had not gotten on well, not since his mother died. If he could trust the memories he stored as a child, there wasn't much love between them even before her death. His mother was the parent who wanted children. Their father worked. Served the One God. Produced heirs not because he wanted them but because his religion told him he must.

But as Caleb stood at the edge of the grave, looking

down upon his father's wooden coffin, he realized how alone he truly was. He had loved his father, even through the beatings. But he hated his father as strongly as he loved him. At times feared him.

Caleb knew he had to say goodbye. He *wanted* to say goodbye.

But he didn't know how.

A shuddered breath pulled through his lungs. They still ached from the smoke of the fire, but Dr. Hale said he was certain that Caleb would recover, that he would be fine. *Fine.* As if he could ever be truly all right again. But for Bells? For Blythe? He would try.

Caleb tipped his head in the position of prayer the minister had favored. *I hope you've found peace, Father. Peace and rest with the One God.* As goodbyes went, it was nothing special, but it was the best he could do. He hoped his father would understand.

Unable to meet the eyes of his neighbors, Caleb turned from the gravesite and started the slow trek back to town.

He had another goodbye to deliver.

Dr. Hale caught his gaze but let him leave. They could speak that night over dinner. Though Caleb could return to his childhood home now that his father couldn't bar the door, there were too many memories there. When he was ready, he'd sell the home to someone else. Use the money to travel east, like he and Blythe had planned. In the meantime, the doctor had offered Caleb a home free of painful memories, had offered him a role in Brekham. Instead of the minister's son, Caleb would become the physician's apprentice.

But for now, he needed to be alone. Dr. Hale's look said he understood.

Caleb walked past the carriage. Though the horses

were ready, he needed the walk to reclaim his mind. The doctor could take the carriage alone.

In the cold air, his ruined hands throbbed with each pulse of his heart. Though Dr. Hale assured him he could still work as an apprentice—even with the state of his hands—Caleb was less sure. But he didn't argue the point. They could return to the conversation when his hands had healed and they knew how stiff they would remain.

At the town square, Caleb paused. Smoke lingered in the air and upset his lungs. The courthouse still stood, but the fire had destroyed much of the roof. Rumors spread around town that the building was cursed. That it couldn't be rebuilt, as it would only collapse again.

The gallows were a pile of ash with charred bits of wood sticking up at odd angles. More wood, round pieces the length of his forearm, scattered around the ashes. He kicked a piece, and it rolled over, reveling a pool of blood underneath. Caleb shuddered, wondering who it might have belonged to. Were they among the injured or buried with the rest of his family?

A gentle breeze wound through the square, pulling at his hair, caressing his face. If he listened closely, Caleb could almost hear Blythe calling his name, hear her sigh as if he'd kissed her. It had only been a few days since he'd seen her last, but already he missed her so fiercely it stole his breath.

He missed the sound of her voice. The way she challenged him. The light in her eyes when she discovered something new. Caleb stopped at the edge of the ashes and stared at the mound, a clamp around his heart. It didn't feel real, this world without her. Without Bells.

Shutting his eyes, Caleb fought through the pain to remember what had happened when she fell. The noose was tight, but he felt certain it had not snapped her neck.

But there was no comfort in that knowledge. It seemed almost worse that she lived long enough to feel the lick of fire at her feet. To be burned alive.

"I'm so sorry, Blythe. I should have realized the truth sooner," he whispered to the pile of ash before him. For a moment, he thought he felt her presence in the kiss of wind against his skin. "I miss you."

The breeze changed directions, carving through the buildings and trees. The air swirled the ashes, scattering them across the square. Something near the center caught his attention, uncovered and then hidden again as the ashes danced.

He stepped forward and cupped his ruined hands around it.

What he pulled from the ruins stopped his heart.

Caleb ran his fingers over the carvings. The Eastern Star stared up at him, masquerading as the One God's sun. On the back, he traced the stars that created the Traveler. Somehow, the bit of wood, imbued with his love for Blythe, had survived the fire.

Unblemished.

Caleb clutched it to his chest, wrapped his injured hands around the wood.

"I love you," he said, tears streaming down his face. "Until my dying breath."

Light flashed. His hands stung, but then the pain faded. The amulet sat in his palms, still perfect. But the white bandages around his hands were gone. Burned away.

And underneath, like a final parting kiss of magic, his burned palms were fully healed.

EPILOGUE

Mother says there is no magic stronger than spells born of love.
Love for oneself. Love for others.
And love for those we have lost.

-diary of Blythe Bradbury, age 15

Caleb Walcott walked through Brekham with quiet confidence. In the two years since tragedy tore his world asunder, he had rebuilt his life. He'd found unexpected strength under the weight of his sorrows. Unlike so many in town, he had not succumbed to the bottle. That seemed, more than anything, to have earned him the respect of his neighbors, even if they also feared him. A little.

A few months after the trial, Caleb sold the Walcott home to a family from Rowley. Though he could have purchased a new home, he hid the money away, waiting for the moment he could escape Brekham for good. While he bided his time, Caleb lived with Dr. Hale, learning all he could as Oliver's official apprentice. Over time, Amos and Oliver became something like a surrogate family. Though they could never replace the one he lost, there was rich love in their home. Caleb's frozen heart did eventually thaw, though he never found another to love.

He carried Blythe always in his heart.

But the time had come for Caleb to leave Brekham

behind. Dr. Hale deemed him ready to attend the universities in the east, to rise beyond the role of assistant and become a physician himself. The doctor prepared a grand dinner, and they dined with laughter in their hearts and smiles in their eyes. Caleb was to leave in the morning, journey to the coast, and take a ship across the wide ocean.

He had slipped out of the house after Amos and Oliver —both delightfully tipsy on celebratory wine—retired to the bedroom for a night of private merrymaking. Caleb had further goodbyes to deliver, the types of goodbyes that did not warrant company.

As Caleb stepped into the night, he tipped his face to the sky. As he'd done every night since he lost Blythe, he scanned the blanket of darkness. His heart warmed when he spotted the Traveler, and finally, *finally*, he was following her east.

Under the light of the full moon, Caleb walked through the streets of Brekham. He paused in front of his old home, the first time he'd been back since it sold. "Goodbye, Bells. No one will ever replace the music you brought into my life." He bowed his head and held her memory close to his heart.

He missed her, but these days her memory brought comfort. She was life and energy and music. Caleb had not returned to her grave since the final burial. He didn't need to be there to offer his goodbyes. His family had *lived* in this house. He was there to honor the memory of their lives, not their deaths.

The warm spring breeze danced through the town, threading through his beard and tossing his hair. It seemed like a goodbye, like Bells teasing him one last time before he left. Though this was the last time he'd ever see this home, the finality of it calmed him in a way he didn't expect. His life had fallen apart, but he'd managed to build something new.

Caleb continued into the center of town and paused where the gallows had burned to the ground. Whether the storm had sought to punish Blythe or punish the town that condemned her, no one escaped that night.

Unless… Perhaps *someone* did.

The Traveler charm Caleb had made for Blythe—that he had found in the ashes of the gallows—was buried deep in his pocket. The smooth piece of wood had inexplicably survived the fire that consumed everything else. It had healed the burns on his hands. In the years since, Caleb had often held the charm tight and wondered if Blythe had survived, too, just like her charm.

He often dreamed that Blythe would spirit herself into his bedroom at night, and together they could disappear and journey for a new world. A world where no one had heard of Brekham. A world where they would be safe together, happy together. Where their love could flourish.

But she never came.

And now he had to leave.

There was one final place Caleb wanted to visit before he left this town forever. The superstitions prevailed, and the town never rebuilt the courthouse. Even so, much of the structure was still intact. It was there he would make his final goodbye.

Caleb slipped around the back of the abandoned courthouse and pulled open the door, muscles straining against the rusted hinges. When it swung free, memory gripped his throat, so strong and tight he could hardly breathe. But after another step inside, the feeling passed. Caleb weaved his way to her cell.

It was open.

The guards never bothered to close the door when they

escorted Blythe to the gallows. It seemed no one had come down there since. Caleb stepped inside the final place Blythe had been, the place where they had despaired and loved and fought.

He ran his hands along the smooth stone walls, heedless of the dust and grime.

Except… his fingers brushed against something else. Something decidedly *not* stone.

It felt almost like—

Parchment.

Caleb found the bit of paper wedged between two stones about waist height. With the care of a physician's apprentice, he extracted the folded parchment and unfolded the message. He recognized the curved handwriting instantly.

"Blythe." Her name fell from his lips for the first time in almost two years, and the first line of the message caught him in his chest.

My dearest Caleb,

This letter was for him. Born of her hand. Tears stung sharply as he read through line after line of her final message to him. His heart ached through her declarations of love, through her acceptance of whatever fault he laid at her feet. And though he'd discovered the truth for himself in the end, reading it in her hand was like closing the final chapter on that part of his life.

Yet a flutter of hope picked at his heart. Blythe had kept her promise. She had punished Isaac and Grace and so many others who had lied about her in court. Isaac only survived nine days before infection set in and ended his life. No one in Brekham ever heard from the Pratchett twins again, not even their cousin Edonie.

Caleb ran a shaky hand through his hair and read through her final words again.

The guards are close now. Too close. I hear the keys. I have mere moments left.

I love you, Caleb. Never forget the truth of that. Until my dying breath, I love you, and I will do everything in my power to breathe beyond this day.

Yours forever,

Blythe

Caleb clutched the pages in his hands, fresh tears streaming down his face. He had forgotten how urgently he missed her. Though he had held her charm close the past two years, there was something so precious about carrying her written words. His heart fluttered, desperate to believe in her final promise, to breathe beyond that day at the gallows.

But where was she now?

And how could he leave the only place she might know to find him?

There wasn't time. Caleb had a tight schedule to keep if he wanted to catch his boat across the seas. He carefully folded Blythe's letter, but something else caught his eye. He stepped further into the cell, holding the paper into the tiny bit of light that filtered through the window.

A final message was scrawled in haste across the back.

If I'm able to leave you any reason to hope, come to me.

I will wait until my dying breath.

~

The journey east was longer than Caleb expected, but land was finally on the horizon.

He grasped the wooden charm in his pocket, left behind by Blythe to prove she was still alive. At least, that's what Caleb chose to believe. It's what kept him sane during the tumultuous nights when the ship swayed so much in the swells that he feared it would toss him into the sea. The hope burned hot while he helped tend to sea-sick passengers and a drunken sailor who dropped part of an anchor on his foot.

It was more than the unharmed wooden amulet that gave Caleb hope. He believed in Blythe's power, and the farther he traveled, the more often he thought he heard her voice on the wind.

And now, finally, land was growing larger in the distance.

Caleb wasn't sure how he was supposed to find Blythe—she could be anywhere on the unfamiliar continent—but he would never stop looking. He'd check every university he could find, every bookshop, every library, even if it took him a hundred years.

But Caleb didn't have long to consider his plans. Soon, the captain was shouting orders, and travelers like him were sent to their rooms to gather their things and prepare to disembark. Caleb hadn't brought much. His clothes, a few books, and all the proceeds from the sale of his childhood home. It all fit in two bags, but he liked it that way. He would travel light until he found his love.

More shouting came from above, the sailors rushing around the decks to prepare for docking, and soon someone came to herd all the passengers to prepare to unload. All around him, excitement buzzed in the air, and a strange worry curled in his gut.

Would Blythe recognize him when they met again?

Would she really have waited so long?

What if she didn't like the beard? Maybe he should shave before he began his search.

It was dizzying, feeling this close to her again. Knowing he might find her around any corner.

The boat jostled as it docked, nearly knocking Caleb

off his feet. He managed to right himself and adjust his grip on the bags by the time he reached the edge of the boat. As he descended the gangplank, he searched the shore, desperate for a familiar face. Though it was impossible, he hoped somehow Blythe knew he had finally made it. That she might be waiting for him.

But there were no dark-haired women waiting along the shore.

Caleb tried to suppress the rising disappointment as he made land and headed into the busy seaside town. He had survived two years without her, two years convinced she was dead and gone. He could hold on until he found her. At least he had made it across the sea. He had followed the Traveler east, just like they'd always dreamed.

First, all he needed was a room for the night. He could get his bearings, and then he could begin his search.

He allowed himself to get swallowed into a sea of unfamiliar faces, and searched for an inn. Any place to lay his head where the ground beneath him wouldn't rock.

All around him, vendors hawked their wares. Voices rose and fell, each call blending into the next until it sounded like a wordless cascade of ocean spray.

"It's a lucky thing, that I promised to keep breathing rather than hold my breath."

The voice cut through the chaos of the market, and Caleb froze. He knew that voice, but he had imagined it so many times before. He didn't dare believe.

A soft touch caressed his back, and Caleb dropped both of his bags. Still, he could not turn around.

"Caleb, I—" The teasing fell from her voice, replaced by a deep and abiding sadness. "I missed you so much. I worried you'd never come. I worried I'd lose you to the bottle or to grief or…"

He turned then, and his legs nearly gave out beneath him when he finally laid eyes on her.

She was real.

She was here.

Blythe smiled softly and reached out to touch his face, her fingers brushing through his beard. "This is new."

A laugh interrupted the tears building in his eyes, and he pressed a kiss to her palm. Blythe reached for him, pulling him close, and Caleb let himself get lost in her embrace. He had so many questions and so much to tell her. So many hopes and dreams burst to life inside him.

It would be weeks before Caleb stopped fearing her return was just a dream.

Months before he felt safe in the knowledge that nothing could tear them apart.

His grief for Mirabel faded over time, but it never left.

His love for Blythe grew with each passing season. Forever didn't seem long enough.

And every time they kissed, it was like coming home.

Thank you for reading THE TRIAL! If you enjoyed the book, I would greatly appreciate it if you could consider adding a review on your online bookstore of choice.

Reviews make a huge difference to the success or failure of a book, especially for newer writers like myself. The more reviews a book has, the more people are likely to take a shot on picking it up. The review need only be a line or two, and it really would make the world of difference for me if you could spare the three minutes it takes to leave one.

With all my thanks,

Charlotte Page

INKED
BOOK 1 IN THE DANIKA FROST SERIES
BY CHARLOTTE PAGE & CONNOR ASHLEY

Private detective by day. Demon hunter by night. Danika Frost leads a complicated life.

When Dani accepts a missing person's case, she expects the usual culprits—money, drugs, or secret affair. Instead, she finds herself drawn deeper into Blackthorn city's shadowy underworld.

With the help of the Ink, ancient spirits who live in her skin as tattoos, Dani follows the investigation to the last place she wants to be: a nightclub owned by her ex-boyfriend. Their reunion is explosive, but it's the least of her concerns when bodies start piling up in the city morgue, each branded with the same demonic sigil.

As the evidence points to a rare demon, Dani realizes that she can't solve this case on her own. In order to find the missing girl and stop the necromancers before their demon grows too powerful, Dani must decide who she trusts—the man who broke her heart or the naïve detective who wants to mend it.

Inked is the electrifying first novel in the Danika Frost urban fantasy series, perfect for fans of high-octane action, riveting romance, and unforgettable characters.

Get your copy today and delve into the binge-worthy series everyone is talking about.

www.ingramcontent.com/pod-product-compliance
Lightning Source LLC
Chambersburg PA
CBHW050747190726
48285CB00005B/1559